JAYBEN

AND THE
GOLDEN TORCH

JAYBEN

AND THE
GOLDEN TORCH

THOMAS LEEDS

HODDER CHILDREN'S BOOKS

First published in Great Britain in 2023 by Hodder & Stoughton

1 3 5 7 9 10 8 6 4 2

ISBN 978 1 444 96863 7

Typeset in Sabon by Avon DataSet Ltd, Alcester, Warwickshire

Printed and bound in Great Britain by Clays Ltd, Elcograf S.p.A.

The paper and board used in this book
are made from wood from responsible sources.

Hodder Children's Books
An imprint of
Hachette Children's Group
Part of Hodder & Stoughton Limited
Carmelite House
50 Victoria Embankment
London EC4Y 0DZ

An Hachette UK Company
www.hachette.co.uk

www.hachettechildrens.co.uk

For my parents, Jacqueline and Tony,
whose boundless love and support
made me who I am.

For Sophie, my best one,
who believed in me, no matter what.

And for every child who is living
with an illness or a disability.
Whatever your story, you can
be the hero.

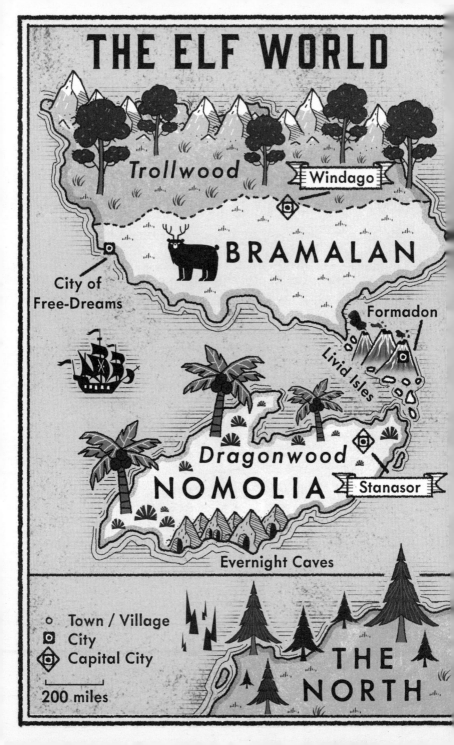

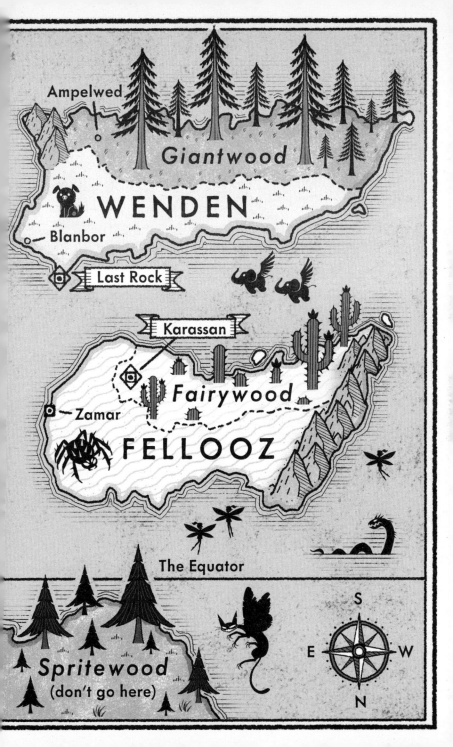

CHAPTER 1

The Greediest Clock of All

Darkness fell on a world far away. A world in which nobody dreams but for a few powerful children.

A hooded woman rode a creature, its hooves clattering up the streets of a ruined city through a thick cloud of smoke, before coming to an abrupt halt at the entrance to a fort. She raised her lantern to illuminate her finely wrinkled face, and the heavy iron gate screeched open before her.

The woman slid from her saddle and used a crooked stick to hobble inside, past a group of armed men, to the foot of a marble staircase which was surrounded by tiny black dragons, hissing at each other and blowing sparks from their razor-sharp beaks.

With her lantern still shining by her face, the old woman looked up to the top of the staircase, where a masked figure stood waiting. 'The lights!' the woman screamed. 'The lights have aligned!'

The figure at the top of the stairs shook with fury.

The woman gagged, and continued. 'Just as the Book said. A Ninth Dreamer is coming—'

'But *I* am the Ninth!' the figure cried, pointing down at one of the dragons, who squealed, then in a bright white flash of light, it turned into a computer.

The other dragons scattered to the shadows to avoid a similar fate. They'd seen too many creatures here magically swapped with objects from the Earth World.

The figure laughed, and stretched its hand out, and the woman hobbled up the stairs to retrieve a purple monocle.

'Make a thousand more of these for our Agents. Any sign of that light from Earth – we must see it first. We must find the child Dreamer before *they* do.'

'Yes,' the woman grinned, cradling the purple monocle in her palm. 'And we will bring the child here alive. We must take its power.'

The figure broke into a cackle, then raised both arms, and used a force to throw the other dragons to the windows, smashing the glass with shrieks of terror.

Somewhere else in the same world, a sleeping boy in a yellow room stirred.

In London, in the Earth World, Ben Thomson was having a nightmare. He'd had this one before.

It always starts in a dark cave filled with shadows and screams. Ben can hear rasping breath, and the heavy footsteps of a monster. He can't see the monster, but he knows he can't escape.

Usually, the dream carries on this way – Ben hunting for a way to escape and never finding it. But tonight, the dream is different. This time, Ben can see a way out of the cave. A shaft of light up ahead. He hurries towards it. The monster behind him hurries too, its footsteps lighten as it moves towards Ben, but he's almost at the light—

BRRRRRRRRRRRRR!

Ben woke to an ear-splitting siren.

'Ugh! Already?' he groaned, hushing his alarm clock with his fist. The time was 5:47am.

He turned his head and something crinkled against his cheek. A piece of paper: on one side was

3

a photocopied checklist and on the other a muddle of scribbles and sketches, an explosion of ideas, drawn freely.

Ben sat up to find more pages scattered around his pillow and duvet. His bedside lamp was on, illuminating a sketch he'd started before he had fallen asleep. He stared at the lines on the page, trying to remember what he'd been drawing. It was a rough sort of pentagon. The front of a house, perhaps? He knew he'd been excited because the lines were light and thin as if he'd sketched in a passionate hurry, but try as he might, nothing came to him.

He felt a strange tingle in his hands and feet, like pins and needles. The clock seemed to be getting louder. 'Shush!' he huffed at his clock, struggling to concentrate through its ticking. Then there was a fainter but much more alarming, yet familiar sound.

'Bone idle!' snarled a voice beneath the floorboards. 'If you're one second late to help me this morning . . .'

Samantha. Ben's aunt and guardian. Ben had been living with her for the past six years. He had only been six when he'd been brought here. He couldn't remember life before he'd been taken into her care, if you could even call it care. He didn't remember his parents or why they had disappeared one day. He just knew that they had. He couldn't remember why Samantha resented him so much. He just knew that she did. Something else he knew for certain was that he'd suffered a brain injury six years ago; and that was the reason for his memory problems.

His aunt seemed determined to keep Ben in the dark about his past. There were no family pictures or keepsakes in the house. Ben longed to find out more, but there was nothing he could do – except eavesdrop or snoop at messages on Samantha's phone, on the rare occasions she put it down unattended. But he was yet to find out anything of interest.

He knew he should get ready for school, especially since Samantha was also his form teacher at Milgrove Manor School, but he was desperate to remember the idea behind his drawing. Surely it was some kind of building – perhaps he had drawn it before. He rolled back on to the bed, reached behind his bedside table, and pulled a wedge of older crumpled drawings of buildings from their hiding place, hoping one might jog his memory.

Ben was fascinated by buildings. For as long as he could remember, he had been bursting with designs for houses, hotels and skyscrapers, though never the boring sort with symmetrical grids of rectangular windows. He loved buildings with lopsided doors, odd-shaped windows, and roofs that looked like they were melting. All of them were functional, in spite of their flaws.

What Ben loved most about his designs was that he could make them complete. They made sense, unlike his life. Until earlier this year, Ben had kept his ideas safe in the one place in the world that belonged to him – his head. He could remember his pictures and redraw them whenever he needed to. But not any more. About a year ago he'd started to have seizures, brought on by his brain injury, the doctor had said. Ben's memory was becoming more and more unreliable. Sometimes he'd find his lunchbox empty at lunchtime but have no memory of eating his sandwich. Often at school he'd forget which classroom he was meant to be in. And now he was frightened of losing his ideas. They had to be drawn on paper and kept hidden somewhere safe.

Flipping through the wedge of paper, Ben found his most precious possession: a postcard that had been handled so often over the years, it had fallen to pieces and been sellotaped back together. On the front was a photograph of Barcelona, four spectacular buildings designed by the famous architect Antoni

Gaudi. They had scaly, curvy, dragon-like roofs, wavy-framed windows and colossal towers.

Ben had found the postcard in the bin when he was nine. Before then he'd never imagined there were buildings so similar to the ones in his mind. Ever since then, he knew he wanted to be an architect when he was older. But that wasn't the reason the postcard was so precious. He flipped it over.

Dear Ben,

Hello from Barcelona! We cannot wait to bring you here next holiday – you will love it! The buildings are out of this world! Just like the ones you come up with. Dad and I have had a lovely anniversary but we can't wait to get home and see you. Be a good boy for Granny. See you soon.

Love from Mum and Dad x

Until he'd found the card three years ago, Ben knew nothing about his parents. It had been posted to him six years ago, when he was six, before he could remember. It was sent the year of his brain injury, the year his parents had disappeared – the year he had moved in with Samantha.

To see some evidence of a happy childhood, of

being special to someone – it gave him hope. Maybe he could be special to someone again one day. Maybe he could be happy again.

He'd hidden the card from Samantha right away. But he had felt brave enough to ask her if they could one day visit Barcelona. She had laughed in his face. When Ben thought of her reaction now, he felt a burning rage bubble up from deep inside. His school friend Emma had invited him to Spain with her family last year, but Samantha wouldn't allow it.

Samantha called from downstairs. 'Do you want to lose your lunch as well as breakfast today?'

Ben glanced at the clock in dismay. It was 5:57am.

He hated clocks. To him they didn't tell the time, they stole it. They made him late. He hated their greedy faces, especially his alarm clock, the greediest clock of all.

He gathered his drawings and the postcard, stashing the half-started sketch in his pocket, and stuffing the rest behind the bedside table.

'Sorry!' he shouted. 'Down in a minute!'

He rolled out of his small, hard bed, still feeling strangely heavy, then whipped off his grey pyjamas and crammed them into a drawer in the middle of his tiny bedroom. There wasn't a single toy on his shelf and no posters on the dark blue walls, only cracks and a patch of mould for decoration.

He hopped with anxiety while pulling on his charcoal school trousers, his arms and legs still tingling, the bedside clock ticking away. *Tick tick tick*. It grew louder still, and the tingles spread to his arms and legs. It was starting to bother him.

What is *that?* he thought, rubbing his arm. But there was no time.

He combed his short coppery hair, straightened his navy-blue tie into his navy-blue sweater, twisted the handle of his door and sighed a long, heavy sigh. This would be a difficult day, like any other.

Almost certainly.

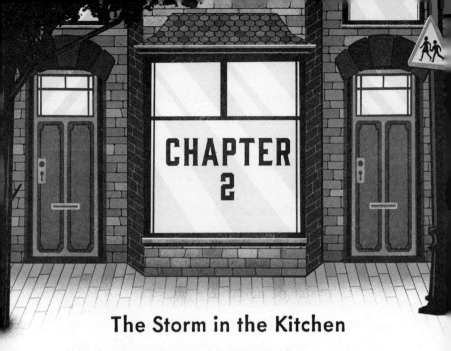

The Storm in the Kitchen

Samantha: an imposingly tall, thin tower of a woman, with tightly pinned black hair, piercing green eyes, and a sallow, frowning face. She stood at the bottom of the stairs, tapping her squeaky leather boots.

'Morning!' Ben said with a brave smile, trying to imagine being eighteen one day, free to stand up for himself and leave.

'What time do you call this?' she said. 'I can already hear those birds twittering out there, and you haven't even *begun* sorting my books for school!'

'Sorry,' he sighed, his bubble of courage bursting. He was only eleven. Eighteen and freedom was another seven years away. Seven long years. 'I'm sorry, I—'

'The time is now 6:03.' She held her wristwatch next to her phone, checking they had precisely the same time. 'You are a person – albeit a pitiful excuse for one – but a person nonetheless, and *people* work to the clock.'

'I'm sorry,' he pleaded. 'I really am—'

He stopped at the sound of someone coming out of the bathroom. It was Marcus, Samantha's boyfriend, his hair glistening with fresh hair gel. He was tall, dark and handsome in a gross kind of way, but most notably he shared her contempt for Ben.

'I'll text you later,' said Marcus, pushing past Ben as if he didn't exist.

Samantha pecked him on the cheek. 'Take out the recycling, would you?'

'This it? No paper today?' asked Marcus, grabbing a near-empty bag of recycling.

Ben froze.

'That's odd,' said Samantha, 'there was lots in there yesterday.' She turned to Ben with a look of derision. 'You know, when I throw something away, that doesn't make it yours. You are a child; nothing belongs to you, and nothing gives you the right to waste my ink on those moronic doodles of yours.'

'Don't let him bug you, Sams,' Marcus scoffed as he

opened the front door. 'It's just Ben. He's not worth it.' He slammed the door and got into his silver sports car, bearing the logo of a company called Lipworth Lettings.

Ben plodded into the kitchen. He was tired of being 'Just Ben'. He had been special once; his parents had cared about his happiness, the postcard was proof of that. One day he would be special again – he'd be successful, travel, go to places beyond his wildest dreams – he'd show them. He'd never be 'Just Ben' again.

He glanced at the clock above the oven, its big face eating up the minutes as if it was starving. *Tick tick tick.* 6:05am. He'd never heard it tick so loudly. The tingles now seemed to be spreading to his chest.

Why can't you count down to something useful, instead of getting me into trouble all the time? he thought. *Why can't you count down to when something good is going to happen? Count down to when I can finally get out of here, and—*

Something stopped his train of thought. A cool, white light shone gently from the window. It was the full moon, peeking for a moment through a narrow break in the otherwise cloudy dawn sky. But the beam of light was distorted, dancing through a stream of

rainwater running down the glass, pouring through the glass like it was too vast to be contained. Ben suddenly had the weirdest feeling. Like he had seen this before, somehow, like déjà vu – or like he was dreaming. Or like he had seen this same light in a dream.

The ticking stopped. The tingling rushed to his head, and the moon disappeared behind a cloud.

What was that? And for how long had he been standing there?

He looked at the kitchen clock and felt goosebumps all over. It really had stopped ticking. He turned to the mantel clock in the sitting room, and the grandfather clock in the hall. They had all stopped.

'For hell's sake!' Samantha snapped. 'Get a move on! If you're quick, you can have that last burnt piece of toast!'

But Ben was starting to worry about the tingling sensation. He sometimes felt like this before a seizure. 'I don't feel good,' he said. 'My head isn't—'

'Nice try,' Samantha tutted, heading upstairs with her breakfast to watch TV in bed, like every morning. 'You won't get a day off that easily.'

Ben sat at the kitchen table chewing a charred piece of cold toast, which even the birds outside would have refused. He loved watching animals through the

 13

window. He felt a sort of kinship with them, especially the local fox who refused to quit raiding the outside bins no matter how much Samantha tried to scare it away.

He looked up at the clocks again. Still nothing. He wondered when Samantha would notice.

Then he saw something else odd, on the kitchen counter, by the plug sockets: a rock the size of an apple – glowing green. It was exactly where Samantha usually kept her tablet. In fact, he was certain he had seen the tablet there, charging, the night before. Now, in its place, was a green rock. Perhaps it was a weird present from Marcus.

But there was no time to think about it. Ben had to organise four bags of Samantha's school books in less than an hour.

He choked down the crust and turned to a mound of grey exercise books and a stack of small, violently orange detention cards for 'bad children'.

Samantha, known as Ms Vaughan to Ben's classmates, did not believe there was any such thing as a good child, but she did believe in success and failure. Her students were not encouraged to try their best; they were required to succeed, and success was not easy in Ms Vaughan's class. She considered any test score below 100% to be a dismal failure.

Ben sighed as he started organising the books. He desperately wanted to do well at school, so he could get a good job one day and get out of here. But over the past year it didn't seem to matter how many hours he spent reading or how carefully he listened in class. He couldn't concentrate. Nothing he learnt seemed to stay in his head.

He flicked open the first page of the top notebook, and noticed his aunt's handwriting labelled with today's date: 15th September. Ben's twelfth birthday. His stomach dropped.

It was his birthday and he hadn't even noticed.

The date did not evoke happy memories of cakes and candles. In fact, Ben only knew it was his birthday because he had seen it on a letter from his doctor a few years ago. He'd found it in the recycling while rummaging for paper to draw on. Samantha didn't do birthdays. Each year, Ben had to pretend it wasn't his birthday at all.

He reached for a second book, his own. There wasn't a single tick from Samantha's green pen of approval. Reluctantly, he flipped through every disappointing page, then he saw a handwritten comment on the last page. Samantha had written in bold red ink:

Benjamin Thomson, you are HOPELESS!

What a birthday! Ben slammed his book shut. His life here was . . . hopeless. Samantha called him lots of unpleasant things, but 'hopeless' was the worst.

Nothing meant more to Ben than hope; hope that a memory of his parents would come back, or that he would recall something of his previous life. Hope that his brain would stop emptying, so he could study and one day build a life – one with a career, and hobbies, and friends, maybe even a family – far away from this lonely, miserable place.

'I'm not!' he muttered through gritted teeth. 'I'm not hopeless! I don't belong here. Maybe I'll go, and – maybe I – maybe—'

He stopped, and that's when it started.

Every noise in the house became louder. Every light was too bright.

A storm was coming.

Ben could hear Samantha clonking down the stairs. She marched through to the kitchen, clutching her phone, her watch and a tiny screwdriver. 'What did you do to the clocks,' she hissed.

'What?' said Ben, standing up. 'I never—'

A sharp pain shot through Ben's tingling head. He gripped the kitchen counter, teeth clenched. Looking down at his reflection in the sink, his jaw tightened with pain. He let out a cry.

'You can cut that out,' she said, switching on the radio. 'It won't work on me. Oh and I found this.'

Ben looked up. She had found one of his sketches.

'These stupid drawings won't get you anywhere,' she smirked, ripping it into tiny pieces. 'You are hopeless.'

Hopeless.

He wanted to answer back but he couldn't concentrate through the pain and the noise and the bright lights.

'Hopeless,' she tutted.

Suddenly he could hear the irritating tick of the kitchen clock again. *Tick tick tick.* But it sounded different somehow, sharper and deeper. He looked up. The clock hands were running *backwards*.

Then he heard the mantel clock in the sitting room, and the grandfather clock from the hall. All of the clocks. All of them ticking and tocking, from every corner of the house. He looked around to the hallway, breathing fast, and then to the living room. They were turning the wrong way.

'For hell's sake!' Samantha shouted. 'What did you do now?'

Samantha's watch sprang back to life too. In an awful chorus of clanging, the grandfather clock and the alarm clocks upstairs began furiously hammering their bells.

The radio screeched like the squeal of a car's brakes.

The tap dripped like falling hail.

'Enough!' she cried. Was that . . . *fear* in her eyes? 'Whatever you're doing – stop it. This instant!'

'I didn't do anything. Please, I'm sorry, I—'

'So am I!' she snarled, grabbing him by the arm. 'I'm sorry you were ever born! I'm sorry your parents spoilt you rotten! I'm sorry that you're still here, poisoning my life! I'm sorry that every single day I have no choice but to . . .'

Ben could no longer make out the words. Not over the tinny screech of the radio and the dripping of the tap and the wild ticking of all those clocks. *Tick tick tick*. He shut his eyes tight, trying to separate out the sounds, but the noises were locking together, swirling around and attracting yet more sounds. A car alarm wailed across the street, a dog barked in next door's garden, a plane passed groaning overhead, and a train rattled over its tracks.

He cupped his hands over his ears, but he couldn't block the noise out. Then he smelt it. The room reeked as if the leftovers inside the fridge were rotting. Now he could *taste* it. It was stinging the back of his throat.

He tried moving a hand from his ear to hold his nose, but his arm wouldn't move. The tingling sensation was like electricity buzzing around his body, and he could feel his heart beating hard.

Thud thud.

Tick tick.

Behind his tightly shut eyelids came pink and yellow dots. They flashed like tiny fireworks in his head, and just when he felt as though he would burst, his arms thrashed out and he fell to the floor. Down and down, as if the ground had opened beneath him. Down he fell, until suddenly, with a loud crack, everything stopped.

There was no sound and no smell here, only stillness and darkness. His heart stopped racing, his breathing slowed. Every muscle in his body was still.

The storm in the kitchen had taken Ben's mind to a world far away.

CHAPTER 3

In the Eyes of the Beast

In the faraway world, a boy opened his eyes.

The boy had no memory. He felt calm at first, but that only lasted a moment. There was a faint jingling sound and a cool breeze against his toes. He strained to focus his eyes on a wood-beamed ceiling. *Where was he?*

The boy bolted upright, and a hundred little bells rattled all around him.

He was sitting on a bed with reels of bells tied to every post. The bed was in the middle of a bright-yellow room, surrounded by dozens of potted trees of various shapes and sizes. Some as big as grown men, others small enough to hold in his hand, and lots in between.

He jumped down to investigate, struck by a wave of dizziness. The bells jingled and he lost his balance, grabbing the metal bedframe to steady himself.

This place didn't seem familiar. It didn't feel right. The boy was starting to feel scared. He noticed a small stuffed toy next to his pillow, with four legs, a trunk, wings, and covered in light blue feathers. He picked up the toy, but then dropped it with a start – there was another boy staring at him through a window.

The other boy's gaze, wide-eyed and wary, made the boy feel uneasy. But it was strange . . . when he flinched so did the other boy.

Maybe he can help. Maybe he knows where I am.

The boy cautiously approached the window.

To his surprise, the other boy copied.

He stopped and scratched his head, so did the boy.

Wait. It wasn't a window. He was looking at his reflection in glass. *How could he not recognise his own face?*

He saw a slight boy, with short coppery hair. His feet were bare and he was wearing a pair of tan brown shorts and a white shirt.

In the mirror, he noticed a thin, silver chain dangling from his left pocket, and pulled it out. On the end was a circular object made of polished black

21

wood with bold silver letters engraved on one side.
It read:

JAYBEN

What – or who – was Jayben?

He flipped the disc over to find a smaller engraving:

AS LONG AS YOU HAVE A HOME TO FIND
YOU WILL NEVER BE LOST.
TO OUR PRECIOUS JAYBEN,
WITH LOVE FROM MUM AND DAD

The boy sounded it out slowly. He could read, but it
was difficult.

'*As long as you have a home to find . . . you – will –
never . . . be lost*. Mum and Dad?' He flipped it over
again, running his thumb across the deep-cut letters,
and looked back at the boy. *Jayben?* Was that his
name, then? Reading it again, it felt strangely familiar,
like his mouth had said it before.

'Jayben,' he whispered. Jayben. The word felt warm
in his mouth.

As long as you have a home to find. Jayben held the

object to his chest and looked around the yellow room again. This unfamiliar place couldn't be his home. He would know it, surely.

He noticed something poking out of his right pocket. He reached in and the depth of the pocket seemed to know no bounds. He pulled out a large object wrapped in sheets of scrunched-up paper. He lifted it to the light, and the papers fell away to reveal another shiny thing. It was long and heavy and gold, some sort of pipe, the length of his forearm, but with a hole at only one end. The other end curled into a swirly spiral, like the shell of a snail. Just above the spiralled end, there were four grooves cut into a golden spout.

Was this from his mum and dad too? Brushing his finger over the indentations, he saw his face reflected in the gleaming gold.

Then he heard a noise. A strange rumbling in the distance. It was getting louder, pounding and vibrating the floorboards beneath his feet. But he couldn't be scared. He needed to leave this mysterious room. He needed to be brave.

He needed to find his home.

Putting the objects back in his strangely deep pockets, he walked towards the door. The noise grew louder still. With a deep breath, he opened the door.

Jayben found himself in a hallway, at the top of a flight of stairs. Downstairs was another door with a window, and sunlight streaming through. The noise was clearly coming from outside. Maybe someone out there would recognise him, and could help him get home.

He stood on tiptoes to peek out of the window, but it was impossible to see anything in the blinding light. He could only hear the thundering from outside, and see the doorknob in front of him, which was beginning to shake.

CLINK! CLINK! CLINK!

The handle rattled as the tremors shook the hallway. It matched the thumping of his heart.

CLINK! CLINK! CLINK!

THUMP! THUMP! THUMP!

Enough waiting. Jayben braced himself, grabbed the handle and flung the door open. He held one hand up to shield his eyes from the direct sun and saw the source of the commotion pass by. It was some kind of animal, enormous and black, chasing a man up a cobbled lane.

He squinted at the creature. It had a swishing tail. He was sure he recognised it. He decided to follow it.

Maybe more memories would come back. Maybe the man would have answers.

Jayben started running barefoot up the cobbled lane, through a busted fence and into the shadows of a forest. He looked up at the trees as he ran, noticing scorched bark and singed branches, and yellow signs with the warning:

DANGER
DREAM THIEVES

Danger? he thought briefly. *Dream Thieves?*

The animal was disappearing into the thickening woods now. Jayben darted after it. He glanced down and saw his feet were scratched but he didn't feel any pain as he ran across the jagged stones and twigs on the forest floor. Weird. He struggled to keep up as the creature bounded up the steep slope, but then, suddenly, the man in front tripped and fell to his knees, letting out a cry.

The animal towered over the man and began circling him.

It hadn't spotted Jayben approach from behind. Now Jayben could see the creature more clearly. It was taller than a grown man and boasted two immense, scorpion-like claws and a series of sharp horns from its head to its long armoured tail. It had four hoofed legs, shiny black skin, and four yellow eyes. It looked pretty cool.

The beast grabbed the man's leg with one of its huge claws and flipped him over, and Jayben saw terror on the man's face.

Jayben froze. He had to help, but what could he do? The man and the beast were so focused on one another, neither of them had noticed him.

In the end Jayben went with, 'Hi.'

The creature dropped the man immediately, startled. The beast backed away, angrily shaking its head.

'Are you okay?' Jayben said to the man on the ground. 'I thought I recognised that thing, but now I'm not so sure . . .'

'Careful, son!' the man cried. 'It'll kill you!'

Kill me? thought Jayben. But there was no time to think, he could already see the shadow of the beast's immense claws and feel its hot breath on the back of his neck. Turning, Jayben saw his reflection in the eyes of the beast.

CHAPTER 4

When a Tree Tells You to Run

Jayben gazed into the creature's four lemon-yellow eyes and the creature gazed back. A moment of calm passed between them, like it understood him, like they understood each other. Time seemed to stand still.

Then all at once, the beast reared, retracting its claws and swiping Jayben with its long tail, before fleeing down the slope.

Jayben felt the wind knocked out of him, as he fell into a pile of dry leaves.

The man on the ground sat up, breathing heavily. 'How did . . . how did you scare it away?'

'I don't know,' said Jayben, pulling himself up. He wasn't hurt but he felt shaken and frustrated. He was

27

no better off than he'd been in the house.

The man clambered to his feet and removed two earplugs made of cork. He was very tall, with scruffy brown trousers held up by an overloaded tool belt and a red plaid shirt that appeared too small for his mountainous shoulders and protruding gut. His eyes were chocolate brown, his skin tanned and freckled, his short brown hair and beard were beginning to grey, and the tops of his ears were pointed. There was something about his presence that Jayben found comforting, though he couldn't explain why.

'Honestly, lad, how did you scare it away?' the man said, dusting the soil from his beard and putting the earplugs in his top pocket. 'I mean, thank you – really – thank you. You saved my life! But . . . *that was a skallabore!*'

Jayben looked at the man blankly. A skallabore?

'Nothing scares 'em,' the man laughed, giddy with relief. 'Horrible things! Feared 'em since I was wee, but never thought I'd meet one. And you're just, well – you're just a lad! Impossible!'

Jayben shrugged. He only knew that when he had locked eyes with the beast, it had seemed to understand it should leave.

Jayben felt a wave of courage for the first time

since he'd woken up. 'I'm looking for my parents. Can you help?'

The man smiled warmly. 'Of course. Least I can do.' He held out a hand and Jayben shook it. 'My name's Tedrik. Tedrik Feller.' Then he looked down at Jayben's wrist and frowned. 'Where's your band?'

'My band?'

Tedrik pointed to a leather band on his own wrist, with a tiny charm on it, a red pine cone.

Jayben shrugged. 'I don't have one. What is it?'

Tedrik looked baffled. 'A clanband. With your family charm. Maybe you dropped it.' He pointed to Jayben's feet. 'Drop something else?'

Jayben looked down and saw the gleaming tip of the golden pipe-like object, poking out of the dry leaves where he had fallen. He quickly picked it up, checking it wasn't damaged. It was a precious clue to who he was. He couldn't lose it.

But Tedrik was staring at the pipe as though transfixed. 'But it can't be,' he whispered. 'That would mean you're the—'

Tedrik broke off, eyes still fixed on the pipe.

'Are you okay?' said Jayben. He put the golden object back in his deep pocket. The low evening sun cast a golden glow over the forest, and shone across a cut in Jayben's left hand. Tiny crystals in his palm shimmered with all the colours of the rainbow.

'Whoa!' said Jayben. He hadn't noticed the rainbow wound before. It looked like a line of tiny crystals embedded in his palm and twinkling in the light. But it didn't hurt at all. Not even when he poked it. 'Look at this,' he said, holding out his palm to Tedrik.

Tedrik's jaw dropped. 'Great Moonmother above us,' he whispered. 'It *is* you.'

'What? What's *me*?' Jayben felt a rush of goosebumps and excitement. 'Do you know my parents? Do you know who I am?'

'I think I do. I might do. I must be going mad!' Tedrik paused. 'It's not safe for you here. I'll walk you back – where do you live?'

Jayben's stomach dropped. 'I thought you knew who I was? Don't *you* know where I live?'

'Oh,' said Tedrik. 'You don't remember, do you? Of course, that's how it works. Don't worry, we can help.'

'Thanks,' said Jayben. He suddenly wasn't sure he trusted this man at all. 'But I'll be okay.' He took one step back, only to realise he had even forgotten which way he had come. 'I'll just go this way—'

'Wait!' Tedrik interrupted. 'Do you hear that?'

Jayben fell silent. He could hear something now and it was coming from a tree beside them, with blackened bark. A low, slow, clicking sound.

Another fire-damaged tree started clicking – as if the trees were *talking* to each other.

Now most of the trees around them had joined in and were making a deep drumming noise.

'What's that music?' Jayben asked.

'That's no music, lad,' said Tedrik. 'That's the worst sound in the world. The trees are warning us. Someone must know you're here.'

'Who?' Jayben asked. 'Who knows I'm here?'

'I'll explain later. For now, we need to go. Where are your boots?'

Jayben looked down at his bare toes in the dirt. 'I don't know.' He shrugged. 'I don't remember.'

He felt something hit his head. Little twigs and leaves had started dropping from the branches above. They were shaking. The clicking and drumming grew louder.

Tedrik popped his earplugs back in his ears and rummaged in his back pockets with a nervous grin. 'Always check your pockets, as I like to say . . .' He pulled out a pair of big leather gloves. 'Here we are. Unusual, but it'll have to do. Stick them on your feet.'

Jayben's toes were getting cold and he gladly slipped them on.

The tree beside him let out a deep groan and Jayben jumped with fright.

'When a tree tells you to run, Jayben – you run.'

Tedrik grabbed Jayben's arm and began to pull him through the forest.

'This way!' Tedrik pointed, running up the slope.

Jayben tugged his arm away and slowed. Did he trust Tedrik? Surely he shouldn't follow him blindly? Suddenly the forest floor came to life with thousands of shiny black bugs, crawling out of the soil and rustling across fallen leaves in all directions. Another tree groaned loudly and that made Jayben's mind up for him.

He set off after Tedrik, struggling to keep up in his gloved feet, stumbling on unearthed roots and rocks.

Over the pounding trees, Jayben heard twigs snapping from behind. Something or someone was coming closer . . .

Then came a flock of winged creatures, a blur of pink, narrowly missing Jayben's head as they shot past with high-pitched croaks of panic.

The woods beat faster and louder.

'They must be close!' cried Tedrik.

Jayben tried not to imagine what Tedrik and the entire forest were afraid of. He focused on putting one foot in front of the other.

As he ran, every flower snapped shut, and every leaf detached itself and fluttered off like a butterfly.

Jayben found Tedrik at a fast-flowing stream. Toadstools formed a path through the water. Tedrik jumped on to the first.

'Take the stepping stools, lad.' Tedrik jumped on to the next stool, waiting for Jayben to catch up. 'Quick! They won't wait!'

Jayben took the gloves off his feet, then ran and jumped.

Slam!

He landed on the first stool, slipping about over the gushing water. It was slimy underfoot. Then the stool began sinking.

Tedrik stepped on to another. It sunk slightly, and Jayben leapt behind him.

Slam!

He made it, but it was coated in wet moss, and he could barely stand; it was too slippery. He eyed up the next one, leapt and—

SPLASH! Jayben felt his body go cold as the white water engulfed him.

'Gotcha!' said Tedrik, grabbing his arm and pulling him on to the bank. They ran towards the foot of a giant red tree, as broad as a house, with huge furry roots. This tree had no sign of fire damage – and between two of its roots was an entrance. Which was fast closing.

Tedrik flung himself forward and held the roots apart with all his might. 'I can't hold it much longer!' Tedrik yelled, his muscles straining. 'Are you coming?'

Tedrik didn't wait for his answer. He jumped through, pulling Jayben behind him, and as the giant tree clamped shut, something leapt in behind them.

CHAPTER 5

This Mischievous House

Jayben stumbled into the dark hollow, and just as quickly saw roots opening on the other side. As he crawled out, he noticed a banner of coloured flags above them.

Welcome to Ampelwed
Home to the most modest of giants

Home. Could this be Jayben's home? Or was that ridiculous, given that he wasn't a giant?

'You okay, lad?' said Tedrik, standing in the light. 'You're safe here.'

But Jayben could hear something behind him, a

strange noise – like the bark of a dog or the grunt of a pig, or a mix of the two.

'No we're not,' he said. 'Something got in!'

'Oinff! Oinff!' It was coming closer. 'Oinff! Oinff! Oinff!' it said, and then something green shot past Jayben on three legs and leapt into Tedrik's arms.

'Ah, it's only Russog!' Tedrik beamed fondly. Jayben noticed that the creature had a stump where its right front paw would have been.

Tedrik scratched its belly. 'What were you doing out there, boy? It's too dangerous. Never mind, I've found you a new friend.'

He put Russog down again. The animal trotted over to Jayben. It had a short piggy snout and a curly tail, with the body and paws of a dog, covered in thick, green hair and brown spots.

'What is it?' Jayben asked, relieved to see that the creature was harmless.

'A skoggle. His name's Russog.'

Jayben crouched and stroked the skoggle's fuzzy head, receiving a face full of wet snout. He felt better here, away from the drumming trees, but he couldn't relax. 'What happened back there? Who were we running from?'

'Wicked people,' Tedrik said. 'The trees were

warning us to run.' He patted the furry bark of the tree, one of a long line of giant trees tightly interwoven to form a barrier between this place and the wider woods. 'These big reds should keep them out.'

The drumming sound was muffled now. The skoggle's ears pricked up to the distant sound of a woman's voice calling, 'Russog! Dinner!'

'Oinff!' Russog bolted ahead, down a path of turquoise pebbles, his three little paws barely brushing the ground.

'Come on. We'll get you fed and cleaned up,' said Tedrik. 'Then we can talk.'

Jayben's stomach grumbled. It was enough to sway him. Strangely now he couldn't remember anything before he had entered the woods. He tried to think but it quickly faded. He was so lost. If Tedrik really did know something about him, then he needed to find out what.

The path curved into the dense forest. The woods were different here. It was quiet, and the air was dizzyingly fresh, peppered with the welcoming scent of wood smoke.

They turned left off the lane, passing a yellow mailbox that was floating in mid-air. Beyond it was a large, red wooden house in a colourful garden. Wisps of white smoke rose from its chimneys, and its mossy roof reached all the way down to the ground, speckled with the nests of the winged pink frog-like animals, cheerfully croaking.

Tedrik led Jayben past a stable to the front door of the house, where he wiped his boots and stepped inside.

Jayben followed, admiring the hovering baskets of flowers over the decking and the wavy lines of the roof. The design of this peculiar house felt comforting, familiar somehow. He was so busy looking up, he didn't notice a thin branch protruding from the bottom of the door-frame, which nearly sent him flying. He steadied himself on the door.

'Excuse the house, lad – no manners!' Tedrik bent down, grabbed the twig and tied it in a knot, out of the way. 'Doesn't mean any harm.'

The logs of the house walls were dripping with sticky sap, and one of them was engraved:

Always check your pockets
Before you search the woods

Jayben was intrigued. 'What does that mean?' he asked.

Tedrik explained, 'It's our Feller family motto. It's saying that sometimes what we need is closer to home

than we think. It's also good for when you can't find your keys.' He chuckled.

Jayben hoped that finding out who he was and getting home would be as easy as finding lost keys, but given the day he'd had so far, he wasn't so sure. He followed Tedrik into a large living room with sloping wooden beams for a roof, cabinets spilling with old books, colourful paintings on the walls and a crackling fire where a tall woman was sitting with a blanket, reading a book. She wore a teal dress and had red hair to her shoulders, straight with a flick. Her eyes were green, her cheeks pink, and she wore a charm bracelet on her wrist. Jayben warmed to her immediately.

'Whatever happened to you? I was beginning to worry,' she said, sweeping her hair behind her pointy ears and closing her book. 'Where did you— Oh!' She noticed Jayben in the doorway. 'And who's this?'

'This is Jayben,' said Tedrik, bolting the front door behind them. 'He's lost.'

'You poor thing,' the woman said, crouching down to his eye level. 'We'll get you home, don't worry. But you're very welcome to stay while we figure out where you need to go. Our last foster boy has just left – there's plenty of space. I'm Larnie.'

'Thanks,' Jayben replied. He was grateful for their

kindness, but at the same time he felt a strong sense of urgency. That message from his parents had lit something inside of him. He longed to feel the comfort and familiarity of home – if only he could remember what it was like. 'I won't stay long,' he said, trying not to fall over Russog, who was bouncing excitedly at his feet. 'I just need some information and then I'll go.'

Larnie looked surprised. 'Well, the sun's going down. You can at least stay for tonight.'

Jayben glanced around. The warm, cosy house did seem like a good place to stay, and it *was* getting dark. And if Tedrik was right about 'wicked people' out there, then Jayben didn't want to leave until he understood who they were and why they were after him. *Just till it's safe*, he thought. Then his stomach rumbled loudly.

'Hungry?' said Larnie, her eyes twinkling.

He nodded with a grin.

Russog let out a long, loud fart. Then, from his snout came a deep man's voice: 'Who farted?'

Larnie rolled her eyes.

'Did . . . Russog just . . . *talk*?' said Jayben. 'And fart?'

'Sorry,' said Larnie laughing. 'He was raised in the wild. Oh, and here comes our other little one . . . Well,

she's thirteen now, I don't know where the time goes.'

A girl, a bit taller than Jayben, came down the staircase bouncing a ball with one hand. She had her father's dark freckles, brown eyes and brown hair, tied in a ponytail, and her ears were also slightly pointed. She wore a bright-green shirt and shorts, bearing the tan of someone with little time for life indoors, and Jayben noticed a thin leather charm bracelet on her wrist – the clanband Tedrik had mentioned earlier.

'Great,' she muttered sarcastically, catching her ball and rolling her eyes in Jayben's direction. 'Another one.'

'Jayben,' said Tedrik, 'this is Pheetrix, who is mostly lovely . . . when she's not being a giant pain.'

'Hi, Pheetrix,' Jayben said politely.

'Hey,' she replied shortly, shooting daggers at her dad. 'It's Phee. I mean, call me Phee. What's your— Oh!' She stopped, dropping the ball to hold her nose. 'Russog, you are disgusting!'

Russog jumped up at her. '*Breakfaaast!*' he sang in Larnie's voice.

'It's dinner,' said Phee. 'How many times?'

'He really does talk!' said Jayben.

'Yeah,' said Phee. 'Skoggles imitate people. You have to be careful what you say around them.'

Russog opened his snout again, and in Phee's voice, he moaned, 'Why is Mum so annoying?'

'See what I mean? Mind your business, Stinkbomb!'

Larnie kissed Russog on the head. 'Such an imagination for such a tiny little brain.'

Tedrik laughed. Then his expression turned more serious. 'A quick word with you in the kitchen, love?' he said to Larnie.

'Oh,' said Larnie. 'Dinner is ready. Couldn't we—'

'It'll only take a moment,' he said. 'And Jayben here's had a long old trek, I'm sure he's bursting for the shed. Can you show him, Phee?'

Phee led Jayben to a small, draughty room at the back of the house.

'This is the shed, where we do our business. Wash your hands over there.' She pointed to a bowl of soapy water and left him to it.

Jayben hesitated. Then he dunked his hands quickly. He wiped the drips on his shirt, walking hurriedly back to the sitting room. Then paused. He could hear Tedrik, Larnie and Phee whispering behind the kitchen door.

'But, Dad,' murmured Phee, 'the *Torch*? Are you sure?'

Larnie whispered, 'And a skallabore? One of those

monsters, in these woods? What if it comes back? You mustn't go out there from now on!'

'I know it's scary, love,' said Tedrik. 'But the lad walked right up to it! Spooked it something fierce. And he has no memory. It has to be him. He has the Torch, and the Rainbow. We all saw the lights aligning last night, didn't we? Everyone did.'

'Lights?' Jayben asked, opening the door. 'What lights?'

'Oh!' Larnie gasped, trying to compose herself, looking pale. 'Just in time for dinner. Who's hungry?'

'*Breakfaaast!*' Russog sang loudly again before licking a dribble of sap from the wall.

Jayben scowled. What weren't they telling him? What were they hiding – and why?

'I need to know,' said Jayben, clenching his fists.

'Of course,' said Larnie, nervously closing the curtains. The sun was setting, casting a soft red-golden light through the trees. 'But you look like you haven't eaten all summer. Come and have something and then we'll all have a nice chat.'

Jayben kept his fists closed. He felt wary but his stomach was rumbling and everything smelt delicious. 'Okay,' he said with a sigh.

Tedrik lit the candles on the table and everyone

took their seats. There was barely space for the plates on the table, loaded as it was with various steaming pots of stews and sizzling pans of sauces.

Larnie held a small bottle upside down over a heavy corked vessel. She removed the cork, and pink liquid poured upwards into the bottle. Then she fastened it with a straw and passed it to Jayben.

'Well,' she said, 'Wherever you're from, for now you're our guest.'

'Yes,' said Tedrik, raising his own bottle. 'Welcome to Ampelwed. The loveliest village in all the Memory Woods.'

Larnie chuckled. 'Home to the most modest of giants.'

Jayben was intrigued. 'Giants?'

'Giants were very big people,' Larnie explained. 'Back in the olden days, when there was enough magic to grow so big, they planted this forest. We don't grow so tall these days.'

'Easy on the flumjuice, Russog,' said Tedrik.

'Oinff!' said the skoggle, guzzling on his bottle so fast that he was beginning to float.

The three Fellers paused for a moment, taking hold of their bracelets, which each bore the same charm: a little red pine cone. They exchanged glances, then smiled.

'Let's eat!' said Larnie.

Jayben didn't hold back. He hadn't realised how hungry he was until he'd started. He had seconds and thirds of every dish. He even ate the blue shadowgrass salad, which Phee and her father would only touch when smothered in Mrs Feller's glowing eight-bean sauce. The only thing slowing him down was the distraction of a small twig from the table leg, tickling his shin with its leaves.

'What's it doing?' he said, bending to see.

'Sorry, lad,' said Tedrik, tapping the table. 'Lottal! Leave him be.'

The playful branch retreated, until Tedrik looked away. Then it crept back and started tickling Jayben again.

'Don't worry,' said Phee, grinning at Jayben's bewildered expression. 'Not many people would understand our cheeky furniture – not even other folk in this wood.'

'Yes,' said Larnie. 'This mischievous house is Tedrik's unique version of tree-taming.'

'Tree-taming?' asked Jayben.

'It's what I do,' explained Tedrik. 'I make things from the trees, the old-fashioned way.'

'So you chop them down?' asked Jayben.

'Oh no! No, I don't kill 'em, just tame 'em. It's an old art, talking to trees and listening to what they say back. Then I sell what I make down at market. The better-behaved ones, that is. My father was a tamer. Grandpa too. Back when anyone in the towns would buy tamed forest goods.'

'Cool,' said Jayben.

'*Cool?*' said Phee.

'Yes,' he said, downing his fourth bottle of juice and letting out a loud burp of pink bubbles. 'Tree-taming sounds cool.'

'Well,' said Tedrik, looking confused, 'it can be cool out there, in the spring and autumn. In the winter, it's freezing.'

'Oh.' Jayben laughed. 'No, I meant cool as in *good*. It sounds like fun.'

The family looked puzzled.

'Well,' Tedrik continued, 'it's fun when trees understand you. Takes years of practice. You can't just tell a tree to become a set of chairs, can you? Not if you want them to last. You have to get to know a tree and care for it, and listen. All my furniture told me what they wanted to be, and I carved them into it. A tree never forgets. If you're good to it, it will never let you down.'

'A tree never forgets?' said Jayben. He liked the sound of that, since he had forgotten *everything*.

There was a deep groan from the wooden beams of the house, and the candles flickered. The air was perfectly still, but they were dancing as if blown by a breeze.

Tedrik looked uneasy.

'Oinff! Oinff!' said Russog, running to hide under Larnie's chair.

There was another groan.

'Are the trees warning us again?' said Jayben. 'I *need* to know what's going on. I've waited long enough.'

Larnie looked at Tedrik, who gave a slight nod, and then seemed to decide something. 'You're right,' she said, standing. 'You deserve to know. Come through.'

Before Jayben followed Larnie through to the sitting room, he noticed Tedrik had gone to the window. He was peeking through the curtains. Then he double-checked the doors were locked.

What was he looking for out there in the woods? He said we would be safer here, didn't he?

CHAPTER 6

A Chord Between Worlds

Jayben sat down on a patchwork armchair by the fire. The chair's frame began to fidget and move, adjusting itself until it was the perfect size and shape for him.

Tedrik took a large tin from a shelf that was just out of skoggle-hopping range. It was full of brown nuts, the size of his fist.

'Help yourself, Jayben,' he said, placing them on the hearth of the fireplace. 'Best gribblenuts in this wood.'

Tedrik and Phee took a gribblenut each, gave them a shake and a good, hard whack on the bricks, cracking them in two. They held each half like a little cup, and the soft filling instantly fizzed and foamed into a steaming liquid.

'Amazing!' said Jayben, doing the same. He gulped his down so quickly he was left with a frothy moustache. It tasted like nutty hot chocolate.

'Aren't you gonna eat the shell?' said Tedrik, and to Jayben's surprise, they chomped into the outside, handing Russog a piece.

Jayben gobbled up the sweet, buttery shells. They were delicious, but sat heavily in his stomach as he waited for what the Fellers were about to tell him.

Larnie went to fetch something from a bookcase that was trembling.

'Here it is,' said Larnie, carrying a red leather-bound book over to him, with a title embossed in gold. 'In here is everything you need to know—'

The Book Of Dreamers

By The Scholars of Formadon

'What are Dreamers?' said Jayben, tracing his fingers over the lettering.

'Did you not wonder how you scared off a skallabore?' said Phee.

'Yes,' said Larnie, sitting down between them with her own gribblenut. 'What happened earlier, with that monster, the way it behaved with you is extremely, extremely – well, it's unheard of. Almost.'

There was another deep groan from the house, the fire faltered, and Tedrik lost the glow in his cheeks.

'What do you mean?' said Jayben, confused.

'Well,' said Tedrik, clutching the clanband on his wrist. 'Unheard of, for everyone but Dreamers.'

Everyone stared at Jayben, then Larnie pointed at the red book.

Below the title there was a gold symbol: a pipe-like object with a swirl at one end.

'Wait,' said Jayben. 'That looks just like—' He reached into his deep pocket and pulled out the slender object.

Larnie and Phee inhaled sharply.

'Told you.' Tedrik grinned, perched on Jayben's armrest. 'Jayben, now show 'em your hand. Go on.'

Jayben opened his left palm, and in the gentle firelight, the strange crystals sparkled red, blue, green and yellow.

'Plodding hoks!' whispered Larnie.

'It's okay.' Tedrik chuckled. 'He won't bite, will you, lad?'

Jayben said nothing. He was too busy comparing the mysterious thing from his pocket to the picture on the book's cover.

Phee's eyes were full of wonder. 'I can't believe I'm looking at it.'

'What?' said Jayben. 'What *is* it?'

Gently, Larnie took the book from Jayben and opened it to Chapter One:

The First Dreamer

'We call it the Golden Torch,' Larnie explained, 'but it's not just a Torch. There is a pipeline from this world to the Earth World, through which the Energy flows. And that object you hold there is one end of it.

'Both worlds need this Energy. It's a powerful memory force. It's what allows our brains, in Earth World and here in the Elf World, to access memory. Without it, people in either world forget who they are and struggle to think or form ideas. They become gullible and vulnerable and easily exploited. The Energy must flow equally and it only works if it comes from the opposite world.'

Larnie pointed to an old illustration of two parallel worlds, carefully drawn in pen and ink. Two spheres were joined by a long object – the same as the object held in Jayben's hand.

One sphere was labelled Earth World, the other Elf World. The slender stream connecting them was labelled the Golden Torch.

'Earth needs Energy from Elf World, and the Elf World needs it from Earth. We have always been connected, since the beginning of time. Our Energies must work together.'

Jayben pointed to Elf World. 'So this is where we are?'

'Yes,' Larnie said. 'This book was written by ancient scholars six centuries ago, at the end of the Magic Ages, one hundred years before the First Dreamer. It explains the long and binding connection between the two worlds. Now, buckle up, it's quite a long story, but you must listen carefully.' Larnie turned the page, settled more comfortably in her chair, and began to read.

The Earth and the Elf World have a relationship that reaches far back in history. In the **Magic Ages,** *the Energy flowed through the Golden Torch in both directions, allowing everyone in the Elf World and Earth World alike to remember, think and dream.*

Here, the Torch blazed day and night, with its dazzling violet flame.

But one dark day an angry giant took control of the Torch. He used a magic spell to put out the violet flame; only an invisible charge remained through the torch. And when the Torch is not lit with a fierce violet light, the Energy stream will only flow one way – to Earth.

The giant then hid the Torch away.

With the Torch now extinguished, Energy in the Elf World began to run out. The elves became forgetful. This worried their leaders. They began to use the trees to preserve jars of their memories and their history.

And so the five forests of the Elf World became the five **Memory Woods**.

Gradually, over time, the memories stored in the woods became less and less.

Elves forgot how to dream and so lost their old magic.

It was the end of the **Magic Ages**.

But there is hope. There is always hope. For a prophecy has been foretold. A prophecy of the Dreamers.

The **First Dreamer** shall come one hundred years from now, in the time of a tyrannical king, a ruler who will fear his people growing in power and so decide to destroy his people's remaining memories. He shall begin to burn the Memory Woods.

Then, upon a full moon night a young girl shall start to dream, seeing glimpses of another world – the Earth World. Rainbow crystals shall appear on her feet. People around her shall regain their memories.

Through these magical rainbow crystals, the girl shall draw Energy directly from the Earth World.

This is the First Dreamer. The Dreamer's name shall be **Sojan**.

Sojan shall find the **Golden Torch**. She will find a way to light it and the purple flames will release bursts of Energy to help her fellow elves restore their memories.

But the giant's spell is strong, and Sojan cannot keep the Torch alight for long. And when the Torch is not lit, the Energy stream will only flow one way – to Earth.

Soon after, Sojan shall see something in the woods – a chord between worlds, a doorway. Her dreams about the Earth World will become more vivid.

Sojan will gain the greatest power: the power to **Free-Dream**.

Free-Dreaming is to obtain objects from Earth –

and send Elf objects in return. With each object will come some Energy. Those nearby can regain their memories.

Sojan will spend her life travelling the world, Free-Dreaming Earthly objects. The tyrant shall be overthrown. Sojan shall become Queen, and all the objects she Free-Dreams shall continue to provide Energy even after she is gone, so that all elves may remember and think for themselves.

Larnie fell silent. Jayben was horrified and intrigued. He stared down at the illustration of Sojan, the blazing torch in her hand.

'She's cool,' he breathed.

Phee smiled. 'She was.'

'And that was just the beginning,' said Tedrik, turning the pages.

'Shall I carry on?' said Larnie.

And she began to read from Chapter Two.

The Second Dreamer

After Sojan's death, there shall be peace under her son King Malton. Elves will manage with what memories they have. But gradually greedy folk shall begin to

steal Sojan's Free-Dreams, to exploit new technologies from Earth and to guard the Energy for themselves, instead of sharing it freely. These wicked people shall leave communities to forget again and to live in fear. The world shall be ruled by these few greedy **Dream Thieves**.

Until, a decade after Sojan's death there shall come a Second Dreamer.

Another girl shall find rainbow crystals on her body. She shall light the Golden Torch with its purple flame and Free-Dream new objects from Earth, continuing Sojan's legacy. But like Sojan, she cannot keep the Torch alight for long.

Her name shall be **Vimajin**.

Through the centuries, there shall be many more Dream Thieves. And each time the Elf World is threatened, another child shall become a Dreamer, destined to put things right. They shall all light the Golden Torch, but keeping it lit will prove difficult. The giant's spell must be broken.

Larnie fell silent again. Jayben flicked through the book to pictures of each prophesied Dreamer in action, stopping at Chapter Eight.

The Eighth Dreamer

The image showed the Elf World and Earth World as spheres again – only this time they were in darkness.

'What happened there?' he asked.

'Maejac,' Larnie explained, 'the Eighth Dreamer, just a century ago – the poor boy made a terrible mistake. In an attempt to break the spell and fix the Golden Torch, he briefly closed the pipeline completely, for a moment leaving both worlds to forget. Thankfully his rainbow crystals meant that he was unaffected and was able to reactivate the pipeline, though it would still only flow one way. Once again, our world had to rely on what little Energy the remaining Free-Dreamed objects were giving off. Poor Maejac had rotten luck. He always struggled to control his power, which caused nightmares for those around him – people's worst fears coming true.

'Our current queen is a descendent of Sojan. When she first came to the throne as a young queen, she ordered her council to hide Free-Dreams across every realm in the Elf World, to keep them safe from any future Dream Thieves.'

'And what happened to the Golden Torch?' said

Jayben eagerly.

'Horrified by his mistake, Maejac never lit the Torch again, and had it locked away before he died. Then it went missing, all those decades ago. Nobody has seen it since.'

'Nobody?' asked Jayben, turning to page 142, the final chapter.

This time, Tedrik was the one to read.

The Ninth Dreamer

*Evil shall threaten the elves once more. A dark force will rise and plot to wipe every mind in the world. When all seems lost, **One Final Dreamer** shall appear with the Blue Moon, when the Southern Lights are aligned.*

On Earth a child shall see a Chord, and his mind will be taken far away, to the brain of his elfling self, in the Elf World.

He shall awaken a powerful Dreamer, with the Rainbow held in his hand. He shall find the Golden Torch, and harness his power to Free-Dream.

He alone must save every elf's mind from being wiped.

The Ninth Dreamer shall be the final Dreamer.

And this final Dreamer must light the Torch and

keep it burning with its violet flame, and break the giant's spell for good, so the Energy flows to both worlds, restoring memory to all and beginning a New Magic Age.

'Everyone's been waiting for the Ninth,' said Larnie. 'And last night, the night of a Blue Moon, we saw the Southern Lights. They aligned, just as the Book said. Now everybody knows there's a new Dreamer, somewhere. A child, like all the others in the Book.'

'It's you,' said Tedrik. 'You found the Golden Torch.'

Jayben inspected the Torch. 'But . . . I didn't find it. It was just in my pocket,' he said.

'Doesn't matter, lad,' said Tedrik. 'Maybe you found it and you've forgotten, we're not supposed to know how it came to you. Only that it's yours.'

'And you have the Rainbow,' said Phee. 'In your hand!'

Jayben looked closer at the crystals in the firelight, every colour glistening.

'We never imagined you would show up here in Ampelwed Village,' said Tedrik, 'and be sitting here in *our house*. But it has to be you, Jayben. You are the Ninth Dreamer. You will save our world from evil, to stop our memories being wiped for good.'

The logs on the fire hissed.

Jayben wasn't sure what he'd expected the Fellers to tell him, but it certainly wasn't this. How could he be this Dreamer who everyone had been waiting for? How could he save the world from evil— Wait . . .

'What evil?' he asked, his throat suddenly dry. It was one thing reading these stories in a book, but quite another to think that they might be real. 'What is the Ninth Dreamer supposed to save the world from?'

'A Dreamer,' said Tedrik. 'But no Dreamer of the Book. It's somebody wicked, using their power for evil.'

Larnie looked uneasy. 'The boy must be tired. We can talk more in the morning.'

But Jayben needed to know. 'Is that who was chasing us through the woods?'

Tedrik nodded slowly.

'But . . . I would know if I was a Dreamer, wouldn't I? I don't remember these Rainbow crystals,' he said. 'Or the Torch. Or anything.'

'I'm afraid that's how it works,' said Tedrik. He turned to page 143 and read the words aloud.

Like every Dreamer before him, his memory and power will be withheld. To unlock it he must find the chord, the same chord seen by his earthling on Earth.

*He must find it before the **Fifth Sundown** after he wakes, or both he and his earthling shall perish, and darkness shall reign ever after.*

'*Perish?*' said Jayben, his stomach turning. 'Fifth Sundown? But . . . the sun's already gone down tonight. Does that mean—' He broke off. It meant he had just four days to save a world he knew nothing about or he would die a horrible death. He put his head in his hands.

'It's all right,' said Larnie. 'You've got plenty of time.' She passed him another gribblenut.

'So, I'm here in the Elf World,' said Jayben, trying to make sense of this. 'But I have an earthling as well?'

'Yes. Your earthling is someone in the Earth World, who looks like you, born on the same day. The ancient scholars said we all have an earthling self but our minds are never connected, unless our earthling sees a chord.'

Jayben dropped the gribblenut, trying to imagine another version of himself, going about his life on earth, completely unaware that he existed in the Elf World. He had so many questions. 'What's a chord?'

'A chord between worlds, like in Sojan's story. It connects the two worlds. It's usually something that appears suddenly and doesn't quite make sense – it could be an extra room in your house that wasn't there before, or your school switching places with the local shop. If a person sees a chord on Earth, a doorway between the worlds opens, taking their mind far away, into the head of their elfling, here. The Rainbow crystals appear and they see glimpses of Earth, only in their sleep. They become a Dreamer. But their memories are temporarily lost in the process.'

'That's why you can't remember, lad,' said Tedrik. 'But don't worry, it's all in there. Your memory and your earthling's. They're just locked away. And it's vital you restore 'em.'

Jayben was comforted to know the memories weren't gone for ever, but that didn't get him any closer to finding them.

'To unlock 'em,' Tedrik continued, 'you need to find your chord, the one your earthling saw. It's the key to your memory – and your power. When the other Dreamers found theirs, they remembered their dreams, clear as day – memories from their Earth life.'

'Which meant they could Free-Dream!' said Phee. 'They only had to think of something from Earth World and they could bring it here!'

Jayben couldn't help feeling excited by the idea of bringing objects from another world. 'But . . . how can I find the chord if it's in the other world?'

Larnie bent over the Book again. 'Chords are identical in both worlds; two sides of a doorway.'

Jayben thought for a minute. He had no idea where to begin looking. The Book would have a clue. After all, the other Dreamers had been written about, so surely he would be in there as well. He turned to the last page in the book. It was completely blank but for the page number '144'.

'Where's the rest?' he asked, feeling panicked. 'Where's the picture of me, and my name?'

'This isn't the original Book,' Larnie explained. 'It's a copy, one of many. Most elf households have one. When the original Book was found, there were eighteen pages torn out. Every chapter was missing at least one. No one knows who removed them or why, nor what was written on them. So when these copies were printed, they left blank pages for the missing ones.'

'Why would someone tear them out?' said Jayben,

frustrated. There wasn't a single clue to help him find his chord.

'I reckon there was something important on those missing pages,' said Phee. 'Something big, something someone didn't want us to know.'

Russog raised his green snout and said in a toddler's voice, 'Bum stink!'

Larnie rolled her eyes. 'Yes, thank you, Russog. There are many theories about the missing pages, Jayben, though we may never know the truth of it. The original book was written by scholars six centuries ago, a hundred years before Sojan, the First Dreamer. It was discovered in the ruins of the Formadon palace. I understand that it is hard to trust something incomplete. But the Book has never been wrong. It has correctly predicted everything about the other eight Dreamers.'

Jayben suddenly felt exhausted. He yawned, rubbing his eyes.

'You need a good rest,' said Tedrik. 'A lot to do tomorrow.'

'Yes,' said Larnie, 'we'll take you to the Jarmaster. He can tell you a lot more than us, and he can help you in ways we can't.'

'Jarmaster?' asked Jayben.

She nodded. 'You need to hear the rest from him.'

'But,' said Phee, 'couldn't we tell him a bit more about—'

'In the morning,' said her mother firmly. 'You'll need all your energy, Jayben. There's a long journey ahead of you.' She closed the Book, stood up and put it back on the trembling bookcase.

'A journey to where?' said Jayben, putting the Torch back in his pocket.

'Last Rock,' said Tedrik. 'The capital city of Wenden, this realm of the Elf World. Where you'll find the Chordian Guard. They've helped all the other Dreamers find their chords. If anyone can help you find your chord, it's the Guard.'

'But first you need to get there,' said Larnie. 'The Jarmaster can help you with that, and tell you what you need to know. We'll set off first thing in the morning.'

Phee led Jayben up the stairs by a flickering lamplight.

He noticed halfway up that every step had a little carving beside it in the banister. Each carving was a different scene, intricately cut into the wood, and framed inside a circle, and each seemed to be alive, moving.

Phee explained they were her father's 'memorings,' one for every year since he had built the house. Each ring had a different memory from that year inside it, recorded by the wood that Tedrik had tamed. Jayben noticed that Phee was in each ring, but there were other children there too.

'Oh,' said Jayben, stopping on the seventeenth step. 'This one's not finished.' The circle was incomplete and there was no picture inside it.

'Yeah, that's this year. There won't be a picture inside until the last day of the year.'

'Cool,' he said, brushing past the leaves that were growing out of the banister. He wished there was a staircase capturing memories of *his* life. Maybe there was, in his parents' house. 'You're growing taller in each ring,' he said to Phee.

'Yeah,' she sighed. 'Caught in the same wood every year. What I would give to leave the forest for just one day, and not just be stuck at home because it's "safe".'

Jayben thought that Phee didn't know how lucky she was. To have parents who loved her and wanted to keep her safe at home with them.

She took him past the attic stairs and into a neat bedroom. It had wild leaves sprouting from its sloping roof, and everything was pink: pink walls and a pink

wardrobe, a pink vase of flowers on a pink dressing table and a little bed, neatly made with frilly blankets.

'This is Gram's old room,' said Phee, drawing the curtains. 'She liked pink – a lot. The last kid who stayed here wanted my room instead.'

'Thanks,' said Jayben, longing to fall into the bed.

Phee paused. 'Sorry, if I came off rude earlier. The last couple of foster kids were a bit of a handful. But you're . . . well, you're different.' She paused and smiled. 'I'm glad you're here, Ben. Sorry, I mean Jayben.'

Ben. Somehow the name Ben felt familiar; he liked it. 'You can call me Ben if you want, I don't mind.'

'Oh. Okay.' She put the lamp down and walked to the door. 'And thanks, for saving my dad today.'

'All comfy there?' said Larnie from the doorway, kissing her daughter goodnight.

'Good, thanks,' said Jayben, sitting on the bed. Exhaustion was clouding his thoughts, but his mind was buzzing.

'You're safe here,' said Larnie, pulling the curtains tightly shut. 'Have a good night's sleep, little one. Long day tomorrow.'

Tedrik grinned from the hall. 'G'night, lad.'

Jayben got into bed, fully clothed. The bed's frame contracted around him until it was perfectly

Jayben-sized. He turned, eyes still open. The bed hugged him tighter. He yawned and turned again, still pondering in the lamplight. He allowed himself to wish for a moment that he were a normal boy, with a memory and a home, not a Dreamer on a dangerous quest, with such a high risk of death.

But there was no wishing his way out of who he had to be.

The bed started to hum, gently vibrating his soft pillow. He took out the black disc from his pocket, engraved with his parents' message.

'As long as you have a home to find,' he read it again, 'you will never be lost.' Then he closed his eyes, falling into the sleep where he would find his first dream.

CHAPTER 7

A Spiral Village

Jayben stands amid trees and there is water running nearby, but he can't see it. Instead, he sees an archway with a wide frame. It's covered with tiny, white glowing gems, their lights piercing the mist . . .

He walks through it and finds himself in a dark cave of shadows and screams. There's a noise behind him. Somehow he knows it's a monster, though he can't see it. He hears its rasping breath, its heavy footsteps. Somehow he knows it's hunting him. He runs. His heart's pounding. He can see a faint light ahead. The monster is getting closer. In the distance he can hear singing. He runs towards the light—

Jayben woke.

He took deep breaths, heart still thumping loudly at the memory of his dream. He looked around at the pink bedroom. Light beamed through the curtains from the early morning sunshine, swaying in the gentle breeze. The singing he'd heard in his dream was coming from behind the door, and there was a delicious smell too.

Then the house groaned around him and everything he'd been told the night before came back to him. He felt a knot in his stomach. But the sun was up. At last he could get on his way and get some answers from the Jarmaster, whoever they might be. He couldn't say he was looking forward to hearing more about this evil Dreamer he had to face, but on balance he felt it was better to know than to not.

He leapt out of bed, still dressed, and opened the door to a bleary-eyed Phee with spectacularly messy hair.

'Morning, Ben,' she grinned, heading down the stairs.

He followed her down and into the kitchen, where he was greeted by the perky little skoggle.

'Oinff! Oinff!'

'Morning, Russog,' he said, and his stomach rumbled.

'Ah!' said Larnie in the kitchen, bright-eyed and wearing a mint-green dress. 'Good morning. I was just coming to wake you. Did you sleep well?'

'Yes, thanks.'

'Fabulous! Do you remember where you are?'

He nodded. *There was that at least*, he thought wryly to himself, even if he couldn't remember any of the important stuff. He'd dreamt last night, he was sure of it, something about a monster in a cave – but it was misting up already, retreating to some corner of his mind. Something told him it might be important and he should hang on to it, but it was difficult.

His stomach rumbled again.

'Come and have some breakfast,' said Larnie, rushing to the open front door. 'Tedrik!' she called, 'Jayben's up! Tedrik's just outside feeding the animals.'

Jayben sat down and got stuck into the morning feast, guzzling three bottles of flumjuice and wolfing down a buttery waffle dripping with syrup. Every taste and texture was a welcome distraction from the stress building in his head.

'Morning, lad!' said Tedrik, wiping his big boots at the front door and joining them at the table. 'Plodding hoks! You don't mess about with breakfast, do you, Jayben?'

The same twig of the cheeky table was tickling Jayben's leg again. 'What animals were you feeding?' he said, devouring his third berry muffin with a slice of cheese.

'Trox,' said Tedrik. 'Not much between their antlers but they've got steady hooves. I'll take you to meet 'em when we're done.'

Russog looked up from his bowl and said in Larnie's voice, 'You left Maddle behind at market?'

'What's that?' said Phee, tying her hair back in a ponytail. 'Is Maddle okay?'

Tedrik sighed, shaking his head at Russog. 'Thank you, fluff-nugget. Didn't know you were listening last night . . . Maddle's fine, love, I just didn't want her to get injured protecting me so I left her behind. She was back home this morning. Nothing a few nomseeds couldn't fix.'

'I assumed she'd come back with you and Jayben,' she said, jumping up from the table. She turned to Jayben. 'Maddle is one of our pet trox, I'll introduce you.' She turned back to her father. 'Actually, can I show Jayben Maddle now?'

'When you're ready for school,' said Larnie, scraping leftovers into Russog's bowl. 'Could you help Jayben find some spare clothes?'

Jayben shook his head. This was not what he'd had in mind. 'I thought we were going to that Jarmaster person? You said they'd tell me everything and help me get to the city.'

Larnie smiled. 'Don't worry. We'll find him near the village school, where I teach.'

'My mentor,' said Tedrik, 'the Jarmaster. He'll know how to get you to Last Rock. And you never know, he might even have a jar of memories under your name, if you're from around this wood.'

Jayben felt a flutter of excitement. *'Memories? Of mine?'*

Tedrik shrugged. 'Worth checking. You deserve a bit of luck, with everything ahead of you.'

Jayben leapt to his feet. 'I'm ready,' he said. 'Thanks for breakfast. Which way is school? Beyond the big red trees?'

'Goodness, no!' said Larnie. Then she chuckled, pointing at his bare feet. 'You might need boots too. Come on, let's get you sorted . . .'

Phee went off to change into a pale-yellow shirt and shorts. She found some fresh clothes and boots for Jayben, left by one of the previous foster boys. The sky-blue shirt almost fitted, and the boots weren't too tight. Jayben checked the Golden Torch and the black engraved object were safely buttoned up in the brown cargo shorts.

Then Larnie bandaged his hand to hide the Rainbow crystals. 'We don't want everyone knowing who you are yet,' she explained. 'Not until you've got your power.' She tied a plain brown string around his wrist in place of a clanband, to help him blend in.

Phee insisted on checking on the trox before school.

Jayben waited at the stable door, keen to leave. It was a tall, dim hut. A musky, leathery smell hit him before three enormous four-legged creatures with antlers and thick fur stepped out of the shadows.

'They're massive!' he said, intrigued. There was something about animals; he found their presence calming.

'Yeah,' Phee agreed. 'They're bred for speed and stamina and can run for a long time.'

Phee introduced him to the trox. They were all female. The biggest was Maddle, whose coat was chocolate brown, and stood two feet taller than Tedrik. The other two trox were Keylo, a redhead speckled with white spots, and Woodge, who was golden brown.

Phee led the creatures out to graze. 'They're stubborn as old trees, but they can't talk, which I like.'

Jayben opened a bucket of their favourite nomseeds, and soon the trox were happily blowing hot air on to his face from their furry nostrils.

'It tickles!' he said, walking back to the path. 'Are they coming with us?'

'Not to school,' said Tedrik, saddling Maddle. 'I'm going to ride back to market, for the wagon. We'll need it later.'

'You're going back *already*?' said Phee. 'After the skallabore? And what if you hear whispering again?'

'Whispering?' said Jayben. The knot in his stomach twisted.

'Trees will warn me.' Tedrik shrugged and put his arm around Phee. 'The drumming's stopped. I'm sure it's safer now, especially now Jayben is here with us. I'll be back before you know it.'

Tedrik popped a pair of earplugs into his ears and climbed on to Maddle's back. 'Honestly, I'll be fine, love. Won't hear any whispers with these in.' He smiled. 'Love you. Take care of Jayben. I'll see you back here later.' And Maddle trotted down the lane, until they were out of sight.

Jayben bombarded Larnie and Phee with questions about Ampelwed and the realm of Wenden, all the way to school. If he wasn't talking or listening, his mind was dwelling on the lines from the Book about perishing and darkness reigning ever after.

The lane never straightened, curving to the right between the enormous trees. Soon, there were more floating mailboxes, and thatched cottages knitted closer together. Jayben discovered that Ampelwed was a spiral village, and they were nearing the middle: a winding parade of shops and bakeries, and cheerful Ampelwedians busy doing their morning chores.

Admiring the cottages and shops with their lopsided doors and odd-shaped windows, Jayben felt that same sense of comfort and familiarity he had felt on first seeing the Feller house. These unusual buildings felt *right* to him.

They passed a fruit shop, where a man held a bunch of floating pink flums on strings. They passed a pet shop, where a woman held two baskets of baby skoggles, just hatched with bits of blue eggshell stuck to their green fluff.

One of the baskets had a sign attached reading:

Half Price!
(May already know rude words)

Jayben noticed a man in a bookshop window, taking down a banner that read:

Happy Blue Moon Day!
Dreamers of History on sale here!

An old woman was talking to the man inside as they walked past. 'Didn't you hear them trees last night?' she said. 'Something was trying to get in from the other side.'

'Really?' said the man.

Jayben paused, listening.

'Oh, yes,' she said. 'Haven't heard a racket like it since the last time them wicked lot tried getting through the big reds. They'll be after the Ninth all right. The Book is never wrong.'

Jayben's gut turned. What wicked lot? People working for the evil Dreamer?

The man laughed. 'You don't really think the Ninth will have appeared up this neck of the woods?'

'I'm telling you, someone was trying to get in. I reckon the poor kid's closer than you think.'

CHAPTER 8

What Null Wants

'Here we are,' said Larnie. They had reached a brass sundial at the foot of a gigantic tree with helical branches: the centre of the spiral village. It was bustling with children who were making their way up a ramp that curled around the tree's broad red trunk.

'This is our helicorn tree,' explained Phee, following the other children.

Jayben's apprehension was building. He followed her to the top, where the children followed a deck around the sap-dripping treehouse, but Jayben stopped with Phee and Larnie outside the entrance. Larnie knocked on the door. A sign read:

JARMASTERY

'Hello! Hello!' came a cheerful voice, and the door swung itself open.

'Good morning, Jarmaster,' said Larnie. 'A moment, please?'

A jolly-looking little man stood inside. 'A pleasure to see you, always, Mrs Feller,' he said, straightening his mustard bow-tie and shifting one of two pairs of glasses on to his bald head, hooked on by his pointy ears. 'Come in, come in.'

Jayben's eye was drawn to the man's white beard. It was *moving*. Three little red seeds were nestled in the thick hair, tickling each other with their tiny shoots. Was this strange man really the one who could help?

Jayben stepped into a trove of treasures. Hundreds of glass jars in various colours hung on wires stretching in through windows on one side, and out through the windows on the other. Each jar had a label and inside were all sorts of things – jewels, coins, old tickets, sticks and shells. Some were glowing, others hummed, and there were no two alike.

'This is where family memories are kept safe,' Larnie explained, 'where the spirit of an elf's life can be drawn out of personal keepsakes and absorbed by family charms, to be worn by the next generation.'

What if Jayben *was* from this wood? What if he *did* have a jar in this tree? He desperately hoped he could be so lucky.

Larnie smiled. 'This is Jayben. Any chance we might have a jar under that name?'

'Pleased to meet you,' said the Jarmaster, spinning a wooden wheel, and with a few loud clinks and clangs the wires began moving and the jars rattled around the tree and in through the window, until labels with names beginning with 'J' started rolling in.

Jamfred . . . Jexie . . . Jimothy . . . They tinkled through. Jonnifer . . . Jorbet . . . Juxton . . . and then Kayzie.

The Jarmaster stopped the wheel and shook his head. Jayben's heart sank.

Larnie sighed. 'Thank you for checking. We're going to need a new one.'

'New foster boy?' said the Jarmaster. He took an empty jar from a shelf and handed it to Jayben.

'He has nothing to jar yet,' said Larnie, 'but we need your help with something else. Something big. This cannot leave the treehouse, Jarmaster.'

The Jarmaster sat down as they explained.

He even stopped fiddling with his bow-tie. He looked flabbergasted by the time they'd finished.

He stared at Jayben. '*You* are the Ninth Dreamer?' he said wonderingly. 'I must have eaten one too many dragonflakes this morning.'

'He doesn't have a clanband either,' said Phee. 'He can't remember anything at all.'

'Well that's to be expected, if he's the Dreamer,' said the Jarmaster. 'We can find him a charm though.'

'I guess,' said Jayben. 'What are these charms for?'

'For luck,' the Jarmaster explained. He glanced at a wooden chest and whistled. A drawer opened, spilling dozens of glasses and bow-ties in every colour. He tutted at the chest. 'Not that one, you daft old thing.'

Phee laughed, then covered her mouth when she saw her mother glaring.

'Has your father been tinkering with this?' the Jarmaster joked. He whistled again and another drawer opened with five compartments, containing hundreds of tiny charms. 'These are from the five elf clans of the five Memory Woods. Your clan is named after the wood where your family lived, back in the Magic Ages. Pity you don't know what charm you wore before. You're going to need a lot of luck.'

Jayben shrugged again. He put his empty jar down

and pulled the shiny black object from his pocket. 'Well, I have this from my mum and dad.'

'What a superb compass!' said the Jarmaster, flipping it open to reveal a silver navigational dial inside. 'Black nortwood. Very rare.'

Jayben gasped. He hadn't known it could open. 'What's a compass?'

'Golly!' said the Jarmaster. 'You really have forgotten everything, haven't you? A compass shows you which way to go. But this is an interesting one. Usually South is at the top of the dial – but it's North on here. Look.' He tapped the little disc.

'What a beautiful message from your parents,' said Larnie, reading the engraving.

Phee peered eagerly at the words. 'I bet they're explorers, Ben! Maybe that's why you're not with them.'

Jayben took the compass back and put it in his pocket. 'Is that my charm, then?'

'Afraid not,' said the Jarmaster. 'A charm must hold the spirit of a relative who has died. It brings us luck from the old magic in our blood. And of course, only the seeds of five types of helicorn tree can hold spirits: the old trees of the five Memory Woods.'

Jayben sighed. Everything seemed so difficult. He'd

thought that coming here would give him answers, not make him feel even more lost. Then he noticed something colourful on the wall, a map of the Elf World.

It was divided into five realms, and within each realm there was a forest – one of the Memory Woods. One forest was called Trollwood, another was Dragonwood. Then there was Spritewood and Fairywood.

But it was Giantwood that caught his eye, in the realm called Wenden. There was the village of Ampelwed, beside an illustration of a green skoggle. Wait. *Did the skoggle just blink?*

'We didn't tell him yet,' said Larnie, drawing Jayben's attention back to the Jarmaster, 'about the other Dreamer. You were so tired last night, Jayben.' She blushed. 'And we thought that you, Jarmaster, would be the best person to—'

'It's quite all right,' said the Jarmaster, taking both pairs of glasses off his head. 'It's hard to tell a child something like that.'

'Tell me what?' said Jayben, his frustration building again.

'He is an adult Dreamer,' said the Jarmaster. 'Using his power for evil.'

Jayben was dumbfounded. 'An *adult*? But . . . I thought Dreamers were always kids?'

The Jarmaster nodded, and the three seeds in his beard hid.

'Six years ago,' he explained, 'a masked adult appeared in this world, with Rainbow crystals on their arm. Never seen without the mask but reportedly male, he became known in the woods as "Null". Nobody knows his real name. Null found a chord. He was able to harness the power of Free-Dreaming and connect to his earthling.

'We Jarmasters span every realm, overseeing personal memories of every elf. Ordinarily we would never share the secrets of the jars. But these are not ordinary times, and we've been passing critical information between the woods. We know it was a witch from the North called Snaggis, of Spritewood, who helped Null find his chord. They are working together, both hungry for power. Null argues that *he* is the Ninth Dreamer.'

'So, then . . . if Null is the Ninth Dreamer, what does that make me?' said Jayben.

'Well,' said the Jarmaster. 'Null is not the Ninth Dreamer the Book tells us of.'

'He's a fraud.' Phee frowned. 'A liar. Those town

idiots might believe him and call him the Ninth but up here, we called him Null.'

Jayben was puzzled. 'But if he could Dream before me, then he *is* the Ninth, isn't he?'

'Yes and no,' said the Jarmaster. 'According to the Book, the final Dreamer will mend the Torch, so that Energy flows to both worlds, restoring memory and thought to all and beginning a New Magic Age. We Jarmasters believe that Null wants to do the opposite.'

Larnie put her arm around her daughter.

'You mean he wants to *break* the Torch?' said Jayben. 'And end the flow of Energy for ever? But why?'

'Null wants total control,' said the Jarmaster, 'and we believe he has a dark plan to conquer both worlds.'

'Both worlds?' said Larnie, sitting down on a stool.

'What do you mean?' said Phee.

The Jarmaster whispered, 'According to our Jarmasters in the realm of Bramalan, Null plans to find the Torch and close it like the Eighth Dreamer did, closing the pipeline, only this time permanently. With the Rainbow crystals on his arm, Null alone would still receive Energy. He would still be able to remember and form ideas. Everyone else's memories would be wiped. Both worlds in darkness. Null and his earthling free to rule them both.'

'But that's horrible,' whispered Jayben.

'Yes,' said the Jarmaster. 'But Null doesn't have the Torch. It's been missing for decades. While he's been hunting for it, he's found other ways to cause harm and take control . . .

'Null whispers a spell on the wind everywhere he goes. Any adult who hears it can no longer absorb the Energy from Free-Dreams and is left all but brain-dead. Then they start whispering the same spell, spreading the curse to any adult listening.'

'We call them nullheads,' said Phee. 'And their spells are the whispers. They don't affect children, only adults. That's why grown-ups have to wear earplugs if they leave the forest.'

Jayben felt sick. 'That's horrible,' he said.

'It is,' said the Jarmaster. 'And that's not all. Null has told the townspeople a terrible lie. He's told them that their loved ones have become nullheads, or "stupids" as he calls them, because us forestfolk have stolen the hidden Free-Dreams from their towns and are hoarding them in the woods. He calls us Dream Thieves.'

'So dumb,' said Phee. 'Who would believe that?'

'Frightened people will believe many things,

Pheetrix. Enraged, the nullheads' families set forest fires, burning our Memory Wood. We keep putting them out as best we can, but they strike again. So many stories lost. Null has promised the nullheads' families that if they help him find the Golden Torch and gather every existing Free-Dream, Energy will be restored for them. They will live rich and happy in the city of Free-Dreams he's building in Bramalan, while the forestfolk will be enslaved.

'These people are now his "Agents of the Ninth", searching the realms for the Golden Torch.'

The wicked people, thought Jayben.

'Forestfolk do not believe this new Dreamer is the true Ninth. He did not appear with a Blue Moon and the Southern Lights like the other Dreamers. He doesn't have the Torch. We know him to be a fraud. We've been waiting for the true Ninth to come and defeat him, and now – here you are.'

Jayben felt goosebumps all over and he sat up straight. He'd asked for the truth and now he'd got it. This was all on him.

'We all knew the Blue Moon was coming,' the Jarmaster continued, 'and to see the Southern Lights aligning the other night – pure elation! Now the forestfolk know there is a new Dreamer, somewhere, just like our eight great heroes in history. It's given hope to every elf in the woods. The Queen and the Chordian Guard will be readying themselves—'

'Who are these Chordian Guard people?' Jayben asked.

'An ancient society of scholars charged with protecting the Dreamer. I know one of them. They can help you find your chord, and learn how to Free-Dream.'

'But Null's Agents of the Ninth will be ready too,' said Larnie. 'Null is terrified the true Ninth Dreamer of the Book will reveal themselves. He's set all his Agents hunting for you – the imposter, he calls you.'

'So are they the wicked people Tedrik talked about?' asked Jayben.

She nodded.

'Dreamers give off a purple light, or so the Book says,' said Jarmaster. 'The Guard made special purple lenses to help them spot Dreamers from a distance – but Null has stolen some of these glasses and given them to his Agents.'

'You mean I'm giving off purple light?' Jayben looked around at the windows, wondering if it could be seen from outside. 'How can I hide it?'

'It'll be very dim until you find your chord, almost

impossible to spot deep in this wood – but you should still be careful.'

It wasn't much reassurance. However dim, giving off a light only visible to the Agents hunting him was a terrifying thought.

'It is best you know,' said the Jarmaster slowly. 'You have the power to turn the Torch back on again. Once you find your chord you will be just as powerful as Null and that, I'm afraid, is why he wants you—' The Jarmaster broke off, looking pained.

'What is it?' said Jayben. 'Please tell me.'

The Jarmaster sighed. 'He'll want you brought to him alive so that your Rainbow crystals are active. He will want to fuse them with his own. It would make him twice as powerful, and it would kill you. Then there will be nobody to stop him ruling two worlds.' The Jarmaster put his hand on Jayben's shoulder. 'What Null wants is the Torch, your crystals, and then you – dead.'

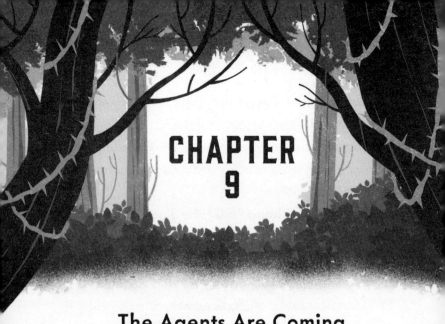

CHAPTER 9

The Agents Are Coming

Jayben was frozen in shock. He was only a kid and the most powerful and evil person in the world wanted him dead.

He glanced up and saw the fearful expressions on Phee and Larnie's faces. It helped him focus. Failure was not an option. He had to think not just of himself but of everyone else in this world – and on Earth. He had no choice but to swallow his worries and face the challenge.

'You have the Golden Torch, don't you?' said the Jarmaster.

Jayben pulled it out of his pocket. He saw himself reflected in it again. He looked at his bandaged hand,

concealing his Rainbow crystals, and tried to remember his strange dream. 'I am a Dreamer,' he said. 'I know that now. But the Torch . . . what if I close it, by accident, like the Eighth Dreamer did? What if I close the pipeline?'

'The Guard will show you how to use it. You can't control it yet, so don't worry. Once you've found your chord, then you can light it.'

Jayben fought down panic. 'The Book says it must be found before the Fifth Sundown or I'll perish! It could be anywhere!'

'The Guard will help you,' the Jarmaster said firmly. 'If it is somewhere, then it can be found. To quote Sojan, the First Dreamer: *If it's not impossible, then you can do it.*'

The words spoke to something deep inside Jayben, a fierce determination to overcome hopelessness. It would be hard, but that didn't mean it was impossible. He'd be following in the footsteps of eight great Dreamers before him.

'Okay,' he said, rising to his feet. 'Where do I start?'

The Jarmaster stood too, beaming. 'I'll fetch the marshal. We need to get you to the city as safely and quickly as possible. It'll take three whole days. Last Rock is the northernmost point of this realm, Wenden.

Once there, the Guard will help you find your chord.'

'Before Null finds *you*,' said Phee.

The Jarmaster hooked Jayben's empty jar on the line between Jamfred and Jexie. 'We must all act normally to avoid any suspicion. Mrs Feller, you take them to school and I'll bring the marshal to you.'

'But . . .' said Jayben, frustrated that it could take days just to reach the Chordian Guard, when he only had four days left to find the chord, 'can't I come with you to the marshal?'

The Jarmaster chuckled. 'A boy out of school in the morning? With no memory?' He shook his head. 'It's too much of a red flag. There could be Agents undercover in these woods. Don't you worry, I'll be as quick as a pippit. I know the marshal was dealing with something just outside the village. You're safe here. Well, as safe as you can be . . .'

The Jarmaster took his charm off his clanband, a tiny, square blue nutshell, and handed it to Jayben. 'Today, you're an honorary Trollwood. Whatever magic's in your blood, I'm sure the old trolls will gladly lend you some luck.'

Jayben grinned, admiring the scratched little charm. 'Thank you,' he said. 'I'll find that chord.'

'By the Fifth Sundown,' the Jarmaster said, nodding.

'Plenty of time. Like the eight greats before you. Fear not, the Book is never wrong.'

'This way,' said Larnie, leading Phee out of the door.

Jayben went to follow them, but the Jarmaster caught his arm. 'Two more things,' the Jarmaster said to Jayben, putting both pairs of glasses back on his head. 'Rainbow crystals draw the old magic from your blood, and from the blood of those closest to you. Our ancestors had magic abilities, different for each clan. In the wrong hands this power could do great harm. Take care when choosing your friends.'

'Okay,' said Jayben uneasily. He heard Larnie greeting her students outside.

'And lastly,' said the Jarmaster, as the little seeds poked their shoots back out of his beard, 'once you can recall Dreams vividly, mind what you bring to this world, and what you send to the other. For you are swapping one thing for another. Your predecessors told of Free-Dreams causing much trouble for their earthlings: fierce creatures appearing in Earth classrooms, cursed crystals on the shelves of Earth shops . . . Free-Dreaming is the greatest power we know. It must never be used lightly.'

And with that, the Jarmaster dismissed him.

Jayben followed Larnie and Phee outside and around the treehouse, his mind full of everything he had just learnt. They were met by a noisy rabble of children coming up the ramp.

Phee held Jayben back a few paces and lowered her voice. 'Don't say a word about any of this, okay? There are still grown-ups coming in and out of the giant reds, for work. There's always a risk news could spread. The whole village would be so excited! Especially the kids.' She smiled wistfully. 'We've been stuck here for so long, knowing that terrible things are happening outside and not being able to do anything to help. You're lucky, you get to *do* something, while all we can do is wait.'

Jayben nodded, but he couldn't help wishing, once again, that he had what Phee seemed to take for granted: the stability and comfort of a home and loving parents.

'I remember when we could go anywhere,' said Phee dreamily, 'even out of the woods. That was before Null, of course. Before the townsfolk hated us, before grown-ups had to wear earplugs to leave the forest. I'm not saying I'm not grateful. Those big red trees around the village protect us. Their furry bark stops the whispers and fires coming in.'

Jayben recalled seeing trees with scorched bark

and singed branches in the forest before he had passed through the big red tree. Those trees had protected the village.

'That's why I wish Dad would stop leaving to sell his chairs. We've lost too many grown-ups already – to the fires and to the whispers.'

'So why don't *you* go to sell the chairs? If kids aren't affected by the whispers?'

'I wish! But everywhere is dangerous if you're from the woods.'

She subtly pointed to some of her classmates coming up the ramp.

'Dax has a foster family now,' she said, gesturing to a broad-shouldered boy in a wheelchair. 'He lost his when the townsfolk started burning the forest.' She nodded at another boy and a girl. 'Norwin lost his dad too, over in Jonningwed. Pannabell lives with her grandmother. They all moved up here, away from the fires. So many families and memories gone.'

Jayben swallowed. He couldn't remember his family – but at least he had the hope of finding them. If that was taken away from him . . . well, he didn't want to think about it. He couldn't imagine how awful it would be to know they were gone for ever.

Jayben watched Norwin trailing along, aggressively

ripping flowers from the tree, Pannabell stumbling behind him, her face buried in her book. He felt their pain, frustration, and anger.

He could stop others suffering like them – if he could find his chord.

'Come on!' Larnie called. She was standing at the rear of the Jarmastery, at the top of a very long slide, woven through the helical branches. Beside it was a stack of old doormats. She grabbed a mat, placed it on the slide, sat down and *WHOOSH!* she zipped off, into the trees.

'Wow!' said Jayben.

Phee chucked a mat down for him, and he followed Larnie, shooting through the branches, the hanging jars clinking all around him.

'*Whoa!*' he yelled in exhilaration, whizzing down over the village rooftops, then crossing a glistening lake, through a hole in a hedge and BAM! He landed sideways on a bed of moss, by a tree stump that was spitting out pencils.

Jayben stood up, laughing. 'What was *that*?'

Larnie grinned, standing and dusting herself off. 'I'm glad you enjoyed it. Some teachers find it a bit much in the morning, but I like my students wide awake.'

Phee shot down behind him, landing on her feet. 'Nice landing, Ben!'

She caught a couple of the pencils spat out by the tree trunk, and handed one to him. Then they followed her classmates along the lake, passing a sign that read:

Don't run!
Skipping is more fun

Ahead of them were several wooden huts – 'Our classroom,' Phee told him cheerfully. And then—

Jayben felt dazed. He looked down to find himself strapped into a wooden cart, spattered with mud, wearing shinpads, kneepads, shoulderpads and a helmet on top of his head. The trees were quiet. *What just happened? Where was he? Where was Phee?*

He felt his heart rate quicken, and his palms were sweating. Then he heard a cheer, which pulled him back into the present. It was Phee's friend Dax, from another cart, a gold medal around his neck. 'That was awesome, Jayben! How many d'ya get?'

Jayben didn't answer. He tried to, but he couldn't. He couldn't move. He kept staring down in the dirt, holding in the rising panic.

Everything felt heavy and fuzzy. Like Jayben was somehow outside of himself, trapped.

'Ben?' asked Phee, unstrapping herself from her own cart, and coming to his side wearing a yellow helmet with two antlers on top. 'You okay?'

And then, just like that, Jayben was free. He could move his eyes and head. He turned to face the others.

'Are you all right?' Phee repeated, looking concerned.

'I don't know,' he said. His cheeks were hot, his eyes welling with tears. He looked around at his cart. 'What were we doing?'

Phee looked confused. 'We just crossed the finish

line, remember? Playing Rackem? You were great!'

Jayben felt a rush of fear and the panic he'd pushed down earlier rose up again. *He couldn't remember.* The last thing he remembered was arriving at Larnie's classroom this morning. What time was it now?

'Don't worry,' Phee said. 'This probably wasn't a good idea. Let's get you back to Mum.'

All Jayben knew was that he had lost more time, time he couldn't afford. He tried to get his head together, looking around. There was a large barn full of carts and sports equipment. He could see the lake, still half-shaded by the trees. Their shadows were long, so he knew the sun hadn't risen much. *It's still morning,* he thought, trying to calm himself. *It will be okay.*

'One more race?' said Dax, rolling back and forth in his cart. 'Let's hit the Koji Track!'

'No,' said Phee. 'Mum said one quick game while she gets the Jarmaster. Ben needs to get back now so—' She stopped, distracted as she tipped her face up towards the sun and inhaled.

Jayben felt a wave of hot air and a strange, bitter smell filled his nostrils. 'What is that?' asked Jayben.

Suddenly Pannabell came running from the barn, her eyes wide and frightened.

'*Run!*' she cried. 'The Agents are coming!'

CHAPTER 10

The Dreaded Whispers

Jayben tugged off his straps, questions racing through his head. Where were the Agents? Had they spotted his faint purple light through the trees? Were they coming for him? For the Torch? He checked his pocket. It was still there.

The wind changed direction, churning the leaves and blowing tiny hot embers around them, and everyone was visibly petrified.

Then the wind dropped, there was an ominous rumble, and—

SMASH!

The windows of the barn shattered and they could hear something – the crackle of flames. Smoke began

to fill the barn. The roof was on fire.

'NO!' cried Dax, wheeling himself towards the enormous doors.

'This place is meant to be safe!' said Norwin.

Every tree started drumming loudly, hammering the alarm, sending it deep into the woods.

A window shattered and the sudden rush of air ignited the hot dust inside, exploding and throwing Dax from his cart on to the cobbles.

'Dax!' cried Phee, rushing to help him as more explosions ripped through the barn.

Phee leapt from her cart, grabbed Dax and pulled him back to the others.

Everything dimmed as the smoke thickened. They watched helplessly as the roof of the old building of treasures groaned and collapsed.

'Back to school!' said Jayben, adrenalin racing.

Phee helped Jayben unbuckle himself and brought Dax his wheelchair.

Norwin got out of his cart and put his helmet back on. Dax pulled himself into his chair and everyone hurried to a red-brick gate. As they reached it, there was a loud crack, and a tree fell, crushing their exit. The forest behind it was burning up.

Pannabell panicked. 'No. No. No. No.' She covered

her ears to block out the beating trees and the whining barn as the heat from the fire intensified. 'Not again,' she whimpered.

Phee put her arm around her. 'We'll go the long way. Down past the—'

'There!' A woman's voice hollered from behind.

They spun around to see a woman in a red coat charging towards them on a white trox, and Mrs Feller clinging to the back of her saddle. Larnie jumped down and swiftly counted the children.

'Thank goodness you're all right,' said Larnie. Her eyes met the awful site of the Rackem barn, reduced to rubble. 'Plodding hoks!' she cried. 'This cannot be happening. We were always safe inside the ring of giant reds.'

The woman in the red coat nodded grimly. 'They are getting bolder – or more desperate.' She nodded at Jayben. 'I'm the marshal. You must be the new boy.'

'Can we go back to the school?' asked Jayben.

'No,' said Larnie. 'Well, I – we – we can't go back there. Not now.'

'Sure we can,' said Norwin. 'If we go past the old—'

'There is no school,' said the marshal bluntly, her spurs rattling as she jumped down from her saddle.

'Agents,' she said. 'Must be. The school is gone.'

Phee was horrified. 'But the big reds? They wouldn't let Agents in, would they?'

'We can go round the lake,' Larnie said, gathering herself.

The marshal nodded. 'Mrs Feller, you take my trox. Get the children home as fast as you can. Jayben, come with me.' She drew her sword from its holster and marched towards the other gate. Then she stopped at the sight of an old man on the other side. 'Out of the way, sir!' she called. 'You need to get back to safety!'

'It's Mr Triffit,' said Larnie, frowning. 'What's he doing out here?'

The old man didn't respond. He was staring at them, shuffling slowly through the gate as if nothing was happening. His face wore no expression but his mouth was moving, the words drowned out by the noise of the fire and the frantic trees.

The marshal froze. 'He's one of them, get back—' Then she broke off and dropped her sword.

'What's wrong?' said Jayben, grabbing the marshal by the arm. It was limp.

The old man shuffled closer, eyes vacant, and that's when Jayben heard it from his lips, a few words in some other language: the dreaded whispers.

'No!' he said, grabbing the marshal to pull her back, but it was too late.

All emotion had gone from her face. She stumbled but didn't blink, then turned slowly to face the others. Her mouth began to form words.

'Cover your ears, Larnie!' Jayben shouted.

Larnie was already screwing her earplugs in, backing away from the null-headed marshal. She held the bridle of the white trox, her other arm around the other children, leading them away from the terrible figure. 'Jayben, come!' she called.

Jayben looked back at the marshal, at her expressionless face. She had been the one who was going to guide him to the city, to the Guards – and now she was a nullhead. He tried to control his breathing as his heart thumped in his chest. He felt in his pocket, reassured by the heavy weight of the Torch and the compass. Then he remembered the Jarmaster's words: '*Last Rock . . . the northernmost point of this realm.*'

Suddenly he realised. *The furthest north.* The compass was more than reassurance; it could show him the way. The bandage on his hand had come loose, exposing the Rainbow, which gleamed in the light.

I can do this.

'Go!' said Jayben, raising his hand so that his crystals flashed at the others. 'Get everyone safe, Larnie. I'm going to find that chord. I'm going to Last Rock.'

'But the Jarmaster—' said Larnie.

'No!' he said. 'Just me. I'm putting you all in danger just by being here. I'm leaving the big reds, the way I came in.'

'I know a shortcut, Ben,' said Phee, pointing to the carts they had ridden for the game. 'I can get you there faster than a trox. Up the cart lift.'

'Good!' he said, hurrying to the carts.

Larnie held her daughter's eye, then nodded. She took a deep breath. 'All right,' she said, helping Pannabell on to the large white trox. 'But I will see you at home, Phee,' she said, and she hurried out through the gate.

Phee didn't reply, running back to her cart, still wearing her yellow helmet. She leapt inside.

'Over there,' she said, using her arms to wheel herself in the direction of a watermill at the bottom of the hill.

'How does this work?' said Jayben, jumping into his cart and spinning his wheels beside her.

She grabbed a rope hanging from a chain and hooked it to her cart. Jayben copied and the chain

pulled them forward, powered by the watermill. They travelled up the hill, between the trees, their wheels rolling over old roots, and soon they escaped the smoke, reaching a ledge at the top of the lift.

'This way!' she shouted, jumping from her cart.

Jayben leapt out, next to a sign reading:

Rackem Tracks
Helmets on!

The sign pointed right. Phee went left, towards a rockface. She climbed up, wedging her hands and feet in familiar cracks. Jayben followed her clumsily to the top, where they stopped and looked back towards the school. The fire looked like it was dying down. He saw Phee wipe tears from her eyes, before she turned away. They continued to climb into the higher woods, through blue shadowgrass, until a tall red chimney came into view. It was the back of the Feller house.

'I thought we were going to the big reds?' said Jayben.

'We are,' Phee said. 'But first you're gonna need some supplies.'

'Jayben!' Tedrik called from the garden, buckling saddles to the backs of the three trox. 'Phee! What happened? Where's your mother?'

The house gave a groan, the trees were drumming again, and the trox retreated to their stable.

'The school was attacked,' Phee told her father as he led them indoors. 'The marshal has been null-headed, but Mum's fine. Jayben's going to the city.'

Jayben nodded. 'They're after me – I'm the reason they're here. I'm going to find my chord and end this.'

Tedrik looked horrified. 'You can't travel to the city without protection, lad. You need to wait, we'll send for another marshal.'

The air felt thick and tingly, as if a storm was brewing.

'There's no time,' said Jayben, grabbing a bottle of flumjuice. 'And what if they just get null-headed. I don't want anyone else to suffer because of me.'

'Null's curse isn't the only thing to be frightened of out there. Besides, if the Agents can find you then so can the Guard. They could be coming for you right now – you need to stay—'

'I need to go, Tedrik! There's no time. Only five sundowns, remember? I'm one down already. I can't wait any longer.' Jayben flipped open his black compass. 'Last Rock,' he said. 'If that's where the Guard are based, that's where I need to be. I have to find my chord in four days. That's all that matters.' He took a swig of flumjuice, grabbed a gribblenut, and headed to the front door.

Tedrik looked surprised. 'You'll need more than that!'

'I'm okay, thanks.' He stuffed the nut in his pocket and walked out of the house.

Phee picked up her backpack and her dad's map of the wood, and hurried after him. 'Wait!' she said, strapping a leather belt around her waist, loaded with tools. 'We'll need a tent.'

'We?' said Jayben, going into the stable. 'You can't come, Phee. It's too dangerous.'

Phee followed, to find Russog hiding, nervously burping, clearly frightened by the noise.

'Come here, Stinkbomb,' she said, giving him a cuddle.

'Poor Russog,' said Jayben, feeding Keylo a nomseed and taking her by the bridle to lead her outside. She wouldn't budge. She was too scared. 'Come on, it's going to be okay,' he said, patting her white-speckled red fur.

Phee lifted her skoggle into the top of her backpack. 'You'll need a night guard.'

'You're not listening, Phee,' said Jayben, leading a

nervous Keylo outside. 'Only I can do this.' He awkwardly climbed into Keylo's saddle. He had no idea how to ride a trox but they seemed comfortable with him, and he'd seen the marshal do it. How hard could it be?

'Don't be stupid, you'll need help,' said Phee, pulling Woodge out behind him, with Russog in her backpack and a sack of camping gear on her shoulder. 'You don't know anything about the world. Do you even know how to ride? Or how to get out of the woods?'

'Well, I got *into* the woods,' he said, sitting in the saddle and taking the reins.

The house moaned and thick sap came oozing from its logs.

Tedrik came out, carrying two wicker boxes. 'Got some food, clothes and a couple of blankets,' he said. 'The wagon is busted so this'll have to do.' He put one of the boxes down so he could fasten one to the back of Keylo's saddle.

Phee unfolded the map. 'You need to head straight down to the coast, Ben,' she said, like she'd been planning it all morning. 'To Blanbor, where my aunt Gwennal and cousin Nilthan have a boat. You can avoid most of the towns and Agents if you sail the rest of the way to the city.'

'Thanks,' said Jayben, flipping his compass open to check he was facing north. 'If I get lost on my way there I'll just ask someone.'

'Are you kidding?' Phee laughed, cramming the camping gear into the other box and lifting it on to Woodge's back. 'You can't just go talking to townsfolk!'

'We're not welcome down there,' said Tedrik, going into the stable to fetch Maddle. 'And there'll be Agents everywhere, looking for you and the Torch. You're giving off a purple light to anyone with a glass. Phee, you're staying here – I'll take him.'

'No,' said Jayben stubbornly and nudged Keylo with his heels. 'Go!'

Keylo didn't move.

Phee rolled her eyes. 'You're gonna die before your second sundown – never mind your fifth!'

The steady drumming from the trees changed and became erratic. The same alarm they had sounded the night before.

Jayben gritted his teeth. 'Why won't she go?'

'They're a pair,' said Phee, climbing on to Woodge's back. 'Keylo won't go anywhere without Woodge.' She folded her arms, her expression resolute.

'No,' Jayben insisted. 'You can't come. I won't put

 111

you in danger, not after everything your family has done for me.'

'He's right, Phee,' said Tedrik. 'I'll take him. It's too dangerous out there.'

'It's worse here!' Phee groaned with frustration. 'The Agents got in, Dad, nullheads too. They burned down the school! Nowhere is safe, and it's only going to get worse unless we do something. I'm not gonna hide in the woods any more.'

'But you're just kids,' Tedrik said helplessly.

'Exactly,' she said. 'The whispers won't affect us. They've taken too many grown-ups already . . . I can't lose you and Mum.'

She attached a handheld contraption to her tool belt, similar to a crossbow, and checked that there were arrows in the pouch beside it. 'Won't be leaving the woods without my fishdart.'

The trees drummed faster and the hovering baskets sank down.

Russog was shaking on Phee's back.

Phee looked down at her father. 'Mum needs you here, with Maddle, just in case. We've got Russog, who can keep watch. I'll keep him close. Get inside and keep those earplugs with you. Okay?'

Tedrik scratched his head, but didn't have time to

answer. Phee turned Woodge around and gave her a kick. Keylo sprang into action beside her.

Jayben's heart raced. He was ready.

'Let's go!' he said, gripping the reins. And he and Phee charged down the path, on to the lane to the big red trees. The giant roots opened and they thundered through, the trox leaping over the stools in the stream, and far out into the open woods.

CHAPTER 11

The Mighty Grannix

'Keep that compass open!' Phee called. She was trying to read her dad's map in one hand as they galloped through the forest. 'We need to keep east to avoid the towns, then there's a river we can follow out of the woods. This is just a map of the Giantwood, but on the big map of the whole realm at school Blanbor is north-east of here. That's where we can get the boat.'

'Got it!' said Jayben, clutching his black compass, its silver dial twitching as they zigzagged between the trees. In spite of his resistance, he was glad of Phee's company, and glad not to be alone with his thoughts. Something kept niggling at him though – his strange loss of memory earlier.

'I still don't understand what happened,' he said to Phee. 'I don't remember putting on that helmet or playing a game of – what was it called – Rackem?'

'Yes. I don't know,' said Phee, distracted. 'Maybe it was the stress. Or a Dreamer thing.' She gently encouraged Woodge. 'Come on, we need to speed up. It's a long journey to Blanbor.'

'How long?'

'Dad said it took him two days.'

'*Two days*? And then it's another day to get to the city?' *The Chordian Guard had better have a quick trick for finding my chord*, he thought.

They came to a clearing and the river. A huge waterfall cascaded down from the mountain, filling the air with a fine mist that glinted in the sunshine. They trotted up to a bridge but stopped suddenly at the sound of a loud roar.

Phee froze. She squinted through the mist, up at the highest point of the waterfall from where something large and shiny and monstrous-looking was descending.

'What is that?' said Jayben, going cold. They hadn't even made it out of the woods before they'd run into danger.

Then they heard the screams. Jayben could just

make out the shape of a little girl across the river. The deep roar bellowed again. A creature was making its way towards the screaming.

Russog started burping, nervously trying to hide in Phee's backpack. 'Easy, boy,' he said in Tedrik's voice.

'GRANNIX!' cried Phee, as the creature emerged from the mist. It was huge, a silver, bear-like beast with a crown of golden antlers. 'Ben! It's a grannix!'

'A what?' He could see now that the girl was struggling to free a small boy whose foot was stuck in the ground.

The animal was bounding down the rocks, heading straight for the small children. Its bone-chilling roar shook the trees.

'It's gonna kill them, Ben! Can you stop it? Like you did with the skallabore?'

Jayben had never heard of a grannix, but he could see the fear on Phee's face and hear the screams of the girl. He remembered the look in the skallabore's eyes before it fled, like he had somehow disarmed it. It was worth a try, he thought. He gave Keylo a tap, and they crossed the bridge over the gushing river.

'We're coming!' Phee called to the children, as they reached the other side. 'Careful, Ben!'

Keylo refused to face the approaching grannix and

116

Jayben swung himself down from the saddle, moving into the creature's path. Phee dismounted too, then ran to the children, bending down to free the boy's leg.

The grannix had reached the bottom rocks. Jayben approached slowly, trying to keep his nerve. He was buzzing with adrenalin as the grannix came nearer, and felt a surge of energy coursing through his veins. *I can do this. I can do this*, he thought, slowing his breathing to appear relaxed. He remembered his calm face reflected in the skallabore's eyes. *I need to be that brave boy again*, he thought, pausing a few paces from the beast.

The grannix stopped and turned to face him.

Jayben took another step forward. *Ignore its teeth and claws*, he thought, standing his ground. *Look at its cool antlers and shiny fur. Incredible!*

The grannix rose on its hind legs, roaring and thumping its chest with its paws.

Jayben held his breath and didn't blink, instead he held the creature's gaze.

One . . . two . . . three . . .

The mighty grannix dropped to all fours, growling and sniffing the air.

Jayben looked it coolly in the eye.

Suddenly the grannix raised its antlers and bounded

across the river, and disappeared into the wild mist.

Jayben exhaled, laughing, giddy with relief. He turned to see Phee and the two children staring open-mouthed.

'That was amazing!' said the girl. 'It's gone, Peggro! Did you know a kid could scare them away? You can write about it in your log.'

The boy nervously scratched at his neat blond hair, lifting his glasses and rubbing his green eyes. Pink was gradually returning to his pale cheeks. 'Not if I'm mauled to death I can't. Let's get out of here.'

'But you're an explorer,' the girl said.

'I'm a scientist,' he said, clutching the green charm around his neck. 'Totally different.'

The little girl ignored him and beamed, her brown eyes full of wonder as she turned to face Phee and Jayben. 'You saved us! How did you do it?'

'Long story,' said Phee, looking at Jayben.

'Are you guys hurt?' said Jayben, glancing towards the waiting trox. They couldn't afford a delay. Even if Blanbor was too far to reach before nightfall, they needed to get as far as possible.

'I'm fine,' said the girl. 'That was super brave of you. Who are you anyway?'

'Brave or foolish,' said the boy, 'one of the two.'

118

'You're funny, Peggro,' she said with a giggle.

Peggro sighed. 'I'm not funny. Anyway, who are you people?'

'I'm Phee,' said Phee, handing a nomseed to Russog.

'I'm Jayben,' said Jayben, retrieving Keylo and Woodge from the bushes. 'We're kind of in a hurry. Are you sure you're okay?'

'Fine,' said Peggro, clinging to his brown leather satchel as if it might be snatched from him at any moment. It was bursting with books and papers. Even the pockets of his olive-green blazer and trousers were crammed full of crumpled notes. 'I'm Peggro Clotts.'

'Nice to meet you, Peggro,' said Phee. 'Who's your friend?'

'She's not my friend,' said Peggro, shifting away from the girl.

'My name's Maybie!' the girl announced, skipping forward to shake their hands. 'I'm seven and a quarter, and Peggro's nine. And he *is* my friend, really. He's just shy. We've been friends for a *whole* morning already!'

Peggro kept quiet and stared at the ground, looking uncomfortable. Jayben noticed that everything Maybie wore was fuchsia pink: her sparkly shoes, rings, frilly dress with pockets, and the flower in her curly black hair – everything but the tiny, golden nutshell charm around her neck, glistening against her brown skin.

'Did you say your name was Maybie?' asked Phee.

'Yep,' said the girl. 'M-A-Y-B-I-E. That's me!'

'She's from Fellooz,' muttered Peggro, rolling his eyes.

'Yup!' said Maybie. 'Not supposed to come so far into Wenden – or stay on the ground. But I couldn't leave you alone, Peggro. Now that you're okay, and you have these guys, I'll be off.' She took a tiny pink dress out of her pocket and wandered into the shade. With a quick sniff of her golden nutshell, she hid behind a broad tree trunk.

'Wait, what?' said Jayben, climbing on to Keylo's back. 'Sorry, um, Peggro – but we can't take anyone else. You need to stay together and get to the village—'

He broke off. He could hear a volley of sneezing from behind the tree.

'She's shrinking,' Peggro explained.

'What?' said Jayben, confused.

'It's how Fairywoods fly,' said Phee. 'A throwback to the old fairies.'

Five sneezes later, a miniature Maybie appeared, wearing an identical, yet tiny, version of her dress. She strained to fold her regular-sized dress like a

sack to carry her regular shoes, hair band and things from her pockets. She fluttered in mid-air on four silver wings, no more than seven inches tall, tightening her charm necklace.

'Wow!' said Jayben. 'Is that old magic?'

'Oinff!' said Russog, standing in Phee's backpack and batting his paws like he wanted to chase her.

'Magic?' Maybie giggled, flying higher above Russog. 'There's nothing magic about flying. I mean in the old, old days proper fairies could do spells!' She sighed. 'If only we could be proper fairies . . .'

'I'd say flying is pretty great,' said Phee, climbing into Woodge's saddle. 'Sorry we can't stay to help. Can you take Peggro to Ampelwed, before you go home?'

'Where's Ampelwed?' said Peggro, pulling a map of the realm from his bag. 'I was with my dad, we were travelling to a town near a market. Then we got separated this morning. My dad – the nullheads . . .' Peggro stopped himself and fiddled with his glasses, like he couldn't talk about it.

But Jayben saw the emotion in Peggro's eyes. He knew that sadness, of being lost with no family. 'I'm really sorry, Peggro,' he said.

Peggro hid behind his map. 'I'm fine,' he snapped. 'Just annoyed. My dad has our compass.'

Clearly Peggro wasn't fine. He had just lost his dad. But he'd made it clear he didn't want to talk about it.

'I have a compass,' said Jayben.

'But we do need a proper map of Wenden,' said Phee thoughtfully, looking at Peggro. 'Oooh!' said Maybie, buzzing around the map. 'It's one of those hidden Free-Dream maps!'

'What?' said Peggro, frowning. 'There's nothing on here about Free-Dreams.'

Maybie laughed. 'Silly Peggro. That's because you're reading it the right way up!' She turned it upside down and dozens of little gold X marks appeared all over Wenden, wherever Maybie breathed.

Peggro looked gobsmacked.

'Every X is a Free-Dream from Earth World!' she said. 'And the number beside it tells you which of the first eight Dreamers Free-Dreamed it here! Mamma says they use fairy ink for treasure maps sometimes, so that other people can't see.'

'How did I not know about this?' Peggro blushed. 'The guy who sold it to my dad must have known it was special.'

Jayben's eyes lit up. If he could locate the items from the Earth World that had been Free-Dreamed here, maybe it might jog some memories of his own.

As Maybie continued to breathe on the map, Jayben spotted a number 8 next to the moor between Ampelwed and Blanbor. 'There's one on our way, Phee!'

Phee bit her lip. 'What if there are Agents there?'

'Well,' said Maybie continuing, 'there's no harm in looking. "8" means the Eighth Dreamer Free-Dreamed it, nearly a hundred years ago! I wonder what it could be?'

'It would be amazing to see it,' said Jayben longingly. He knew they didn't have long – but it was on their route and he wanted to know everything about his eight famous predecessors. Besides, it might offer a clue to his mysterious past or earthling self. Might it even be his chord? He looked at Phee and blurted out. 'It might bring a memory back!'

Phee shook her head. 'It's too risky, Jayben,' she said gently. 'Thanks for showing us your map, Peggro, but we have to leave now.'

As Jayben took the reins, his Rainbow crystals flashed in the sunlight.

'*Oh, my wings!*' said Maybie, catching a glimpse and hovering closer, 'Is that what I think it is?'

'We have to go,' he said, quickly closing his fist. 'It was nice to meet you. Glad you're safe!'

Peggro backed away, putting his map back in his satchel. 'Wait, what did you mean, it might bring a memory back?'

'Oinff! Oinff!' said Russog, suddenly squirming about.

The tree behind them made the deep clicking sound. The woods started drumming.

Phee looked around. 'Who's that, over there?'

The group turned towards the bridge to see a woman riding a grey trox, wearing a grey coat and glasses. Even from where he stood, Jayben could make out that the lenses were tinted purple.

Peggro gasped. 'Agent!' he cried, rushing into the trees. 'Run!'

Jayben tapped Keylo and sped past Peggro and Maybie's hiding spot, leaping over a fallen tree with Phee, Woodge and Russog close behind. He had to get away!

'STOP!' the woman yelled, chasing them on troxback.

Jayben looked back and saw Peggro struggling to keep up, with Maybie fluttering at his shoulder. The woman was closing in fast behind them.

Jayben hesitated. He and Phee could escape now, if they let the Agent catch Peggro and Maybie, and they could be on their way again. But no. He couldn't leave them. Especially not Peggro, having just lost his dad.

'He'll never make it, Phee!' said Jayben.

Phee took her fishdart weapon off her belt.

Jayben turned Keylo around, riding back just as Peggro stumbled and fell to the ground. Jayben pulled the reins sharply and came to a halt. 'Peggro, climb up!' he cried.

The woods pounded their alarm and Maybie buzzed anxiously as Peggro reached up to the saddle.

The Agent galloped ever closer.

Phee took an arrow from her belt and armed her weapon.

Jayben grabbed Peggro's shaking arms, pulling him awkwardly on to Keylo's neck before turning the trox and galloping away fast.

'Come back!' the woman shouted. 'Dreamer, come back!'

Maybie blew a raspberry as she flew beside the others, racing away, watching the woman get smaller behind them until she was nothing but a dot in the dense woods.

When they were some distance away, they stopped and Phee helped Peggro rearrange himself in the saddle to sit behind Jayben.

'Thank you!' said Peggro, gripping his satchel, his face pale green. 'I thought I was done for.'

'That's okay,' said Jayben. 'We'll find somewhere safe to drop you off.'

They rode on. Maybie flew alongside with a grin from ear to ear. 'Are you really *him*? Are you really the Ninth Dreamer?' she asked, gently landing on his palm to peer at the crystals.

Jayben looked awkwardly at Phee, unsure what to say.

She smiled. 'How do you think he tamed that grannix?'

Peggro looked shocked. 'Wait – no – you can't mean . . .'

'You can't tell anyone,' Jayben said.

Maybie beamed. 'Magical!'

'We need to find his chord before he can be truly magical,' Phee said firmly.

Peggro sighed. 'I'm sorry you have to be the one, Jayben.'

Jayben tried not to think any more about it; there wasn't time. They seemed to have shaken off the Agent. He gripped the reins and nodded at Phee.

Together they rode north, to the ghost village of Jonningwed. Jayben slowed Keylo down as they walked through the eerie, lifeless place, full of fire-ravaged cottages. He wondered what it would have been like once. Ordinary people, on their way to school or work, families arguing, laughing, living. Now it was all lost, thanks to Null and his lies.

They eventually found themselves back in the deep forest and Jayben was glad of it. There was too much sorrow in Jonningwed. The group fell into a comfortable silence.

THUD!

One of the trees just ahead of them turned to crackling ice, its branches white and frozen.

It was suddenly freezing cold. 'What was *that*?' said Jayben, seeing his breath in the air.

There was a flash of darkness.

'Darkning!' cried Maybie, trembling. 'It's striking at us!'

THUD!

Another flash of black, and a second tree turned ice-white, then shattered like glass.

The trox panicked and Phee drove them down the slope, dodging two more strikes.

'What's darkning?' shouted Jayben as another dark spike of air narrowly missed the boys, leaving frost on Keylo's mane.

'It's an underground storm!' said Peggro. 'From the North. Snatches all energy wherever it strikes. I didn't know it happened here in the South!'

THUD!

'But it never strikes the same place twice,' he added, clutching tight to the saddle. 'Go to the place where it just struck!'

Maybie zoomed up high. 'I can see the end of the woods!' she shouted. 'Over there!'

Jayben and Phee steered from one frozen tree to the next, dodging the darkning strikes and riding hard until they reached the edge of the Giantwood forest, where the air was warm again.

'We did it, guys,' said Jayben, shaking with relief.

Phee was shivering. 'I've always feared darkning,' she said, 'but never seen it.'

Peggro shrugged. 'It's caused by a curse.'

'Horrible!' said Maybie.

'Well, it might not be over,' said Jayben. He spotted the chimneys of a town ahead – but a town was exactly what they needed to avoid. 'You still got your map there, Peggro?'

'Got it,' said Peggro. He looked small and vulnerable.

'We should all stick together for now,' Jayben decided.

Maybe it wouldn't be so bad, travelling together. They could help one another. They'd made a good team, with Maybie directing them out of the wood.

'We need to avoid the towns and move quickly,' he said. 'That Agent had those purple glasses. They must have seen that weird invisible light from me. We need to stay out of sight. Maybie, can you keep a look out?'

Maybie slung her bundle of clothes on to Woodge's back, then zoomed up high. 'All clear!' she said.

'And Peggro, can you find a safe way to the moors? We have to cross them to get to Blanbor and I have to see that Free-Dream. It's on our route and it could be my chord!'

Peggro unfolded his map and plotted a route, to the 'X8' hidden Free-Dream.

Phee buckled her fishdart back on to her belt, still loaded with an arrow. 'Any more Agents, they can answer to this.'

Jayben brushed ice crystals off the trox antlers and flipped his compass open. 'Let's go!' he said and they were off, riding fast across the meadows of Wenden.

Phee grinned. 'Considering we've almost been killed twice, this is kinda fun!'

Jayben rolled his eyes at her. He couldn't stop thinking about the Fifth Sundown and what might happen if he couldn't find his chord within four days. Would Ampelwed become like Jonningwed? 'We need to go faster!' he said through gritted teeth.

'Faster than *this*?' Peggro gulped, clinging to his straps.

'Sounds good!' said Maybie, zipping through the air.

Russog gave an 'Oinff!' of agreement and Phee leant forward.

The trox started to run, leaving the smoke, the drumming trees and the darkning far behind. The wind whistled in their ears, blowing the horror and sadness to the back of their minds, and soon, despite himself, Jayben was laughing with the others, wondering what strange dreams he might have, and what incredible magic he might be capable of, when he got his memories back.

CHAPTER 12

The Gramophone in the Ground

The shadows of the running trox drew longer as the afternoon hurried away, until they reached the moors. Keylo and Woodge slowed as they climbed to the top of a hill, panting and stumbling, exhausted.

'Good girl,' said Phee, ruffling Woodge's mane.

'Wow!' Maybie cheered from above, her wings sparkling in the evening sun.

The weary trox reached the top of the moor, the highest point for miles, looking out over a colourful patchwork of fields and farms stretching north. Their eyes met the spectacular sight of a tall arch of sandstone, speckled with dozens of white moonstone gems.

Jayben felt a memory tug at him. An arch? With tiny lights? It was just like the one in his dream. 'I've seen this before!' he said, jumping down from the saddle and looking up with wide eyes. 'In a dream!' Then he recalled the dream had been scary but couldn't remember more details. He was just excited to have remembered.

'What?' said Phee. 'A memorial arch? They have them in Earth World too? I mean, you will only see Earth memories in dreams, right?'

'I don't know,' said Jayben, shrugging.

'Or maybe it's your chord!' said Maybie. 'Maybe sometimes you can dream about things *here* too? Who knows?'

'Great!' said Peggro. 'Will you remember everything now?'

The gems looked like the lights on the arch in his dream – surely it was the same. Jayben allowed himself to hope. Could this really be his chord? Was it that easy? Was this the key to all his memories, to finding his family, and unlocking the power to defeat Null? His stomach fluttered with anticipation.

Phee and Peggro climbed down from the trox.

'Anything coming back to you?' asked Maybie, buzzing by his side. 'Can you Free-Dream now?'

Jayben walked towards the structure, focusing on it with every ounce of his energy. *Please work.*

But no memories came. Nothing felt different, and no objects from the Earth World magically appeared. 'I don't think so. Maybe it takes a while to work?'

Peggro scratched his head. 'Sorry, but if the arch was your chord, you'd just have to see it for it to work. Then you'd remember everything. It says so in the Book. Page twenty-three, I think.'

'Okay,' Jayben said, taking a deep breath, trying to fight a sinking sense of disappointment. He squatted to the ground next to the arch. 'But if this isn't my chord, it must be a clue, at least. Right? I definitely saw it in a dream last night.'

'Amazing!' said Phee. 'That's the spirit!'

Maybie persisted. 'Are you sure you can't Free-Dream? Try looking at that rock over there and thinking of something we won't have seen. Something your earthling self might know.'

Peggro ducked down with his hands over his ears. 'Something small, please – nothing dangerous.'

Jayben looked at the rock but no Earthly memories came to him. All he could think of was Tedrik's cheeky furniture, the Rackem helmets, and all the other new and exciting things he'd seen here . . . The rock stayed the same.

He shook his head. Had the dream been important? The arch clearly wasn't his chord.

He sat down on the rock and took out the Torch, trying to gather himself. He looked at his reflection in its golden spout and recalled the words of Sojan: *If it's not impossible, then you can do it.* He knew the chord was somewhere. He still had four sundowns left. It wasn't impossible.

'I can do this,' he said out loud. The first step was to remember.

He thought hard, concentrating on remembering the details of his dream: there had been a blurry archway with a wide frame, covered with tiny white glowing gems . . . and water . . . it was beside some water!

He stood up quickly. 'There was water in my dream too!' he said. 'The arch was by some water. There's no water here. This isn't the same arch.' He shook his head in frustration. 'We need to meet the Chordian Guard at Last Rock and then it will be clearer.'

Phee nodded. 'Yes. We need to press on to my aunt Gwennal and cousin Nilthan in Blanbor. Then we can sail to the city on their boat.'

'Cool,' he said, his hopes lifted again. The arch had

been a dead-end – but it had jogged his memory of the dream, which was a start.

'Cool?' said Maybie.

Phee chuckled. 'You'll get used to it.'

'Fascinating,' said Peggro, reaching for his logbook and scribbling in it. '"Cool". Meaning "good".'

Does nobody say 'cool' like that here? thought Jayben. It must be an Earth World phrase. *Maybe I'm remembering something from my earthling?*

As he turned back to the trox, Jayben spotted something behind the arch: seven stacks of rocks in a row, slowly turning by themselves. Beside them was a shallow hole in the ground.

'What are those?' said Jayben.

'Turnstones,' said Phee. 'Enchanted rocks that spin where there is lots of Energy. They were left by old trolls in the Magic Ages. But what is *this*?'

She walked over and crouched down by the hole. There were piles of dirt to one side, like it had been dug recently. And inside there was a strange half-exposed glass dome. She wiped its smeared glass to see a brass horn inside, resting on a wooden box.

Peggro joined her. 'The gramophone!' he cheered with great excitement. 'It's one of the objects from Maejac's Free-Dreams! It played music, apparently.'

Jayben felt strange, looking at the gramophone in the ground; odd as the object was, it seemed to make *sense*. He was intrigued by a shiny black disc on the wooden box, connected to the brass horn by a long needle. Somehow he knew the disc was supposed to turn, and then music would play from the horn.

'It's like I've seen one of these before,' he said. Was it a memory? *A real memory?* He felt hope balloon inside him.

'Oh, my wings!' said Maybie, buzzing around them. 'It's from magical Earth World! And the Eighth Dreamer was right here. Like, a hundred years ago!'

Jayben dusted soil off a notice beside the glass dome. It read:

PROPERTY OF THE CROWN
Thieves will be <u>imprisoned</u>

Then he noticed little cracks in the dome, like someone had tried to smash it open, unsuccessfully. 'Did an Agent try digging this up?'

Phee shrugged. 'Whoever it was, they clearly gave up,' she said, tapping the dome. 'This is no ordinary glass.' She smiled. 'I've always wanted to see a Free-Dream. I wonder what object was sent to Earth in its place?'

'There would have been an eighth stack of turnstones here,' said Peggro, 'because the old trolls always left things in even numbers. So, I guess that other stack of stones must be in the Earth World now? Swapped for this music machine?'

'Wow,' said Jayben, gently touching the rotating rocks. 'How did trolls make them move like this?'

'That was their old magic,' said Phee. 'They could move rocks and metal with their minds. The same old magic in any Trollwood's blood today.'

'Really?' said Jayben. His mind was racing. 'I wonder whether I'm a Trollwood. The Jarmaster said Rainbow crystals can draw old magic from my blood. And the blood of those closest to me.'

Peggro backed away, looking like he was afraid of such powers.

Maybie fluttered forward and sat on Jayben's shoulder. 'I didn't know that could happen. It's not in the Book, is it?'

Phee shivered. 'Those closest to you, Ben? You mean *we* might get old magic powers from our ancestors? I'm a Giantwood. Am I going to be able to lift tree trunks, like the old giants? And will Peggro be able to go invisible like the old Dragonwood folk?'

'Oh!' said Maybie, 'You mean I'll be able to do *spells*?'

Jayben grinned at the gramophone. 'That's just the start of it! Imagine swapping things between worlds! I can't wait to get my memory back.' He looked up at the horizon. 'I can't wait to know more about *this* world, and all your clans.'

Maybie laughed. 'Well here's one way to start.' She whizzed over to Woodge and retrieved a map of her own from her folded dress pocket.

Peggro helped her unfold it and the others gathered around.

THE ELF WORLD

'The whole world?' said Peggro. 'All five realms in one map?'

'Did that bit just *move*?' asked Jayben. He was fascinated. 'It's just like the one on the Jarmaster's wall!' He pointed to the clusters of trees on the map, and the sparkling seas between each realm. 'All the Memory Woods!'

'Almost,' said Maybie. 'No one knows much about the fifth realm.'

South was at the top of the map.

Maybie explained each realm in turn.

Wenden was home to the Giantwood. Some of which was obscured by patches of miniature clouds – real ones, drifting over the enchanted map.

Bramalan was home to the Trollwood, with colossal mountains near the South Pole and great plains stretching north.

Nomolia was home to the Dragonwood, a mysterious jungle land, rich with unexplored caves. Jayben's eye was drawn to a moving illustration of a yellow dragon attacking an explorer.

Fellooz was home to the Fairywood. It was mostly desert. Jayben could see tiny flashes of lightning from thunder clouds along its coast, and fairies buzzing about.

At the bottom of the map there was a bold, grey line, the equator, and below it, the tip of a dark forest of mysterious moving shadows. In tiny print, it simply read:

The North

Spritewood

(Don't go here)

'Don't ask about that fifth realm,' said Maybie.

'Why not?' asked Jayben. 'What's so dangerous about it?'

'Nobody ever tells us.' Peggro shrugged. 'The books are so vague. We're only told there's sorcery there. Not old magic but dangerous spells that we don't understand, used by corrupt wizards and witches.'

'One day I'm going to find out,' said Phee, lifting her chin determinedly.

Jayben shook his head in disbelief. This world was incredible. 'Tell me about the charms you all wear,' he said.

Peggro explained that the five different kinds of charms worn by elves on their clanbands showed which of the five Memory Woods their families had lived in, back in the Magic Ages.

Dragonwoods wore oval green nutshells, like Peggro's.

Fairywoods wore gold nutshells, like Maybie's.

Giantwoods wore red pine cones, like Phee's.

Spritewoods wore silver star-shaped husks.

And **Trollwoods** wore blue square nutshells, like the one on Jayben's wrist.

'I'm half-Dragonwood, half-Trollwood,' said Peggro. 'So my Jarmaster will have decided which charm suited me best, from our family jars.'

Phee explained further. 'Before we're born, Ben, our charms are kept in jars on the local helicorn tree, like the ones you saw today. In a jar full of mementos from an old relative's life.'

'So, Jayben, you're Trollwood?' said Peggro, glancing at the blue square charm on Jayben's wrist.

Jayben shrugged. 'I don't know. The Jarmaster lent me this.' He looked down at the borrowed charm and remembered his empty jar – the empty feeling of not having a family like everyone else. Once he'd found his chord, he'd remember everything – his family, his home, his life. Of course, he'd also have to work out how to defeat a powerful evil Dreamer, but he was trying not to think about exactly what that would entail. The Book of Dreamers had been quite vague about it.

'Your charm will be somewhere, Ben,' said Phee, taking off her backpack and letting Russog down for a sniff about. 'Maybe your parents have it.'

'I wonder what clan you are,' said Peggro.

'Definitely not a Spritewood,' said Maybie. 'I met one once. He was very grumpy. Wouldn't tell me anything about the North. I only know it's where horrible things like darkning storms come from.'

Why would people keep a whole realm secret? Jayben wondered. 'Fellooz looks cool,' he said instead. 'I'd love to go there some day.'

'I love it here in Wenden,' said Maybie. Her eyes were suddenly sad. 'I don't want to go home.'

'Why not?' Jayben asked.

'We've got the whispers there too now,' she said quietly.

'Oh,' said Jayben.

'Pappa heard them,' she said, 'but Mamma says everything will be fixed soon. And at least we have wings. I don't have to be there every day.'

'I'm sorry,' said Jayben.

Maybie pointed to Nomolia on the map, changing the subject. 'Apparently the yellow dragons are really stinky. But there's treasure in their poop! What about your home, Peggro?'

Peggro pointed at Bramalan on the map, then he took off his satchel and delved into a side pocket. 'Aha! My dad's monocular . . .' He pulled out a small, silver tube and held it to his eye, looking east to the horizon. 'Look,' he said, handing it to Jayben. 'Can you see the mountains?'

Jayben peered into it and spotted some dark bumps in the distance. 'Wow! It makes them bigger!'

'That's where we lived, until a few days ago. Me and my dad. We've always moved about a lot. My dad's a doctor. Every time we settled, Dad would start treating nullheads. He would get the townsfolk to calm down. He'd tell them that turning against the forestfolk would solve nothing. Null's Agents didn't like that, so we'd have to move again. This summer we couldn't find anywhere safe from all the undercover Agents. That's why we came here, but then—' He cleared his throat. 'Dad heard the whispers, Null's curse. Anyway . . .' He rifled through his books like he was trying to tidy away his emotions.

'We should camp here for the night,' said Phee gently.

She wandered back to the trox, who were busy munching on the knee-high purple shrubs of the moor. Their rich colour was dazzling in the gold evening sun. She unbuckled their saddles for the night and the others joined her to take in the view.

'Your pappa sounds like a good man, Peggro,' said Maybie. 'I'm gonna be a doctor when I'm grown up. I will look after nullheads too.'

'Thanks,' Peggro said. 'Null has gained so much support in Bramalan. So many nullheads in the towns – and he's convinced them all it's the forestfolk's fault. The families of the nullheads were happy to become his Agents. He's given them new technologies from the Earth World, like those horrible flashpin weapons. And somehow they're making loads of them, as if they have old Spritewood magic!'

'Spritewood magic?' said Jayben.

Phee nodded. 'The old sprites could duplicate things,' she said, 'make copies of the same object.'

'So Null's a Spritewood?' said Jayben. 'His Rainbow crystals are bringing out his old magic?' Then he remembered something the Jarmaster had said. 'Or maybe the witch is doing it?'

'What witch?' said Maybie.

'The Jarmaster said Null was working with a witch from the North, called Snaggis – a Spritewood. She helped him to find his chord. And since she's close to a Dreamer she might gain her old magic powers, right? So maybe she's the one making all these flashpin weapons.'

Phee nodded. They all looked worried.

'That's it,' said Jayben. 'That's how he's making so many weapons for his Agents. So many of those purple glasses.'

'That witch is the worst,' said Maybie, shaking her fist to the north of the horizon. 'The Agents are powerful enough already without old Spritewood magic!'

'That explains how Null's building that city so fast,' said Peggro. 'His so-called City of Free-Dreams, in Bramalan, where he's promised his Agents they can live and where their loved ones will get their memories back.'

'Except it's a lie,' said Jayben. 'Isn't it, Phee? The Jarmaster said Null's only promising his Agents that new city so that they help him hunt for the Torch. And now they're coming for me too, because I can stop Null breaking the Torch, and I have crystals myself. I could be more powerful than him – if only I could find my chord.'

Phee nodded. 'It's all a trick,' she said sadly. 'Null doesn't want to help nullheads. He wants to take over this world and Earth World by null-heading everyone!'

Peggro dropped his satchel, looking horrified to hear the full extent of Null's plan.

Maybie frowned with her hands on her hips. 'He really is the baddest baddie ever!' she said. 'I can't imagine how scared all the forest elves are in Bramalan, if that's where Null is.'

'That's why we came back here,' said Peggro. 'My grandma lives somewhere in Wenden. We were on our way to her. Dad never wrote down her address in case the Agents found it. It was safely in his head, until today. When he heard the whispers, and they took him. Now he's gone. And I don't know where she is . . .'

Jayben looked back at the distant Giantwood forest, now punctured by black plumes of smoke. His anger burned inside. 'I know it must be horrible for the townsfolk, seeing people they love becoming null-headed – but how could they actually start those fires?'

Phee sat down. 'Stupid townsfolk, believing *we* are to blame.'

Maybie pointed to Last Rock on the map, the capital city of Wenden, built on an enormous rock, gleaming with purple crystals. 'The Queen's castle garden is full of Free-Dreamed objects. Won't be long before Null and his Agents try to take all that Energy away, for Null's horrible city.'

Phee groaned with anger. 'Idiots probably think the Queen's a Dream Thief herself, hoarding those Free-Dreams! They'd better not try to burn that castle garden tree. It's the oldest helicorn in the world.'

'It won't happen,' said Jayben. 'We won't let it. I'll get to the capital soon, and get the Guard's help, and find my chord. Then we can stop this once and for all.'

Peggro pointed to the map, to a building in Last Rock that looked like something between a museum and a castle. It was labelled *The Observatory*. 'That's where you'll find the Guard. Dad told me.'

Maybie folded her map away. 'What about your mamma, Peggro?' she asked.

Peggro looked down. 'She died when I was three, Dad said. I don't remember how. I was hoping my grandma would tell me, but now I'm not sure I'll ever know.'

Jayben shared his pain, and was desperate to comfort him. He put his hand on Peggro's shoulder.

Peggro shrugged it off. 'Thanks,' he said, clenching his jaw. 'But I'm fine. I don't remember my mum. It's always just been my dad and me.'

'You're funny, Jayben!' Maybie laughed. 'What else did you see in Ampelwed?'

Jayben blinked, staring at his boots. He couldn't answer. He couldn't move. He felt heavy, stuck. Trapped outside of himself. Panic swept through him, he could hear a buzzing sound, but he couldn't call out—

'Ben?' said Phee.

'You okay, Jay-Jay?' asked Maybie.

Russog was sitting at his feet and licking his leg with his green snout. 'There, there, little one,' he said in Larnie's voice.

Slowly, Jayben realised he could move his eyes and head. 'What happened?' he said, looking up at Phee.

'It's okay,' said Phee, putting her arm around him. 'It happened this morning at the Rackem barn, remember? But you were fine afterwards. Let's sit down.'

Jayben sat on a rock, still dazed. He felt a wave of sadness and worry, and suddenly tears were rolling down his cheeks. What was causing this? How much time had passed without him realising?

'It was only a moment, Ben,' said Phee, reading his expression. 'We were just chatting.'

He glanced around. The trox were resting over by

the arch and it wasn't dark yet, so he couldn't have missed much. But it wasn't much comfort. Losing track of himself made him feel scared and powerless.

'It sounds like you had an absence,' said Peggro, taking another book from his satchel. 'My dad had a patient once who had absences. It's a kind of seizure.'

'What's a seizure?' asked Jayben.

Peggro found the right page and sat on the rock next to him, then read him a section from his dad's book about seizure symptoms. It described exactly what had happened to him twice today.

Tears stung Jayben's eyes. It was too much. He had enough to deal with already. 'Is it a Dreamer thing? Will it stop when I find my chord?'

'Afraid not,' said Peggro. 'It's medical. The other Dreamers didn't have them. But lots of people do.'

'It's okay,' said Phee, squeezing his hand. 'You're all right now.'

Jayben put on a brave smile but the tears wouldn't stop. What if the next time it happened he was in the middle of something – something important? What if it had stopped him saving Tedrik from the skallabore, or Peggro from the grannix . . . and worst of all, what if it stopped him from defeating Null? He held his head in his hands.

Maybie perched on his shoulder. 'Don't worry, Jay-Jay,' she said. 'It's okay to be sad.'

Jayben said nothing.

'No need to talk about it,' said Peggro, putting his book away and ushering Maybie over to him. 'If he doesn't want to.'

Russog jumped into Jayben's lap and said in Tedrik's voice, 'Who farted?'

Phee laughed, which set Jayben off, and soon the whole group were in fits of giggles. Jayben felt a bit better.

'We're here for you, Ben,' said Phee. 'We'll help you get through this.'

Jayben smiled weakly. There was only so much they could do. But having the others here did make him feel stronger. 'Thanks,' he said, stroking Russog's head.

Phee looked at the sinking sun on the horizon. 'The trox are exhausted,' she said. 'We're high up. If that Agent catches up with us, Russog can give us plenty of warning. Right, Stinkbomb?'

'Oinff!'

'We'll set off at dawn. Plenty of time, Ben – three whole days.'

Jayben knew he had to stay positive. Anything else wasn't an option. 'At least we're getting closer,' he

said. 'I know I can do this. I know I can find my chord.'

If he told himself often enough, he hoped he'd start believing it.

CHAPTER 13

Both Sides of the Moon

Phee fetched the wicker boxes of food and blankets, then they led Keylo and Woodge down the slope to a small pool of water for a much-needed drink.

'Perfect!' said Maybie, when she saw the pool. She took her bigger clothes and buzzed down to join the trox.

Russog followed, playfully jumping up at her. 'Leave them be, Stinkbomb!' he said in Tedrik's voice.

'Nobody look!' said Maybie, unfolding her regular-sized dress and dropping it on the grass with her regular shoes and hairband. She took a deep breath, closed her eyes, and dived into the water.

Jayben looked away.

POOMF!

There was a bright flash of white light. Keylo, Woodge and Russog jumped back.

Everyone turned, and there was Maybie, full size again, back in her bigger clothes and shoes, putting her miniature dress and map into her pocket.

'Wow!' said Jayben. 'How did you do that?'

'Easy-peasy!' she beamed, restyling her hair. 'Just add water. De-shrinking is *so* much easier than shrinking.'

'How often can you do it?' asked Peggro.

She shrugged. 'It's never not worked. So long as there's nice bright sunshine.'

'Won't your mum worry if you're not home tonight?' said Phee, hammering a tent peg into the ground.

'Meh,' Maybie said, rejoining them and sitting on the grass next to Russog. 'She knows sometimes I'll be gone a while, but she doesn't worry too much. She's glad we can escape!'

Phee laughed. 'I can't imagine Giantwood parents letting seven-year-olds go travelling on their own. I wish we could shrink and fly!'

Russog trotted over to Peggro, who raised his arms defensively, trying to avoid the skoggle's wet snout.

Jayben grinned, helping Phee with another peg. 'I think he likes you, Peggro.'

The tent was up and the sun was slowly sinking. Phee built a mound of bark and moss from their stores, then took a tool from her belt and pushed it into a clump of grass, twisting it in her hands, back and forth. 'This grass isn't dry enough for a fire,' she groaned. 'Or maybe it's the wind.' She carried it to the side of the arch to try lighting it there.

Jayben noticed the moonstones in the arch were glowing slightly. He squinted, trying to get a better look. Something about it felt familiar. Was it . . . Could it be a memory coming through? He reached out for it with his mind—

Pop!

A spark flashed in the shrub next to Maybie.

Pop! Pop!

More sparks flashing. Russog darted off, followed by the trox.

Phee looked up. 'What the—'

BANG!

Every shrub around them burst into flames.

Peggro and the girls dashed for cover.

Jayben couldn't believe his eyes. 'I didn't know plants could do that!'

The girls poked their heads up from behind the crates to see the shrubs reduced to smouldering ash.

Peggro was still hiding his eyes. 'Is Jayben burnt?' he said. 'Is there anything left of him?'

'He seems to be in one piece. What happened?' said Phee, walking back to Jayben cautiously.

'I don't know.' Jayben shrugged. 'I was looking at the arch and I felt like I almost remembered something. Then those plants caught on fire.'

'Magical!' Maybie cheered. 'Oh, Jay-Jay, you must be close to getting your powers!'

'His name is Jayben, not Jay-Jay or Ben,' said Peggro, standing up with his arms crossed. 'And he could have killed us all!'

'But he didn't,' said Phee, lighting the grass from one of the shrubs for the campfire. 'Everyone's okay, and I've got to say, Ben, that was pretty . . . cool?'

'So cool!' said Jayben. He felt elated. 'I can't believe I did that. Sorry, Peggro, I didn't know it would happen.'

'It's fine,' said Peggro grumpily. 'But if your magic is growing, we need to find your chord so you can control it.'

'Where's Russog?' asked Maybie. 'And the troxes?'

Phee reached into her bag for a handful of nomseeds.

'Hey, Stinkbomb, nibbles!'

'*Breakfaaast!*' sang Russog in Larnie's voice, bounding out from behind the arch.

Jayben gave Russog a reassuring belly scratch. 'Nothing to be scared of, see?'

'Come on, wimps!' said Phee, spotting some antlers behind the arch. 'Coast's clear.'

The quivering trox tip-hoofed over and Phee tied their reins to a spare tent peg for the night, then unpacked the food and blankets. Everyone put on a warm jacket and nestled around the fire. The boys got stuck into their sandwiches, while Maybie went straight for her bag of cookies and one of Larnie's blue cupcakes.

Peggro was bewildered. 'Who packs cupcakes in an emergency?'

Phee laughed. 'Ampelwedians,' she said, taking one for herself.

Jayben opened what looked like a bag of tiny nuts and took a bite. 'Ouch!' he cried, spitting it out.

'You can't eat them, Ben.' Phee chuckled. 'Look.' She retied the bag of kernels before throwing it on the ground.

Crack! Crack! Crack!

Jayben jumped as the bag leapt about, explosions

coming from inside, and then the bag disappeared and a mountain of sweet-smelling popcorn formed in its place.

'Dropcorn!' Maybie grinned. 'I've always wanted to try it. Smells yummy!'

'Seriously, Jayben?' said Peggro. '*Dropcorn* made you jump? But a grannix is fine?'

Jayben grinned sheepishly and shrugged. He took a large handful of dropcorn from the ground and stuffed it in his mouth.

'That was so cool,' said Jayben, when he'd finally swallowed the delicious mouthful.

Phee laughed. 'I had never heard that word before you appeared! Maybe your earthling says it.'

'I wonder what else they say . . .' said Maybie dreamily.

'More to the point, I wonder what new things you'll be able to bring from Earth World,' said Peggro. 'Null is Free-Dreaming those weapons here, but the Dreamers in the Book brought us so many other things – better than weapons. I mean, we wouldn't all have copies of the Book of Dreamers, if Sojan hadn't Free-Dreamed the first printing press five hundred years ago. Tujo, the Third Dreamer, brought us the telescope.'

Phee nodded. 'And Ziloji, the Fifth, brought us the temperature scale.'

'Yes,' said Maybie, stroking her dress, 'and Junas, the Seventh Dreamer, Free-Dreamed the first ever sewing machine!'

Jayben liked thinking about the other Dreamers. He found it comforting. If they had succeeded, why wouldn't he? And who knew what wonders he might bring to the world? Would there be comparable stories written about him? Would his story one day be told in the Book? He hoped so.

If he managed to stop Null and fix the Torch.

'It's so exciting!' said Maybie. 'I mean, *cool*.'

Jayben laughed and gazed up in wonder at the dizzying sea of stars, twinkling in their millions. For the first time since he arrived in the woods, he didn't only feel anxious about what he'd forgotten, but also excited about everything he was going to remember.

Peggro shifted next to him. 'What if someone sees the fire? Or Jayben's light? What if the Agents find us tonight?'

'It's okay,' said Phee, chomping on an empty gribblenut shell. 'Russog will warn us if anyone comes. Plus the tent is thick so I think your light will be hidden, Ben. We lost that Agent miles away. Russog will keep watch and he doesn't miss a thing, do you, Stinkbomb? Is there anything else interesting in your bag, Peggro? From your travels?'

Peggro rummaged through the various compartments. 'This is a book I've been reading, about the North . . . This one's all about Nomolian medicines, and this one's—'

'Oooh!' Maybie interrupted, pointing at something shiny in Peggro's satchel. 'What's *that*?'

'The portapedium?' he said, taking a metal cylindrical object out to show everyone. 'Haven't you seen one before?'

Everyone shook their heads. Peggro looked delighted. It seemed if there was one thing Peggro enjoyed more than knowing everything about something, it was knowing everything about something before anybody else.

'It's a very special device,' he explained proudly. 'It's like carrying twenty-six books in one single tube. Any time I need to know something, I can look it up in here.'

They all leant in for a closer look. The brass tube had a line of twenty-six tiny holes from one end to the other, one for each letter of the alphabet. At one end, there was a dial, and at the other end

was a small glass lens, which could be slid along the line of holes.

'Pick something,' said Peggro. 'Any topic.'

'Anything?' said Maybie. 'Oh! How about zalbanopes?'

'What are zalbanopes?' said Jayben.

'I'll show you,' said Peggro with a smile. He slid the lens along the tube, held it up to the firelight, peered into the lens and gently turned the dial, then handed the portapedium to Maybie.

'Wow!' she gasped, peering inside.

She passed it to Jayben. Inside, he saw a tiny article and an illustration of a blue winged creature with four legs.

'This thing is magical!' said Maybie.

'No, it isn't,' said Peggro. 'It's science. The people who make them have some incredible tools – thanks to the Eighth Dreamer.'

'Hey,' said Jayben, his eye to the portapedium. Another memory was niggling away at the edge of his mind. A memory of him waking up in this world . . . Something blue and small, with four legs, a trunk, wings, and covered in light blue feathers . . . 'I think I've seen one of these animals before. With that long blue nose . . .'

'A zalbanope?' said Peggro. 'You've seen a zalbanope?'

'I think so. It was the day I woke up, before I met you, Phee. I'm not sure, it was so small.'

'Small?' said Peggro. 'They're huge! You sure it wasn't a toy? Oh, and it's called a trunk. Not a nose.'

Jayben frowned. Maybe it *had* been a toy. It was all so hazy.

'Wait,' said Phee. 'What else do you remember?'

Jayben paused, thinking as hard as he could. There was definitely a fuzzy memory of the toy now, blue and feathered, but everything else was a blur. It was frustrating but remembering the toy gave him hope that he might remember the rest. He shook his head. 'Just the zalbanope.'

'I saw a real one flying in the sky once,' said Phee. 'It was massive! But they're extremely rare.'

'They need a lot of the Energy.' Peggro nodded. 'They're intelligent – have large brains – so they tend to nest near Free-Dreams. I've got a book on migrating creatures . . .' He rifled through his bag, and two fat reels of gold ribbon fell out.

Phee was stunned. 'You carry all that cash around with you?'

'Not normally,' he said, stuffing them back in. 'But

we had to bring our savings with us, and my dad didn't want it all in his bag – just in case.'

'*Two whole reels?*'

'Yes. Forty-four yards.'

'Wenden money looks funny,' said Maybie. Then she noticed one of Peggro's trouser pockets was glowing. 'What's that light?'

He pulled out a silver gadget about the size of Jayben's compass. The light was coming from a round white stone set in the centre of it. It was encircled by a series of silver dials, engraved with numbers.

'It's a moondial,' he said. 'It measures time.'

'Like a sundial?' asked Phee.

'Sort of. But a moondial doesn't measure the time of day. It's a tiny calendar, for your pocket. It turns automatically as the days pass.'

'I can't see it turning,' said Maybie, pressing her nose against its glass face.

'It only turns once a day,' he explained. 'Every night, when the moon rises, the moonstone reacts. Then at midnight, it moves one notch to the next day of the year.'

'Cool!' said Phee. 'Look, Ben, it says "8" for this year, and "98" – that's today's date. We're counting down – just eight years and ninety-eight days to go . . .'

Jayben was intrigued. 'Until what?'

'The Miracle, of course,' said Maybie. 'We celebrate getting closer each year with Miraclest. That's why it's called the Miracular Calendar.'

'Not in Bramalan,' said Peggro sadly.

'What?' said Maybie.

'Null doesn't recognise Miracular. He's banned everyone from using it.'

'*What?*' said Phee. 'How do you know what day it is?'

'He has his own calendar, from Earth World. The days count *up* instead of down.'

'How silly,' Maybie giggled. 'How will they know how many days till Miraclest?'

'They don't need to. According to Null, there is no Miraclest.'

'*WHAT?*' both girls gasped.

'But it's the best holiday of the year!' said Maybie. 'And one year closer to the Big Miracle!'

Jayben was fascinated, buttoning his jacket as the evening air cooled. 'What Big Miracle?'

Phee explained. 'At the turn of each century, there's a Miracle, so the calendar counts down to it. Every hundred years, something big is supposed to happen. Something that bends the rules of the worlds, but nobody knows what. Last time, the Fifth Miracle, Maejac Free-Dreamed a person from Earth. A living person! Normally it's impossible to Free-Dream people, only objects.'

'Yes,' said Peggro, 'on the few occasions animals have moved between worlds they haven't lived long. But somehow Maejac brought a person here – an earthling – and they survived!'

Jayben's jaw dropped, trying to imagine physically going to another world different from this one.

'But,' said Phee, 'it's only happened once, at the turn of the century. A Miracle. We have eight years and ninety-eight days left until the Sixth Miracle. That's why today's date is 6 minus 8 : 98

'Exciting!' Jayben said. He loved the idea of counting down to something so exciting. 'Can't people in Bramalan just ignore Null's calendar?'

'His Agents are enforcing it,' Peggro explained. 'It also means no more days off.'

Phee was baffled. 'You mean they take the *even* days off instead of the odd days?'

'No. They work *every* day, whether it's an odd or even number.'

'*My wings!*' Maybie gasped. 'If I never had a day off school, I think I would die!'

'Well,' said Peggro, 'most townsfolk there believe he's the Ninth Dreamer, keeping them safe from forestfolk – what little forest is left in Bramalan. It's all treddolwood in the east.'

Phee crossed her arms with a frown.

'Treddolwood?' said Jayben.

'A treddol is like a tree,' explained Peggro. 'A mutation of a tree.'

'They're evil,' said Phee, stoking the fire with some dry twigs. 'They kill everything around them – any tree that won't be treddolized. So you end up with nothing but a creepy forest of tall, identical treddols with no character.'

'It does make cheaper furniture,' said Peggro. 'Because it grows so fast.'

'But it's basically dead inside. It doesn't last and burns up like dry leaves. They help nobody.'

'Except Null,' said Peggro, 'who needs a lot of fast wood to build all his forts and fences. That's why he's nurturing treddols where his Agents have burned down the old forest.'

Phee looked miserable. Jayben guessed that for the daughter of tree-tamers this was upsetting to hear.

'Didn't you say it burns really fast?' said Jayben. 'Why don't the forestfolk burn his horrible forest down?'

'Forestfolk . . . don't start forest fires,' Phee said brokenly.

At that moment, the moondial in Jayben's hand began to glow brighter, and so did the precious gems in the huge arch.

'Look, Jayben,' said Maybie, pointing east to the horizon. 'She's coming up to see us.'

'Who?' asked Jayben. He squinted in the twilight and saw a soft, silver light on the horizon.

'The Moonmother,' said Phee.

'In her shiny, crystal ball.' Maybie smiled. 'Writing the big story, the story of the worlds and everyone in them.'

Russog let off a loud fart. 'Charming!' he said in Larnie's voice.

'Oi! Stinkbomb!' said Phee. 'Away from the fire!'

Jayben laughed, gobbling the last of the dropcorn and staring at the almost-full moon rising slowly in the sky. 'It was Blue Moon Day a few days ago, wasn't it. Does the moon really turn blue?'

Peggro sniggered. 'No. Blue moons only happen every nineteen years, Jayben. We just celebrate them with Blue Moon Day.'

Nineteen years? thought Jayben. He looked back up at the moon. This time he had an odd sense of déjà vu. 'I think I might have seen this before,' he said.

'The moon?' said Peggro.

'I guess. Although it looks a bit different. Did it used to be fuller? And not so wobbly?'

'It always looks the same. I mean, except for the shadow that moves gradually over its cycle. And it's not wobbling, that's just the atmosphere distorting it.'

'Your earthling can see the moon, perhaps,' said Phee.

'Of course he can!' said Maybie, answering for Jayben. 'The Moonmother watches all the worlds she writes in the big story. Earth World must be somewhere up there in the stars.'

'Wow,' said Phee, wide-eyed. 'You've actually seen both sides of the moon, Ben.'

'Maybe.' Jayben shrugged. That did sound pretty cool, now he thought about it. He wished he could remember it – more than a fragment, anyway.

'To think that our earthlings could be looking at the same moon as us right now,' said Phee, 'not knowing their elflings are looking on this side.'

Peggro smiled.

'I can't wait for you to find that chord, Ben,' said Phee sleepily.

'You'll remember everything,' said Maybie, with a

big yawn, 'and you'll be the best Dreamer ever.'

Jayben shuffled down into his blanket. 'Thanks, guys,' he said. He was glad they were with him, glad not to be alone with it all.

Peggro lay back, shifting his satchel behind his head for a pillow.

'The tent's ready,' Phee yawned, scooching in next to Maybie and Russog.

Jayben gazed up at the moon. The more he looked, the more the sense of familiarity grew. 'I think I did see the moon a bit like this,' he said. 'Maybe in a kitchen . . .'

Nobody responded.

His friends had fallen asleep on the grass outside the tent. Jayben laughed and glanced back up at the moon, thinking about the Moonmother writing the stories of the worlds. 'If you are up there,' he whispered, 'please help me find my chord in time. I know you have the power to help me.' Then he climbed into the tent, and drifted into a dream.

CHAPTER 14

Snaggis

Jayben is walking by water. He is alone. Tiny white lights pierce the mist. There's an archway somewhere close by, though he can't see it. He knows he has to go through it. Then he's in that dark cave again, the cave of shadows and screams. There's something in here with him, something that wants to hurt him. He's scared, he starts to run, but he can hear heavy footsteps behind him . . . they're getting closer, they're going to get him. He can hear screaming—

'*HELP ME!*'

Jayben opened his eyes with a jolt. He sat up. Something wasn't right. He'd heard screaming, he was sure of it.

He stepped outside the tent. It was still dark but there was movement all around – a pack of bald, flying creatures with tatty grey wings and large white eyes swarmed around the camp, screeching and hissing.

Jayben shielded his face with his arms as the monsters swiped at him with their hooked claws. '*What's going on?*' he yelled.

'Hemniks!' cried Peggro, sitting up and putting his glasses on. 'Don't let them bite you!'

'Get off!' said Phee, desperately swatting at them. She held up her fishdart, which was immediately snatched away by one of the creatures.

'That's mine!' shouted Peggro, clinging to the strap of his satchel as one of the snarling pests dragged it from him with its fangs. 'Give it back!'

Then Jayben heard the terrified screams again, the same ones that had pierced his dream. He spun around and peered into the shadows, where a hooded figure was holding Maybie by one wrist, fastening a metal chain around the other.

'*Maybie!*' Jayben yelled, jumping to his feet, running as fast as he could, swatting at the pests. Was that hooded figure Null? His heart hammered with adrenalin. 'Let her go!'

'Oinff! Oinff!' Russog leapt to bite the figure's arm,

when a long stick shot out from the hooded cloak and batted him away. Russog made a pained grunt and hung his head.

'*Russog!*' cried Phee, hurrying to help the little skoggle.

Meanwhile, Peggro held his satchel up like a shield and tore down the sloping moor towards the figure. 'Let Maybie go!'

Jayben managed to grab Maybie's hand, but her other hand was tied to the metal chain, held by the figure.

'HELP!' Maybie screamed, her tiny wings beating desperately.

'Surrender yourself,' the figure hissed at Jayben with a broken, husky voice, 'Or she'll lose her wings.'

The hood of the cloak slipped back to reveal the face of an old woman, with long strands of drool hanging from her dry, cracked mouth. Jayben shook as he looked into her icy-blue eyes – frosted windows to a dark place. Her matted cream-white hair wound all the way down to her ankles, and her pale whiskered skin crinkled loosely over her wiry skeleton, almost as loosely as the silver ring rattling on her finger.

'Greetings, Dreamer,' she hissed, putting a purple

monocle in her pocket and taking out a set of handcuffs. 'You couldn't hide from Snaggis.'

Snaggis? Jayben thought. *The witch!* How had she found him? He looked at her bony wrist to see a silver star-shaped charm – and it was glowing. *Spritewood!*

'Come with me, Dreamer and I'll let her live,' said Snaggis, coughing up a luminous green liquid that steamed as the droplets hit the ground, eroding the soil and rock beneath her.

Jayben thought quickly. If he went with Snaggis he was as good as dead; but he had to free Maybie. Phee didn't have her fishdart. If only he knew how to light the Torch. At least the Torch was something – maybe the sight of it alone would frighten the witch. He reached into his pocket, expecting to touch metal – but it wasn't there.

Then he remembered. It was tucked under his blanket.

From the air came desperate yelps from Russog. One of the hemniks was carrying him up into the swarm of grey skin and jagged bones. Keylo and Woodge were under attack too, swinging their antlers at the relentless savages, before fleeing to hide behind the arch.

'Leave them alone!' shouted Phee, jumping as high

as she could for Russog. 'Put him down!' But they were too high.

'Yes!' Snaggis spat her acidic drool. 'Eat up, babies!' She snapped her bony fingers, her silver charm flashed and suddenly there were twice as many hemniks.

Jayben stumbled backwards.

Seeing his fear, Snaggis broke into a sinister chuckle. 'What's the matter, Dreamer? Didn't find your chord?'

Peggro lunged again for Maybie, but his moondial fell out of his pocket, and three of the creatures swooped down, crashing into each other as they jostled for a look at the light.

'Of course!' Peggro gasped. 'The light, Jayben! They're hemniks. Jayben, do the fire trick again.'

Jayben looked at the shrubs and tried thinking about the arch in his dream, the moonstones glittering in the mist – but nothing happened. Snaggis smirked, amused by his inability. And it triggered something inside him, a rage. He thought of all the suffering she and Null had inflicted. All the suffering they would go on to inflict, unless he could stop them. *I have this power*, he thought, *and I have the Torch*.

Jayben needed to buy some time, to distract Snaggis while he kept trying, but how? He grabbed a handful of pebbles and gave them to Phee. 'Chuck these at her!' he said. 'Keep her busy, I'll be right back!'

He turned, breathing hard, then ran as fast as he could back up to the campsite, where the fluttering scavengers were fighting over boxes and bags. He was bombarded by snapping teeth from all directions. One of the hemniks sank its fangs deep into his arm, and it seemed to send the rest of the pack into a frenzy.

Jayben was pushed to the ground as dozens of the creatures scrambled for a bite. But he felt no pain as they pecked at his skin. It was as if he was watching it happen from a distance. His mind was on something far more important.

He slowly crawled beneath them, reaching into the tent for his blanket, and yanking the Golden Torch free. He turned to face the hemnik swarm, punching one in the face so he could free his other arm.

Then he held the golden stem of the Torch with both hands and closed his eyes. *I'm the Ninth Dreamer,* he thought, *and I can light this Torch.*

He aimed it upwards into the night sky.

Nothing happened.

Jayben could see Snaggis picking up her stick.

'Ben! Help!' Phee screamed in the dark.

'Come on!' he shouted at the Torch as another

hemnik crawled on to his chest. 'How do you work? Light! Just light!'

It was no use.

The hellish creatures pulled his arms and clawed at his face.

'Arrrgh! I wish you would all disappear! I just wish this— wish this—'

Sparks flew from inside the Torch. It made a strange rumbling noise and felt hot.

The hemniks flapped back a little.

'Yeah! Get back!' he said, emboldened and clambering to his feet. He waved the Torch in the air.

BOOOOOM!

'AAAAH!' Jayben yelled.

'NO!' Snaggis screamed.

The Torch roared and shot blinding violet flames into the air, illuminating the moor and the campsite and knocking him against the arch and then back on to the ground. The heat was intense and he broke out in a sweat, his arms shaking, and, for a moment, he felt as trapped as he had done in his absence seizures.

If it's not impossible, then you can do it.

With every ounce of strength in his body, he pushed against the force and climbed to his feet. The flaming Golden Torch was no longer a strange object from his pocket; it was his to bear.

Phee and Maybie were looking up in wonder.

Snaggis was crouching in fear, but her pets didn't seem to be scared. The hemniks were hypnotised by the intense light, their claws unclenched, dropping Russog and Phee's tools to the ground. Peggro covered his eyes.

'Stop!' cried Snaggis. 'Come away, babies!' But the creatures' white eyes were fixed on the violet light, and they slowly hovered towards the flame. The witch hobbled towards Jayben, dragging strands of drool along the ground, and Maybie behind her on the chain. 'Don't do this!'

The hemniks carelessly drifted into the light.

FOOMF!

One was vaporised.

FOOMF!

Another one gone.

Then another, and another . . .

'NO!' the witch screamed, stumbling to her knees as all but three of the pests were consumed in the intense heat.

She snapped her fingers and the three remaining hemniks became six. But none could resist the light.

FOOMF!

Two more were gone.

FOOMF!

Three more.

She snapped again and the last one became two.

FOOMF!

Down to one again.

Snaggis tossed her stick up, knocking the final hemnik out of the sky. The witch caught her last remaining monster, then turned its eyes away from the light and hurled it towards Russog.

Jayben swung the Torch down and the last hemnik was caught in the flame.

Snaggis fell to the ground and didn't seem to notice her clanband slipping off her bony wrist.

'You'll pay for this!' she snarled, tugging a sobbing Maybie by the chain.

Wiping his brow with his elbow, Jayben thrust the Torch forward, shooting the flames above Snaggis's head. 'Let my friend go!' he yelled, looking straight into her stony eyes. 'I'm a Dreamer. You don't scare me.' He crouched and picked up her clanband. 'Set her free or I'll destroy this like I destroyed your monsters.'

Snaggis rattled the handcuffs. 'Not without you, Dreamer. And I can survive without a charm.'

With her long fingernails she snipped a curl of

Maybie's hair. Then she gave a menacing smirk. 'Last chance to come nicely, Dreamer.'

Jayben shook his head, struggling to control the Torch's flames.

'Suit yourself.' She raised her stick's sharp point, aiming it straight at Maybie's head.

'NO!' yelled Jayben and he swung the Torch down and scorched the stick and the witch's fingers.

Snaggis fell back, losing her grip on the chain, and Maybie broke free. She ran to Peggro, who shielded her behind him.

Jayben held Snaggis's glowing silver charm in his hand and pictured the ghost village of Jonningwed. *After what Snaggis and Null have done*, he thought, *it's their turn for a spell of bad luck*. Then he threw the charm into the violet flame.

A bright white flash and the clanband was incinerated.

Snaggis vomited, and as she turned, Jayben noticed a single Rainbow crystal embedded in her stick.

'You'll pay for this, Dreamer,' she whispered. Then she ate the curl of Maybie's hair, pointed her stick to the north and vanished.

CHAPTER 15

What's a Monday?

Jayben doubled over, breathing fast. 'Where did she go?' he said, looking around the moor. 'Did anyone see?' But the others couldn't hear him over the roar of the Torch. He looked up at the flames and for a moment, allowed himself to wonder. *If it was lit, maybe it could stay lit. Maybe he had broken the spell.*

Then quite suddenly the Torch went out with a puff of white smoke.

'Oinff!' said Russog at his feet.

Jayben smiled despite his disappointment, stroking the skoggle's green head in the faint light of dawn.

'Oh, thank you!' said Maybie, running to hug everyone, tears on her cheeks. 'The Torch, Jayben!

You did it! You were so brave!'

Russog said in Peggro's voice, 'Brave or foolish; one of the two.'

Phee laughed. 'It was amazing! How did you do it? Same as the fire trick?'

'No,' Jayben said, giddy from what had happened. 'I tried the fire thing, and it wouldn't work, then somehow I got the Torch to light. But I don't know how.'

'Magical!' Maybie smiled. 'I just know you'll mend it, Jayben. You'll keep it burning.'

Phee shook a bag of nomseeds and Keylo and Woodge gingerly returned from behind the arch. 'She kept multiplying those horrible hemniks,' said Phee, crouching down to hug Russog.

'That was pretty terrifying,' said Peggro, who still looked shaken. 'The old magic of Spritewoods, drawn out from being so close to Null. That must be why her charm was glowing.'

Jayben nodded, glad to have destroyed her clanband. 'Well, she's got no lucky charm now.'

'Thank you, Jay-Jay,' said Maybie, more quietly, taking his hand. 'I've always been scared of hemniks . . . I thought . . .' She stopped, swallowed, and when she spoke again she sounded more like the Maybie he knew. 'Look, she's even messed up my hair! Those witches are always hunting for us Fairywoods for their spells.'

Phee helped Jayben rebandage his hand to hide his Rainbow crystals and his hemnik wounds on his neck and arms. They turned his collar up, in case his purple chordian light attracted any more Agents – or worse.

'Thanks, Phee,' said Jayben. He walked over to the rock where Snaggis had vomited. It was eroding, fizzling into shiny remains. 'Witches use Fairywoods for their spells? Is that why she took some of your hair, Maybie?'

'I guess so,' said Maybie. 'She will have used it to go back north, I guess. Probably to replace that charm.'

Jayben nodded. The elation at having survived the attack was replaced with dread as reality settled on him. Snaggis was only temporarily weakened by the Torch. She would return, with Null. They would be easy to track, now that she knew where they were.

He looked around, suddenly suspicious of every shadow. 'Snaggis must have used one of those purple lenses, she must have seen my chordian light . . . But the Jarmaster said it would be dim until I found my chord. Did the Agent we saw earlier tip her off?

What if she's here?' He sighed. 'This is all my fault. I'm so sorry.'

Peggro looked pale. 'Don't worry, Jayben. We're glad we're with you.'

'Maybe the witch's lens is just really powerful?' said Phee. 'It doesn't necessarily mean the Agent is close by.'

'We need to get out of here,' Jayben said, blowing on the Torch to cool it down. 'And keep going, quicker than yesterday. We need to get to Last Rock.'

'And we will, Ben,' said Phee. Maybie took his hand again and squeezed it.

Jayben watched the fizzling rock settle in the form of a frozen splash shape, glowing blue and green. He remembered something, and turned to Maybie, who was standing next to him. 'Did you see Snaggis's stick? It had a Rainbow crystal inside it, like mine. Why would she have that?'

Maybie looked thoughtful.

Jayben looked up at the moon and suddenly an image popped into his head – a flash of something red – and as it became clearer, the shiny shape at his feet began to shake.

'What the—' he said, leaping back.

CRACK!

In a flash of light, the shaking object turned into a bright-red London postbox.

'A post—' Jayben said, the word coming to him as he reached out to touch it. 'A postbox?'

'Stay away!' cried Peggro, hiding behind Phee. 'It could be anything!'

'What the dune-hoppers?' said Maybie, her eyes full of wonder.

'Now *that* is cool,' Phee grinned, holding Russog, who was burping nervously.

Jayben read the notice on the postbox, below its letter slot.

Last Collection Time:
Monday to Friday
6.00pm

'What's a Monday?' asked Phee.

'You know, a day in the week!' Jayben erupted with excitement. 'And this . . . is a postbox! It's where you post letters for them to be delivered all over the country!'

Phee shook her head in wonder. 'Not like any mailbox I've ever seen.'

Peggro and Maybie agreed.

'So, it *is* from Earth World!' said Jayben, admiring the bold crown emblem below the notice. 'I did a Free-Dream! *I did a Free-Dream!*' He laughed with joy, giving Maybie a hug. 'Straight from my earthling's mind!'

Phee and Maybie beamed at him.

'You've also sent that weird rock to the Earth World,' said Peggro anxiously, 'to wherever this strange red post-thing was. Who knows what poison Snaggis might have left in it!'

Jayben shoved Peggro playfully. 'It would only be a tiny bit of poison. And I can do it, Peggro! I can Free-Dream! Watch . . .' He looked at another rock and tried to picture a postbox in his mind again. But the memory was foggy now. He could only see a red blur. 'I'm losing it. But it's in my head. A memory!' He grinned from ear to ear. 'I just need to find my chord and I'll be able to Free-Dream anything!'

'It's amazing!' said Phee. Then she grimaced. 'Oh Ben – you're bleeding.'

Jayben looked down and saw that blood was running down his legs from his hemnik wounds.

'What the dimmits?' said Peggro, turning white.

Jayben was shocked to see the blood. Looking at it made him feel woozy. But he still felt no pain – not even stinging. Was it a Dreamer thing? Or something to do with his seizures?

'So brave, Jay-Jay!' said Maybie, tears filling her eyes again. 'I wish I could fix you up.'

'Hey,' said Jayben, noticing her gold charm was glowing. 'Look at your band!'

She wiped her eyes and looked down at the little nutshell around her neck. '*Oh, my wings!*' As her tears dried in her hands, they gave off tiny specks of glowing dust that drifted in the air. 'That's never happened before.'

'What is it?' he asked, watching the dust floating towards him, but everyone was lost for words.

The glowing specks gathered around his wounds, then one of the beads of blood on his leg stopped running down. It wobbled. Then slowly began running *up* his leg.

Peggro went pale and looked away.

Another blood drop followed up Jayben's leg, then another, and another. Every drop ran back up over his knee and into his wounds.

Incredibly, the wounds were closing, healing perfectly, as if they had never been.

'It tickles!' Jayben chuckled as the last drop was reabsorbed.

'What was that?' Peggro asked uneasily.

'*Dusthealing?*' said Maybie with great excitement. 'I can do dusthealing spells? Like the old fairies! In the Magic Ages!'

'But how?' said Phee.

'I don't know. It just happened. Nobody can do that nowadays – it's old magic!'

'Of course,' Jayben smiled, giving her a hug. 'Remember, the Jarmaster said that people near me might get their old magic restored, from the Energy in my crystals. Like Snaggis has hers from Null.'

Maybie looked like she might burst with excitement. 'Oh, I can't wait to see what kind of magic you guys will do! And what you'll Free-Dream next, Jay-Jay!'

Peggro seemed afraid of the magic in his blood. 'Will I really turn invisible? What if I don't want to?' He took quick breaths. 'What if I *stay* invisible?'

Maybie gave him a quick squeeze. 'I don't think that'll happen, Peggro.'

Phee tried lifting a large, heavy rock but it wouldn't budge. 'Nope,' she said. 'No Giantwood powers yet. Don't worry, Peggro, it doesn't look like you and me are getting ancient powers any time soon.'

Maybie scratched her head. 'So, why, why did I get mine?'

Jayben thought for a moment. 'The Free-Dream,' he said. 'We were holding hands when I did it. Maybe if we all hold hands next time . . .'

Peggro widened his eyes and backed away. 'I'm all right without mine for now, thanks,' he muttered.

Phee shook herself. 'Okay,' she said, buckling her tools on to her belt. 'Before we even think about our magic, we need to get moving. But we've got to be more careful now, Ben. You need to stay hidden. It's getting light. If we set off now, we could make it to Blanbor before the end of the day. We can stay with my aunt and cousin there tonight and leave by boat tomorrow.'

'Anyone got something I can cover my head with?' asked Jayben. 'To hide the light?'

Phee tied two corners of a white blanket and Jayben slipped it over his head like a hooded cape.

Jayben took a deep breath – he didn't want to say this, but he knew he must. 'We should split up,' he said. 'I'm only going to attract more danger. You guys should find somewhere safe.'

'Where?' said Phee, 'Back to Giantwood, where the Agents are burning everything? No. We're staying together.'

'Just until Blanbor, then,' said Jayben. He would

leave his friends there. He couldn't put them in any more peril.

Peggro inspected the postbox from a safe distance. 'We shouldn't leave this here for a Dream Thief.'

'No time to hide it,' said Phee. 'Plus it's massive! We'll tell the Chordian Guard about it when we get to Last Rock. And you've probably doubled the Energy up here, Ben. Together with the gramophone and that big burst from the Torch, no one's gonna lose their memories for miles. That's a great thing!'

They gathered their belongings and packed up the tent and the other blankets. Jayben put the Torch back in his pocket.

Maybie smiled, looking up. 'Daylight, at last!' She pottered behind the arch to shrink herself.

Phee strapped Russog into her backpack and helped Peggro with his satchel, which had been torn by the hemniks. Some of his smaller books kept falling out.

'How about this?' said Phee, and she used some old rope to fasten it for him.

'Oh,' he said, surprised. 'Thanks a lot.'

'We'll have breakfast on the go,' said Phee, tossing a bag of cookies to the boys as they climbed on to Keylo's back. She mounted her own trox.

Maybie was still behind the arch, sneezing and sneezing.

'You okay back there?' Phee mumbled, in her saddle with a cookie between her teeth.

The sneezing stopped and Maybie shuffled out, still full size. 'It must be this silly cloud,' she sighed, trying to check her reflection in a puddle. 'It's too dark today. I can't fly without sunshine.'

Everyone looked up at the sky. The rising sun was trapped behind a thick blanket of cloud with a greenish tint. Jayben couldn't believe they hadn't noticed before now. They'd been too distracted by the postbox.

'Weird,' said Peggro, sniffing at the air. 'Is it tree gas? Must be from all the woods they're burning.'

Phee bit her lip. 'It's okay, Maybie. You can ride up here with me.'

'But I need to fly. I always fly. What if I need to fly away?' She looked anxious.

Phee helped her up into her saddle and handed her a chocolate cookie. 'You won't need to,' she said reassuringly, 'because we'll stick together.'

Maybie looked down, then brightened. 'I guess I'm still quite high off the ground.' She smiled and bit into her cookie.

'Just to Blanbor,' said Jayben, flipping open his compass, 'then I'll go on alone and—' He paused. Was that a shadow behind the arch? Was it an Agent? Had they been followed? Or was Snaggis back already? He didn't want to find out. 'Let's go!'

Peggro unfolded his map.

'Straight to the coast!' said Phec, tapping Woodge's side, and off they galloped down the misty moors.

CHAPTER 16

The Iron Road

They had reached an orchard and come to the end of a row of trees, their branches drooping with the weight of the plump purple fruit. The sky was still overcast but it felt warm here. A pile of freshly chopped logs lay quietly whining on the ground like they were hurting.

'What is that?' said Phee, pulling on her reins. 'What kind of tools did *that*? You can't just hack at a living tree!'

Peggro peeked through the bushes. 'A railway?' He gasped. 'The Iron Road. It's here?'

'The *what* road?' said Maybie.

'The Iron Road. One of Null's big projects, a

192

road with rails. It's for transporting all the stolen Free-Dreams to his new city. Dad and I saw it back in Bramalan but we thought it was just a rumour that his Agents had built a bridge, to continue it here into Wenden. This must be it!'

A bridge over the sea? thought Jayben, remembering the map of the vast world. *A road across two realms?* He was beginning to realise the enormity of Null's support, and the strength of his army of Agents, and their operation. *Formidable, to say the least*, he thought uneasily.

Phee couldn't block out the whining from the chopped wood. 'I can't believe they've just torn up the countryside for this road. And it's weird. What kind of carts need rails on the road?'

A deep clicking noise came from the short tree beside them. Then another . . .

A warning.

Keylo reared up and Peggro dropped his map.

Jayben saw it drift under a bush by the railway. He jumped down from the trox and chased after it, grabbing it just in time before it landed on the tracks.

The clicks turned to drumming and he thought he saw something move behind a tree.

Russog became agitated. 'Oinff! Oinff! Oinff!'

'Shush, Russog!' said Phee, trying to calm Woodge. 'Hurry, Ben!'

The drumming grew faster.

Someone grabbed him from behind and dragged him backwards.

'*JAYBEN!*' Maybie screamed.

'Let me go!' Jayben shouted, desperately pulling to get away. But whoever had grabbed him had already swiftly tied his hands behind his back and pushed him on to the muddy path.

'Get off him!' said Phee, leaping down with Maybie and whipping her fishdart from her belt.

'Oinff!' cried Russog, trying to wriggle from Phee's backpack.

Peggro got down too, clutching his satchel and trembling behind Phee.

The trees were quiet now. Jayben's captor flipped him over and held a sharp knife to Jayben's face.

It was a man, stocky and stubble-faced. Jayben noticed a logo stitched into the sleeve of his captor's grey jacket: nine white squares, and the words: *Agents of the Ninth*.

It was suddenly very real. Jayben's heart was pounding, and he clenched his bandaged fist. Was the man really going to use his knife? Did he know

Jayben carried the Torch? Would he take him straight to Null?

'Drop your dart,' said the man, pulling the white blanket off Jayben's head, 'or he gets hurt.'

Phee paused then groaned and lowered her shaking weapon.

'What do we have here then?' said the man, sniffing at Jayben's collar. 'Sap? *Forest kids?* I've hit the jackpot with yous, haven't I?'

'Who's Jack Pot?' Jayben mumbled through the Agent's sweaty sausage fingers.

The balding man looked down, grinning with yellow teeth, a battered Trollwood charm on a rusty chain around his neck. 'That's right, son,' he said. 'They pay extra for handing in forest scum. Little Dream Thieves like yous.'

Jayben heaved a sigh of relief. The man didn't seem to know he was a Dreamer. There was no sign of a purple lens on him.

'Let him go!' said Phee.

'Sorry, darling,' he smirked. 'Rules are rules. We can't have little slopheads like you running around, nicking our Free-Dream, dulling our brains. Got enough to do trying to catch the new Dreamer!'

Jayben looked at Phee with trepidation.

The man continued. 'Chief saw a flash of the light not far from here, south I think he said, so I'm just passing through. He doesn't need to waste time on forest scum. Just think of the bonus I'll get for handing yous in!'

Jayben's heart raced faster. If a nearby Agent had a purple lens then they didn't have long to escape, since the light would be brightest wherever Jayben was. Luckily this particular Agent didn't seem the brightest, and he wasn't carrying purple lenses of his own, but nevertheless Jayben needed to be calm and think about how to get them out of here. He thought of the skallabore, and the grannix, and Snaggis retreating. He stopped struggling and straightened up. 'You *have* to let us go,' he said against the man's hand.

The man chortled, removing his hand slightly.

'We're not Dream Thieves, and we won't give you any trouble,' Jayben said clearly.

'Who do you think you are? A little slopper like you giving orders to Deputy Under-Officer Fudd?'

'We just met someone who said they saw a Dreamer, running that way,' said Jayben firmly, 'as your chief said, definitely heading south. Didn't we, guys? They had one of those purple lenses.' The others looked extremely nervous, unsure of Jayben's tactic, but they nodded along.

'Hmm,' said the man, looking tempted. Then he shook his head. 'All very well but I don't have them purple goggles. I'll never catch him before the Chief.' Then he noticed Jayben's bandage. 'What happened to your hand?'

'How much?' said Phee abruptly.

'*Eh?*' said Fudd.

What's she doing? thought Jayben. Whatever her plan, it had drawn the man's eye off his bandage.

'How much will you get for handing us in?' she said. 'Your bonus?'

Fudd howled with laughter. 'More than you can count! You couldn't even—'

'I can count!' she snapped. 'How much?'

He stopped laughing. 'Couple of yards for each of yous. Could even be as much as three yards for an older one like you. Bah! That's, like, seven yards, after fees. I think.'

'Agency fees?' Peggro asked.

'Of course.' Fudd nodded. 'What other fees are there? The Agency takes their cut.'

'So,' said Peggro, clearing his throat, 'after Agency fees, that would be four yards, one foot, and six inches.'

'*Eh?*'

'After fees,' he explained, cautiously peeking out from behind Phee. 'That's all you'll get from nine yards. They'll take exactly half of your bonus.'

Fudd looked blank for a moment. He frowned, as if embarrassed to be corrected by a child. Then he shrugged.

'Yeah,' he said.

'Of course,' said Phee, 'they couldn't halve your bonus if they never knew you'd caught us . . .'

'Eh?' Fudd scratched his shiny head. 'Don't be daft, love! I wasn't born yesterday. They won't pay me an inch if I don't hand nobody in.'

'Of course *they* won't. But what if someone else paid you the reward? Someone who won't charge any fees?'

'Someone else?' said Fudd, looking thoroughly puzzled.

'Oh, for moon's sake!' she snapped. 'Us! We'll pay you.'

The Agent laughed. 'Yous? As if slopheads like yous have that kinda ribbon.'

'We do,' said Phee, with a dead-straight face. 'It's your lucky day. Now, name your price.'

Fudd paused to think again.

Jayben smiled. *I have the best friends*, he thought.

'We have plenty of ribbon,' said Phee. She seemed more angry than scared now, like she was angry that this silly little man, who could be bought so easily, was the reason she'd been shut in the woods for years. In fact, she looked furious.

She reached an open hand back to Peggro, who took a step back.

'But it's *my* money,' he said. 'Why should I—'

'Ever wanna see your dad again?' she whispered.

Peggro looked over at the knife, dangerously close to Jayben's throat. 'Nine yards, then.' He sighed, rummaging in his pocket for one of his reels of gold ribbon.

'But,' said Phee, 'in return, you have to get us safely away from here. Before any other Agents come.'

'I dunno,' he tutted, shaking his head. 'You know what they'd do to me if they found out? Nine yards wouldn't help me then!'

'Right.' She nodded, looking like she wanted to punch him. 'So I guess you'll have to be extra careful.'

'Well, I'll need time to—'

The trees started drumming.

'We don't *have* time!' Jayben said urgently.

Phee nodded. 'Get us across, quickly, and safely, and—'

'Someone's coming!' said Maybie, spying through the branches. 'Two men on some kind of trox.'

'Oinff!' said Russog.

Peggro looked terrified. 'What if they have flashpins?'

'Shush, Russog!' said Phee, turning back to Fudd. 'We'll double it. Okay?'

'*Eighteen yards?*' Peggro gasped.

Fudd's sweaty face lit up.

With a sigh, Peggro started measuring out the ribbon. 'One foot . . . two foot . . . three foot . . . four . . .'

'Lovely!' Fudd chuckled, his yellow grin growing wider with every foot of gold Peggro unravelled.

Phee held the ribbon back. 'Let him go first – unharmed.'

Fudd sniggered, putting his knife on his belt and untying Jayben's hands. 'You kids aren't total dummies, I'll give yous that.'

Jayben and his friends climbed back on to their trox.

Phee raised her fishdart, aiming it at Fudd. 'Here's what's gonna happen,' said Phee, 'you're gonna get us across the railway, staying in front of us, where I can see you, till we're safely away. Got it?'

Fudd opened his mouth to assert himself, but nothing came out, unnerved by Phee's look of fury.

Wow, thought Jayben. For someone who hadn't left Ampelwed for so many years, Phee sure knew how to handle an Agent!

Maybie clung to Phee's backpack, looking more relaxed now that she was off the ground again.

Fudd snapped to it. 'Hide in there!' he said, leading them back the way they had come, through the rows of fruit trees towards a large shed. 'I'll get rid of them.'

Russog was shaking. He said in Tedrik's voice, 'Stay here, boy.'

Keylo and Woodge shot into the shed, cramming themselves inside and Phee, Maybie, Jayben, Peggro and Russog were safe at last. The tips of their tails disappeared into the shadows just as two Agents saddled to two trox-like creatures with boxy legs and curled ram horns came around the corner.

Through a small window inside the shed Jayben saw them draw up beside Fudd, who was fidgeting and sweating, likely reflecting on the danger he had got himself into.

Phee whispered to the others, 'Don't. Breathe.' She stuffed a nomseed into Russog's snout.

One of the Agents stepped down from his saddle.

 201

'Oh dear, oh dear.' He tutted. 'What happened to you this time, Under-Officer?' He wore a similar grey uniform with the same white logo. Hanging on a chain from a top pocket was a purple lens.

'Forest scum,' said Fudd, wheezing and wiping his sweaty brow. 'Little Dream Thieves, stinking of sap.'

Jayben's heart sank. Peggro was shaking. Was Fudd about to betray them after all?

'Where?' asked the other Agent. 'Spit it out, Fudd.'

'On troxback,' he spluttered. 'Two trox.'

Phee gripped her reins.

Jayben pulled his collar up, then put his hands in his pockets, hoping that might hide some of the invisible light.

'Th-they went south,' said Fudd. 'That way. Round the shed, t'wards the moors.'

Jayben let out a breath, but then his heart skipped a beat.

There was a man standing in the dark corner of the shed, looking straight at him.

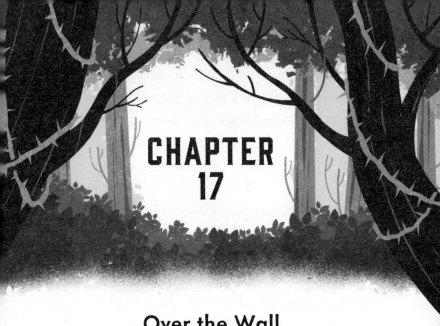

CHAPTER 17

Over the Wall

Jayben pointed to the man in the shadows with a shaking finger. 'Phee?' he whispered.

Phee jolted when she saw the figure and put her hand to her mouth, her fishdart quivering in her other hand. Peggro and Maybie hadn't seen him, and Jayben thought it best to keep it that way.

The Agent outside came closer. 'You sure they went south? Really sure about that, Fudd?'

Jayben wondered why the man in the corner didn't move or alert the Agents. His mouth was moving slightly, though no sound seemed to be coming out, and he showed no emotion.

A *nullhead*, thought Jayben. He knew that nullheads

couldn't harm children but he was terrified the man might make a noise and attract the Agents' attention.

Fudd was pleading outside, 'Of course! Of course! I tried to stop 'em, Guv, I did, but they were too quick, see, but if yous—'

Through the window, Jayben saw one the Agents shove Fudd to the ground. 'Everything's too quick for you, ain't it, Fudd? Not much between your ears.'

'Sort yourself out, Under-Officer!' said the other. 'Ain't much use to the Ninth in that kinda shape. Can't even catch a few filthy tree-scumlets!'

'Yes, Guv. I mean, I'll—'

The nullhead shuffled towards the door, muttering the spell.

Jayben held his breath. Maybie noticed him and gripped Phee's shirt.

'We'll get 'em,' said the senior Agent, climbing back into his saddle and reaching for a handheld weapon different from Phee's. Attached to its wooden handle there was a metal barrel and a trigger.

'See ya back at the unit.' The other Agent smirked. 'You're on watch now, if it ain't too much trouble for ya!'

The nullhead rose up, zombie-like, flung the door open and walked out into the daylight.

'Hang on,' said the first Agent, turning his head to the door. 'What have we here?'

Inside, they all pressed back into the shadows.

Peggro shut his eyes, taking deep breaths. 'Okay, okay, it's just my worst fear coming true. Nothing to worry about . . . Nothing to worry about . . .'

Fudd backed towards the shed door, putting his earplugs in. 'Just a stupid,' he said. 'Ignore him.'

Maybie clung to Phee's backpack, her eyes tightly shut.

The senior Agent looked suspicious, putting his earplugs in. 'Or, maybe . . .' he said, taking his purple lens and raising it towards his eye.

Jayben's heart nearly jumped out of his chest.

Phee grabbed his arm.

Fudd blocked the door as the nullhead wandered off into the bushes. 'It's empty, Guv,' he said, a wobble in his voice. 'All clear in there. I already checked.'

The lens met the senior Agent's eye and he gasped, wincing, as if blinded.

The game was up.

'*Go!*' said Jayben, kicking Keylo's side, and their trox stormed towards the door.

As they swept past, Phee tossed the gold ribbon down to Fudd.

He grabbed it then leapt out of their way, retreating into the shed.

The trees were drumming louder and faster.

The Agents were startled enough that the trox managed to put some distance between them. Phee turned and aimed her fishdart and the men reached for their weapons, turning their animals to give chase.

'Oinff! Oinff!' Russog thrashed about.

The trees were pounding.

Jayben felt a rush of adrenalin, hearing the heavy hooves behind them. *We are not getting caught*, he thought.

BANG!

Something shot past Woodge's ear.

'What the moon was that?' said Phee.

BANG!

Another one, missing Peggro's shoulder by an inch.

Flashpins? Jayben looked back with horror to see the approaching Agents aiming their handheld weapons, their fingers on the metal triggers.

BANG!

A pellet ripped past them and the trox panicked, rearing back, nearly throwing the group from their saddles.

Maybie screamed. 'I wanna fly home!'

'The Torch, Jayben!' cried Peggro. 'Light the Torch!'

Jayben pulled it out and held it up in the air. 'Light!'

BANG!

Another pellet, grazing Keylo's antler.

There wasn't a spark from the Torch. 'Come on!' said Jayben, with a groan of frustration. 'Light! Light!'

'Do it, Jayben. Hurry!' shouted Peggro, clinging to Keylo for his life.

'*Go!*' yelled Phee, regaining control of Woodge.

Their trox put on a burst of speed, outstripping the Agents and their bulkier beasts. Jayben angrily shoved the Torch back in his pocket as they galloped away.

What was the point in having powers, he thought, if he couldn't use them to save himself and his friends.

Nothing much was spoken about that afternoon. Jayben and his friends didn't stop, running and racing on their trox as the sun lowered in the sludgy, overcast sky.

Jayben was trying not to think too hard about the danger they were in. The Agent had been dazzled by his light – clearly it wasn't as dim as the Jarmaster had said it would be, which made him feel dangerously exposed.

They had lost the Agents from the Iron Road.

But there could be other Agents, ready to capture forestfolk, determined to find the new Dreamer. And by now Snaggis would surely be closing in, leading Null to Jayben.

'Another wall, boys!' Phee shouted as they hurtled down a narrow lane. 'Hold on tight!'

'Not again,' Peggro groaned, bracing himself. 'Can't we go around it? Or stop for a bit? I need to pee!'

They neared the wall, and Woodge leapt into the air, clipping the stones with her hooves.

'Weeee!' Maybie squealed, as they thudded down on the other side.

Keylo followed, knocking off several stones.

'STOP!' shouted Phee, yanking on the reins. 'It's a cliff!'

Jayben pulled back as hard as he could and Keylo skidded about, turning her hooves only inches from the drop.

'Let me off NOW!' cried Peggro.

Before Jayben could bring Keylo to a halt, Peggro leapt down, scuffing his knees before clambering back over the wall.

'Peggro?' Phee called, stopping Woodge away from the cliff.

'Where's he going?' said Maybie, buzzing from the

thrill of sort-of flying again.

'You okay?' said Jayben, bringing Keylo alongside Woodge. 'Peggro?'

Jayben climbed over the wall and found Peggro sitting on the other side, his back against the stones, his knees drawn up to his chin, arms wrapped around his satchel.

'Leave me alone!' he replied in a cross voice. 'I've had enough of those stupid animals!'

From the other side of the wall, Maybie giggled. 'But it's fun going fast!'

'How is any of this *fun*?' Peggro snapped, wiping tears from behind his glasses.

'I'm sorry, Peggro,' said Phee. 'You're right. We shouldn't have been going so fast. I know it's been a tough couple of days, but—'

'*A tough couple of days?*' he puffed, tears streaming from his glasses. 'I lost my dad yesterday! I don't know where he is or what might happen to him! Then we were almost eaten by a grannix! Nearly torn to shreds by hemniks! Robbed and shot at by Agents! Not to mention the nullhead in the barn. And now we nearly fell off a cliff!'

Jayben sat down next to Peggro. He took out his last two cookies and held one out to Peggro.

Peggro angrily turned his back. Then he reached back for the cookie. Without a word, and facing away from each other, the two boys sat munching on the sweet, buttery treats. Peggro dried his eyes.

'I'm sorry about everything,' Jayben mumbled through a gooey mouthful. 'And I'm sorry the Torch didn't work today. I can't remember how I did it before, but I did, so once I find my chord—'

'It's fine,' Peggro huffed, between mouthfuls.

'I'm sorry about your money too,' said Jayben. 'Thank you for paying that man. It was very cool that you knew all that stuff about the Agent fees.'

Peggro turned around. 'Well, Dad gave me the money for emergencies.' He shrugged. 'And it was an emergency, and Agency fees aren't exactly stellar science.'

Phee called out over the wall. 'Is he okay?'

'He's fine,' said Jayben. 'Just taking a break.'

Peggro took off his glasses and cleaned them with a handkerchief from his top pocket. 'I'm sorry I got angry,' he said. 'I'm not like the rest of you. I'm not good with animals or weapons. I can't fly or Free-Dream. All I'm good at is being worried, and right now I have a lot to worry about.' He held up his green Dragonwood charm. 'It's in my nature. I mean,

I'm descended from elves who literally turned invisible at the first sign of danger.'

Jayben leant back against the wall. 'You might not know about animals or weapons. But you have your books and machines and your maps, and you know so much about the world. I wouldn't have got this far without you.'

'It's scary when I don't know what's coming next,' said Peggro. 'I don't like not knowing things. I'm not brave like you.'

'You are brave,' said Jayben, licking his sugary fingers. 'And you know so much! I don't even know where I'm from, or who my parents are, or even what clan I belong to! I get scared too. I'm worried about my head and those absences. I'm worried about what will happen if I don't find this chord in three days, about not remembering, about how I'm going to stop Null.' He paused, thinking about their time on the moor. 'But it's been easier to cope, having you and the others with me on my journey. It's made everything less scary. Like, even if it's horrible, I can cope because I'm not alone and we can talk about it afterwards.'

'You mean, like, we're friends?'

Jayben paused, then smiled. 'Yeah, exactly,' he replied.

'I had a friend once,' Peggro sighed. 'But he turned out not to be a friend after all. He only hung around when everyone else was busy, or when he needed to copy my answers in class.'

'Hmm,' said Jayben. 'He sounds pretty rubbish. Well, I can't promise you won't be in danger if you're with me, but I promise I'll be kind. What do you think? Want to be friends?'

'I suppose that would be okay.' Peggro stared down at his now cleaner-than-clean glasses. 'I mean, if you *need* me to be your friend?'

Jayben nodded. 'I really do. I can't remember anything before the last few days. There's so much I don't know – and you seem to know *everything*.'

Peggro smiled for the first time that day. 'I suppose I do know quite a lot,' he said.

'Ben? Peggro?' Phee called out. 'We need to get going if we're gonna make it to Blanbor before dark.'

Jayben stood up, but Peggro stayed put.

'What is it?' said Jayben. 'Did you hurt yourself?'

'Worse,' Peggro said, looking down at his shoes. His face was red. 'You *can't* tell them.'

'Errr, okay. What is it?'

'I said I needed to pee earlier!' said Peggro, turning even more red. 'But we didn't stop and I was going to burst and then the cliff – well. I had an accident.'

Jayben saw his trousers and realised. They were wet. 'It doesn't matter. They'll dry off.'

Peggro put his head in his hands. 'But the others! They'll laugh at me!'

Jayben climbed back over the wall. 'Wait there,' he called behind him.

When Jayben reached the other side, Phee was pacing between the trox, who were shaking their antlers and clomping about restlessly. 'We need to get moving,' she said impatiently. 'Those Agents could still be on our tail.'

'Agreed,' said Jayben, grabbing a bag from the saddle and dropping it over the wall. 'He just needs a moment.'

At last, Peggro re-emerged, wearing Jayben's spare shorts. 'Sorry about that,' he said. 'I'm fine now. But can we go a bit slower from now on?'

'Of course,' said Phee, smiling at Jayben. 'You've been very brave, Peggro. Your dad will be so proud when we find him.'

'Thanks,' Peggro mumbled, tears glistening in his eyes.

Jayben and Phee held the trox by their bridles and led them carefully along a path, casting long shadows as they wound down the cliff, leading the others in a gentle rhythm.

'Look, Jay-Jay!' said Maybie, pointing down from the cliff. 'Another arch! Just like the one in your dream!'

'I bet that's your chord,' said Phee and Peggro together.

Jayben craned his head. He couldn't see much but at the foot of the cliff he could just make out a little white bridge over a canal. Could that really be his chord? He could feel excitement, and hope, rising in him.

Russog poked his head out of Phee's backpack and said in a toddler's voice, 'Are we there yet? When's dinner? My tummy is bored!' Then he let out a fart.

CHAPTER 18

The Sterile Town

Russog's snout was twitching in the fresher air as they wound down the path. As they got closer, Jayben could see that the small white bridge was the same as the other arch, its metal frame encrusted with tiny moonstones. Only this one was over water. Just like his dream!

Jayben turned to the others, his eyes shining. 'That must be it!' he said. 'The wide frame, the tiny white gems – and the water!'

Peggro grinned. 'It's either your chord or a decent clue, perhaps, to where your chord might be. To keep seeing it in your dream, it must mean something.'

'How do we get down there for a better look?' said

Jayben. Then, he looked beyond the bridge.

A town, unlike any he'd seen in Wenden spread out before them. A grid of identical square houses in long, impeccable rows. Each house was the same shape, single storey with a flat roof and a small square lawn. It was strangely uniform – nothing was out of place. It looked neat, but also sterile, like all the joy had been washed out.

'Blanbor,' said Peggro. 'It looks like the drawings in my book.'

Drawings in a book. Houses . . . Jayben felt a shiver run up his spine, and a blurred shape in his mind's eye. A memory of some sort? No sooner than he had the thought it, it was gone.

'Well, this town is even weirder than I remembered,' Phee smirked. 'We came here when I was little. I can't wait to see Nilthan.'

The grid of squares stretched neatly down to sailboats gently rocking in the silver glimmer of the sea. The sky was still overcast, but here it wasn't off-colour. It felt inviting somehow.

Phee took a deep breath, staring at the vast ocean with wide eyes. 'Look, over there – a tiny path to the water,' she pointed. 'That will take us to the arch. Let's follow it!'

'It's still daylight,' said Peggro. 'There are people down there. They'll see us!'

'It's okay, Mum told me there are no nullheads in Blanbor, which means there are probably no Agents either. It's so far from the woods.'

Jayben liked Phee's optimism but he couldn't help agreeing with Peggro. 'Well, Phee, why don't you keep hold of your fishdart for now,' said Jayben, walking Keylo down the slope to the bridge, anxiously looking over his shoulder.

The others followed, edging along the canal-side.

His heart filled with hope as he reached the arch.

Jayben looked up at the white gems in the frame of the bridge. Then he looked around the base of the frame, searching for something meaningful, some memory.

'Anything?' asked Peggro.

Jayben shook his head. He clearly remembered seeing the lights piercing through the mist, tiny white glowing gems on the wide-framed arch, by some water. Surely he had found it, so why was nothing happening?

Then it came to him.

'There were trees next to the arch in my dream,' he said. He looked left and right to the blank space either side of the arch. 'Why didn't I remember that before?'

He sat down, heavy with disappointment.

The others shrugged.

'Don't worry, Jayben,' said Maybie. 'We're on the right track, I'm sure of it.'

Russog added in a toddler's voice, 'My tummy's *really* bored now.'

Jayben put his head in his hands. 'I only have three sundowns left, we're running out of time—' He broke off, gathering himself.

If it's not impossible, then you can do it.

He looked up. 'There must be another arch somewhere,' he said. 'But where?'

'Last Rock!' said Maybie excitedly, in a high-pitched voice. 'I've seen an arch there by the castle, a shrine covered in gems, and a big stream runs down past it – and there are big trees on both sides of it! What if that's the one in your dream, Jayben?'

'Maybe!' said Jayben. He smiled at Maybie. 'Good thinking, Maybie. We might as well try.'

'Yes,' said Peggro. 'And the Guard are there. They'll know what the symbolism of the arch means. They can help you find your chord regardless.'

'Come on,' said Phee, leading the trox over the bridge. The creatures were panting and dragging their hooves from exhaustion. 'Let's go find the boat. I just need to ask my Aunty Gwennal to borrow it. Which won't be easy – she's a bit, well . . . But I'm sure when she sees you, Ben, it'll be okay. We can stay there tonight too.'

'No,' said Jayben, taking his compass out. 'No more stops, I can't afford another sundown. And it's not fair to put you guys in any more danger.' He looked at his friends. 'You should stay here with Phee's aunt. You'll be safer. I'll travel the rest of the way alone.'

He flipped open the compass, more determined than ever.

Phee sighed. 'So you know how to sail a boat, do you?' Jayben was silent and she rolled her eyes. 'Come on . . .' They plodded down a straight path, through a square gate, to a courtyard full of three-wheeled vehicles.

'What are those funny carts?' asked Maybie.

'Tricycles,' Peggro explained with enthusiasm. 'I've seen them in Bramalan. They're fantastic. No need for a trox.'

'No trox?' said Phee. 'A life without trox won't get you very far. No vehicle in the world can replace these loyal, loveable lumps.' Phee stroked Woodge's mane and she whinnied in response.

At the end of the street they stopped.

'We're at Row M,' said Peggro, peering at the street sign. 'It's an excellent system.'

'We need to get to Unit Eight, Row V,' said Phee. 'I remember the address – Dad always sends them a Miraclest card.'

'Are we close?' Maybie yawned.

'Nearly,' said Phee, and they rode on, passing identical square lawns, trimmed and combed to precisely one inch. 'This place gives me the creeps. Everything here is so . . . the same. If we didn't know the exact coordinates, we would never be able to tell these houses apart!'

Everything was in order in the sterile town of Blanbor. Apart from the grass, everything was white. The spotless painted pavements, the houses, even the neatly parked tricycles in front of each white front door.

'It's giving me a headache,' Phee said and Jayben knew exactly what she meant. There was something odd about everything being so neat. As if people didn't live here.

'It's boring,' said Maybie with another yawn.

'Look how tidy everything is,' said Peggro approvingly. 'And it's nice and quiet.'

Jayben noticed a tiny placard on one of the houses and walked across the grass to read it.

> If you can read this you are on my lawn.
> Please use this comb.

'Oh!' he said, looking down at where his feet had crushed the grass. He used the comb to erase his boot prints, only to make new ones as he returned. 'Erm . . .' he said.

Phee laughed. 'Just leave it, Ben. This place is weird. I mean, where is everyone? It's not even dark yet.'

Phee was right. The place was deserted. Not seeing anyone for miles made Jayben uneasy as they continued along the street. It felt like they were on show, as if someone might be lying in wait. 'Are you sure there are no Agents here, Phee?' he said.

'Let's not wait to find out,' she said, hurrying along.

Then Jayben heard something – the clinks of many latches opening at once. He turned in his saddle to see all the Blanborians emerging from their white houses, all dressed in white and clutching white books.

Phee whispered, 'I bet the trox will have rattled them. Blanborians keep their trox outside of town.'

'Here we are,' said Peggro, stopping outside Unit

Eight and pointing to the sign.

At that moment, Keylo moved off the pavement on to the pristine lawn, lifted her golden tail and released the most spectacular dump.

The neighbours gave a collective gasp from their doorsteps. 'Filthy beasts!' one of them said.

Maybie burst out laughing. Peggro turned bright red.

'Errr,' said Phee, with an awkward smile. 'Sorry about that, everyone.'

Suddenly the door of Unit Eight swung open, and a tall woman with short blonde hair stepped out.

'What in logic's name is going on out here?' she said with a grimace. Then her eyes widened in disbelief. '*Pheetrix?*'

CHAPTER 19

Home and Never

'Oh, hello, Aunty Gwennal!' Phee smiled sheepishly.

'Nice to see you, Pheetrix, but what are they *doing here*?' Gwennal cried. 'Get off my grass this instant!' She marched past Phee, Peggro, Maybie and Russog to awkwardly shoo the trox away with her white book, but they just whinnied and stayed put.

Then Gwennal gave a short whistle and a ball of white fluff with a bushy tail, like a cat-rabbit hybrid, came scurrying out of a box beside the house. Then more and more appeared on the lawn.

Russog started wriggling furiously, desperate to chase them. Then he stopped, telling himself in Tedrik's sensible voice, 'Leave them be, Stinkbomb!'

'Clirrets?' said Peggro with great interest. 'I've read about these. Oh, but they're not actually going to—'

The clirrets turned their backsides to the mess, meowing. They lifted their tails and began hoovering it up. Within moments the poop was gone, the creatures' tails brushing the ground for any last traces.

'That. Is. Disgusting,' said Phee, wrinkling her nose.

Jayben couldn't help smiling. She was right – it was disgusting. Maybe this place wasn't so predictable after all.

Gwennal turned to Phee, her hands on her hips as if waiting for an explanation. But before she could open her mouth—

'*Pheetrix!*' an excited voice called from inside the house. A boy Jayben's age, skinny and a couple of inches shorter, with bright blond hair, wearing a blue-and-white striped top, white shorts and a red Giantwood charm on his wrist came bounding outside.

'Nilly!' Phee beamed, rushing to hug him. 'Everyone, this is my cousin Nilthan!'

'I've missed you!' said Nilthan, grinning from ear to ear. 'How come you're out of the woods?'

'*The woods?*' said a neighbour, and there were hushed whisperings before the small gathering retreated to their houses, closing their doors.

'Right!' said Gwennal. 'Everyone inside, before you cause even more of a stir. Seeing as you're family, I suppose we have no choice but to find somewhere for these . . . animals – temporarily.'

Gwennal marched Phee and the trox to a small yard, then ushered the children inside with her nose in the air. 'Well, Nilthan,' she said, stowing their books on a white shelf, 'if we're to stand any chance of conversing with these poor treenips, they'll need hydrating. Would you mind?'

'Yes, Mother,' he said, hurrying to another room.

The visitors went to follow but were blocked in the hallway by Gwennal.

'Shoes off!' she said, wincing down at the eight muddy boots in her hallway.

'No pets, either,' she said, glaring at Russog in Phee's backpack. 'You may hang *that* up here, thank you.' She pointed to the coat hooks on the wall.

Gwennal slipped on a pair of gloves and brought a damp cloth to wipe their faces of any traces of woodland dirt. Jayben noticed that she wore a Dragonwood charm.

'Sorry, Russog,' said Phee after having her face cleaned, reluctantly hanging her backpack up, leaving the sweet skoggle peeking out from between with the coats.

Gwennal took the cloth out to a kitchen and the others wandered through into a sitting room. It was very different from the Fellers' home. White paper blinds filtered the dull evening light through the windows. There were no flowers or pictures or shelves; instead strange, white paper sculptures of different shapes were arranged around the rooms and geometric lampshades hung from the ceiling. And the walls and furniture were straight and still, without a single living branch, which made Jayben feel a pang of sadness and nostalgia for the Fellers' cosy home. He looked at Phee and could tell she was thinking the same thing.

DONK!

'For moon's sake!' cried Phee, hitting her head on a hanging lamp, camouflaged in its blandness. 'Seriously? What's with the lamps?'

Maybie and the boys giggled.

'I know,' said Nilthan, with a smirk. 'Father was always walking into them too.'

'Well,' Phee huffed. 'Maybe if there was something *not* white in here, it would help . . . Hey, where are your toys? And your dad's books you used to bring to ours on the holidays?'

Nilthan bowed his head. 'Mother doesn't want me reading stories any more – just factual books. She can't see Father's things at the moment.' He went to the kitchen to fetch the drinks.

Phee took Jayben aside and whispered: 'My Uncle Hanno died last year, Mum's brother. He was a marshal, stationed near the Giantwood to protect us.'

Jayben's heart went out to Nilthan. It was hard enough not knowing where his parents were. He couldn't imagine losing one. 'I'm sorry,' he said.

'Thanks. Best not say anything to them. Mum says Gwennal hardly mentions him in her letters. I don't think she's ready yet.'

Gwennal called out from the kitchen, '*Sustenance!*'

'What's sus-sta-nance?' asked Maybie.

Phee laughed. 'I think that's Blanborian for dinnertime.'

'Logic!' said Gwennal, joining them in the sitting room. 'In all the commotion, I neglected to introduce myself. I'm Gwennal Dank, and this is Nilthan, Pheetrix's cousin. And where are your parents? No doubt your father is held up, chatting to the trees? It would have been nice to have some prior notice of this holiday . . .' she said sarcastically.

'Oh,' said Phee. 'They're not coming.'

'*Not coming?*'

'No,' said Jayben, his patience wearing thin. 'And we're not staying – well, I'm not. Phee said you might be able to help us with a boat? I need to borrow it, it's important.'

Gwennal tutted, shaking her head. 'What potent berries have they been feeding you? Travelling without adults, for logic's sake! Borrow a boat! Absolutely not. You'll have to stay until—'

'I can't,' Jayben interrupted. He was watching the light fade in the windows; his third sundown. 'It's not safe and I don't have time.'

Phee checked the windows were shut and drew the blinds. 'I know this is hard to believe, Aunty Gwennal,' she whispered, 'but, well – Jayben, show her your hand.'

Jayben nervously unwrapped his bandaged palm.

'Wow!' said Nilthan, eyes wide.

Gwennal lowered her reading glasses. 'Fascinating,' she said. 'Did you have some sort of accident?'

Phee rolled her eyes. 'And the Torch, Ben? It's okay, we can trust them.'

He hesitated but Phee was nodding, so he reached into his pocket and took out the Golden Torch.

Nilthan's mouth dropped open. His eyes lit with wonder.

'That can't be the . . .' said Gwennal. 'Can it?'

At that moment there was a knock at the front door, followed by an 'Oinff!' from the hallway.

'C-come in,' said Gwennal, clearly still in shock.

'What's this?' a deep man's voice bellowed as he entered the living room, a pipe in his hand. 'Finally allowed a pet, Nilthan?'

Jayben panicked, backing towards a window, hiding the Torch behind his back.

The man was as tall as Tedrik, but a slimmer build, and he wore a white cap, white sweater and trousers, a brown leather case belted to his hip, and a Trollwood charm around his neck.

'This is Yespa, the postmaster,' said Gwennal. 'He's a friend.' She smiled awkwardly at Yespa. 'Good evening, Yespa. We have unexpected visitors.'

The man plodded into the sitting room without removing his boots. 'So I see,' he said, fumbling for the leather hip-case on his belt. He retrieved a small silver bottle, unscrewing its cap to take a swig. 'It's all right,' he said, noticing Jayben who had almost disappeared into the blinds. 'I won't bite. I just deliver the letters around here.'

'And you're a good friend to everyone,' said Gwennal, smiling. 'Please have a seat.'

229

But Yespa stayed standing, staring at Jayben's crystal palm, which was reflecting in the glass of the pristine window. Yespa looked more excited than Nilthan. 'It's *you*!' He laughed loudly, taking two big gulps from his hipflask.

'It is!' Nilthan blurted. 'The Ninth Dreamer from the Book! Father and I knew he would come.'

Jayben came out from the corner, feeling slightly reassured.

'Have you found your chord yet?' asked Yespa.

Jayben shook his head.

'Ah,' said Yespa. 'So you might want to hide *that* then.' Yespa pointed to the Torch, which Jayben was still trying to conceal. He moved past Jayben to close the blinds. 'They'll be looking everywhere, including Blanbor. Nowhere is safe now. They all want to be the first to find you. There's a competition amongst all those Agents and a reward . . . nowhere is safe.'

Jayben put the Torch back in his pocket, and sat back on the sofa with his friends. 'That's why I need a boat,' he said. 'Do you know how to sail, Yespa?'

Yespa nodded.

'Absolutely not,' said Gwennal, folding her arms. 'You could be killed for protecting him.'

'But Gwennal,' said Yespa. 'We have to help if we

can. We all saw the lights aligning the other night. Everyone knows the Ninth Dreamer has arrived, and every Agent in the land is looking for him. Some even have those purple glasses. If he was at sea they couldn't get him so easily. The Energy, the light . . . it could be diffused by the water. You know it's the right thing to do.' He glanced at Jayben. 'I take it you're going to find the Guard?'

Jayben nodded, leaning forward. 'Yes. That's why I'm going to Last Rock,' he said. 'To the Chordian Guard. But I don't want to put my friends in danger any more.'

'Don't worry, Ben,' said Phee. 'We're all going with you.'

'Yeah,' said Maybie, 'and what if those angry townsfolk *do* try to take all the old Free-Dreams from the castle? If they do think the Queen's a Dream Thief. We can't let Wenden fall apart. We need to protect it, together.'

Peggro took a deep breath in and out, then grinned nervously at Jayben. 'I'm coming too,' he said.

'Tollywosh!' said Gwennal from her chair. 'There is absolutely no way I'm going to allow all of you to take that boat to Last Rock, for logic's sake. You are children.'

231

Jayben nodded. 'She's right,' he told the others, with a lump in his throat. He was sad to leave his friends but he had always known he would have to face this alone. They had done enough to help him.

Yespa said slowly, 'I know the capital well, Jayben, and where you need to go. I'll take him, Gwennal. First thing tomorrow.'

'Tomorrow?' said Jayben. 'I need to go now. After tonight I have just two more sundowns.'

'The wind's gone, I'm afraid.' said Yespa. 'It'll pick up in the morning. We can sail then.'

Jayben fought his frustration. He had to stay positive. With Yespa's help, there was still time.

Phee was scowling. Jayben knew she hated the idea of being left behind – but he couldn't risk her and the others any more. They'd done enough.

Gwennal straightened her white coffee table. 'I'll send your mother a letter in the morning to let her know you're safe,' she said firmly. 'You may stay here Pheetrix, and your friends, until we can find a way to return you.'

Yespa picked up his pipe and went to lock the back door. 'Let's get some sheets on these blinds,' he said. 'We can't let them see your light.' He smiled at Jayben. 'Welcome, Dreamer.'

Jayben rubbed his eyes and stared up at the white ceiling in the dark. He was exhausted, his arms and hands were tingling, and he couldn't remember falling asleep.

'Huh?' he moaned, slowly pulling himself upright in a stiff white armchair. His head felt heavy as stone.

Peggro's face appeared suddenly in front of him.

'*ARGH!*' Jayben cried, raising his arms defensively.

'It's okay!' said Peggro. He sat back on his heels, his eyes fixed on Jayben. 'It's me. How are you feeling?'

Jayben frowned, scratching his head. Had he been asleep in this armchair? He didn't remember dreaming.

'Morning,' he said, then he noticed a bandage wrapped around his arm. Russog was perched next to him, licking a graze on his knee.

'Morning?' said Peggro. 'But . . . Jayben, don't you remember what happened today?'

Jayben stared blankly, trying to recall, but there was nothing since the evening they had arrived.

But there was more.

'I'm sorry,' said Peggro, holding something out to Jayben.

He took it, numb. It was his precious compass, covered in scratches, and there was a nasty crack across his parents' message, slicing diagonally through the words *home* and *never*.

CHAPTER 20

What Needs To Be Done

Panic struck Jayben like a hammer to his heart. This wasn't like the other absences, it was worse. This time he knew bad things had happened to him, without knowing what or how, or when they might happen again.

'Where's the Torch?' said Jayben, rooting through his empty pockets.

'It's here,' said a voice from a doorway. It was Phee holding the Golden Torch. 'I'm sorry,' she said, approaching him slowly and kneeling down to hand it to him. 'It must be so scary, not remembering.'

'What happened?' he said. 'What happened to my arm? My compass?' He wiped the damaged compass

235

with his sleeve as if he could somehow restore it.

'The wind picked up in the late morning,' she explained. 'You were riding Nilthan's tricycle down to the boats. Then, you sort of, well, you came off. There were other people riding behind us, and they didn't stop in time.'

Jayben lifted his arm to look at his bandage, trying to remember. But nothing came. His eyes stung with tears.

'You had another seizure,' said Peggro, sitting on the arm of the chair. 'It didn't last long but it was a big one. A different sort. When you came round, you didn't seem like yourself. You've been sort of awake, on and off, but really confused. My dad's patient used to do that too – it's normal, with your condition.'

Normal? thought Jayben. *I don't want this to be normal!* He bowed his head, as the panic settled into an anxious sadness. He finally gave up trying to polish the compass. 'I don't like it,' he said. 'I don't want that to ever happen again.'

'Oh, Ben,' said Phee, sitting down beside him. She didn't seem to know what else to say.

'Oinff!' Russog licked Jayben's hand, and in Larnie's voice he said, 'There, there, little one.'

Phee smiled, scratching Russog's fuzzy green chin. 'I know it's scary, Ben, but if it happens again, we'll be there. We'll help you, just like you help us.'

Peggro grinned. 'Phee certainly took care of those girls who ran into you . . .'

'I can't believe those idiots!' she huffed. 'Why would anyone ride those stupid things, anyway?'

'Thanks.' Jayben smiled, letting Russog on to his lap. In spite of his fear, he felt comforted.

Jayben noticed there wasn't a single scratch on the Golden Torch, it was just as he remembered it. Was that part of its magic? Even though it needed fixing internally, on the outside it looked shiny-new. He stashed it in his pocket with his compass, pushing them down as far as they would go. 'Where's Maybie?' he asked.

'Asleep,' said Phee. 'It's been a long day.'

Then suddenly it hit him. 'A *long day*?' he said, looking at the dark windows. They had arrived at sundown, so if it was dark again now . . . 'But that means—' He couldn't finish the sentence. He had been cheated of time – yet again, he'd lost another sundown. He reached for Sojan's words, but right now it was much harder to believe that the task ahead was *not impossible*.

'We're not giving up,' Phee said fiercely. 'We can do a lot in a day.'

Just then Gwennal appeared from the hall, holding a stack of neatly folded white blankets. 'Bedtime, Pheetrix,' she said. 'How are you feeling now, Jayben?'

He shrugged, struggling to find the right words. Words that wouldn't make him want to cry, and he was still so tired, his head felt heavy, as he leant back against the chair.

'You poor child,' Gwennal said, crouching next to him. 'Thank logic you're here.' She tucked a blanket around him. 'The doctor should have some medicine for you in the morning. Plenty of rest now.'

Phee angrily crossed her arms. 'He doesn't have time to rest – he needs to get to Last Rock. The whole world depends on it! It's already been four sundowns. We have to find his chord before the last sundown – tomorrow!'

'We've been over this, Pheetrix,' said Gwennal, neatening the cushions on every chair. 'He is a child and he's not well. He can't go anywhere tonight.' She pointed to the windows, covered in thick blankets. 'Yespa has made sure nobody will find you, Jayben. Now, bedtime.' She combed Nilthan's hair, as if it mattered what he looked like going to bed.

Russog hopped on to a chair and farted into a cushion.

'Logic!' cried Gwennal. 'Outside!'

'Charming!' said Russog in Larnie's voice.

'Come on, Stinkbomb,' said Phee, scooping him up into her arms. 'Jayben doesn't need a bedroom full of skoggle stink right now. So glad you're okay, Ben. Everything's fine. Everything's gonna be fine.'

Jayben appreciated the words, but he could tell by the tears on her cheeks that she was struggling to believe them herself.

He pulled the blanket over him and let the tiredness take him into an uneasy sleep.

Jayben is dreaming again. He can see an archway, there's water somewhere nearby and trees are rustling in the breeze. He needs to get to the arch but he can't quite see his way through the mist.

Now he's in a dark cave. There's screaming. He knows the monster is there before he hears it – the heavy footsteps, the rasping breath – he's already running. But now he can hear something, a man's voice—

'We need to go NOW,' said Yespa, gently shaking him awake. 'Come on.'

Jayben winced as his eyes opened. He watched Yespa creep quietly to the kitchen in the pale light before dawn. He was dressed in his white cap and coat, his sack of letters over his shoulder as he opened cupboards, stuffing a few snacks in a basket.

Peggro whispered, 'You okay, Jayben? Feeling any better? Can you stand up?'

Jayben was confused but pulled himself up, half-asleep, and followed Peggro out to the hall where Phee and Maybie peered out of Nilthan's bedroom door.

'Yespa is going to take you,' whispered Phee. 'We'll explain to my aunt later.'

Yespa crept out of the kitchen with a basket. He put his sack down and cautiously opened the door a crack. The sky was beginning to lighten. 'Clear,' he said, ushering Jayben out. 'Let's go.'

Jayben turned to his friends. They were smiling encouragingly. He knew he had to leave them but it wasn't easy. They felt like home to him. 'How will I find you, after?'

Phee grinned. 'Don't you worry, Ben. We'll find you. I promise.' Then she turned to Yespa. 'He needs to see a doctor.'

Yespa tightened his hip-case. 'Of course. Don't you worry, Jayben. I'm sure the Guard can get you the best doctors in Last Rock.'

Jayben gave his friends a final wave, and then the door shut behind them.

The pair crept down the silent street in the morning twilight. Yespa shielded Jayben as much as he could with his jacket.

Jayben felt glad to be on the move again – he'd stayed too long in Blanbor, and he was grateful for Yespa's presence. 'Thank you, Yespa.'

Yespa nodded. 'It's what needs to be done.'

As they walked in a comfortable silence to the harbour, Jayben couldn't help but think ahead and wonder what was about to happen – if they'd make it in time. And, if they did, whether he'd ever see his friends again.

CHAPTER 21

Escape to the Waves

As Jayben and Yespa quickened their pace through the cool dawn air, Jayben noticed clusters of red fungus on some of the houses. It appeared to be spreading as they passed, spoiling the uniform aesthetic. 'What is that stuff?' he asked, watching three clirrets trying to hoover it away with their backsides.

'Not sure,' said Yespa. 'It started yesterday. Neighbours are pretty upset. It's like their worst nightmare.' He chuckled. 'Even worse than a bunch of forest kids visiting!'

'What's a nightmare?' asked Jayben.

'From the Book of Dreamers? It means your worst fears coming true. It's what we're trying to avoid.'

They came to the end of Row V, crossing an empty cycle lane to reach the boats, gently swaying on the calm waves at the shore.

Jayben paused for a moment, staring at the dark sea in the early light, thinking about his own worst fears. What if he had another seizure and it stopped him from defeating Null? What if the reason that last page in the Book was missing was because he was the one Dreamer who *didn't* stop the tyrant? What if—

'This way!' Yespa beckoned, turning on to a short pier.

Jayben hurried after him.

'Here,' said Yespa, kneeling to untie a rope from a wooden post. He stepped down into the boat and helped Jayben aboard, handing him the basket. 'Supplies. Stash that in the crate,' he said. 'I need to ready the sails.'

Jayben put the basket into the large empty box on the deck, covered by a sheet of frayed canvas. Then he watched Yespa adjusting a mechanism of ropes and chains.

'You hold this one,' said Yespa, grasping a rope.

There was a plonking sound from the stern and they looked back. Was someone there? Then Jayben saw that more red fungus had appeared on the decking, spreading quickly.

'Stay here,' said Yespa, grabbing an oar to push off.

THUD!

A flash of darkness struck the end of the pier.

'Darkning!' cried Jayben as ice needles shattered on the decking.

'Stay down!' shouted Yespa.

THUD!

Another black flash from behind and then another from the street.

Jayben scurried to the base of the mast, and to his horror saw a woman wearing a grey coat running down the pier.

'Agent!' cried Jayben, his heart skipping a beat. 'Yespa, go! Quick!'

As she came closer, Jayben could see her purple glasses.

'Ninth Dreamer!' she shouted. '*Stop!*'

Yespa paddled the oar between the other boats.

A long flash of night, and a patch of water beside them turned to ice.

'Stop!' the woman called. 'We won't hurt you!' But she was too late, they were away. Jayben exhaled, his head in his hands. *What if she knew where his friends*

were? Would the Agent punish them for helping him?

At that moment, he heard a little voice from the stern. 'Is she gone?'

The canvas on the crate wriggled, and out crawled Maybie, followed by Peggro, Phee, and Russog in her backpack.

Jayben was speechless, overcome by a strange mix of emotions.

'*What are you doing?*' he said, fighting his gladness at seeing them again. 'I told you not to come! How the heck did you get here?'

'You can't just sneak on to a boat,' said Yespa with a frown. 'You might have led that Agent right to us.'

Phee crossed her arms. 'We got here by trox, Ben. I wouldn't get on a trike again any time soon. Woodge and Keylo will find their way back to Gwennal's for safety. I know why you told us to stay, but we couldn't let you do this alone. We know the dangers, but this is too important. We got this far together. We're not splitting up now.'

'That's right,' said Peggro, looking more confident than ever before, and Maybie nodded too.

Peggro scrambled to the middle of the yacht's deck, clutching his satchel, his face soon turning a shade of green as they rocked on the water.

Maybie smiled to see the sun poking through the clouds for the first time in days.

'Bath time!' said Russog in Larnie's voice, his snout twitching in the sea air.

Phee laughed, gazing at the ocean. 'It's a very big bath, Russog.'

She let him down on his leash and gripped the side as the wind picked up.

The boat began to tip, catching the wind, and Maybie climbed on top of the crate, her arms in the air.

'Oh, good,' Peggro sighed sarcastically, closing his eyes and hugging the mast as the sails thrashed about. 'More rocking.'

Yespa rolled a bucket down to Peggro. 'Long way to go,' he said. He pulled on a rope, sending two huge silver sails unravelling up the mast. 'Lucky the wind's in our favour. We'll be at the Rock by mid-afternoon in this little racer.'

Jayben took a deep breath. It was cutting it far too close to his last sundown. He hoped the Chordian Guard would know what to do.

At the other end of the deck, bathed in sunshine, Maybie's little wings popped out. 'Hooray!' she gasped. 'That's better!'

'Can you shrink and fly again?' asked Jayben.

'It might take a while.' Then her eyes lit up. 'If my magic's working again, how about I take a look at your arm?'

Jayben removed the bandage to reveal a deep laceration from the trike accident.

'Hmm,' she said, licking her hands and waving them over his arm. 'I remember Gan-Gan said they did this back in the old, old days . . .'

Sure enough, the tiny glowing specks appeared in the air again, and in a matter of moments, his arm was good as new.

'Amazing!' he cheered, seeing her gold nutshell charm glowing. 'Maybie, you're the best!'

Yespa was shocked, his hand to his mouth. '*Old magic?*' he said.

Jayben nodded. 'She got it from being close to me. We were holding hands when I did that Free-Dream. We help each other, don't we, Maybie?' Then he yawned. 'I still feel really tired. Just need to sit down for a bit.'

He moved to the stern of the yacht with Phee, to sit on an old blanket they had laid on the deck. They watched the white roofs of Blanbor disappear behind them, escaping the darkening strikes, the Agent, and the greenish cloud that now covered all of Wenden.

It wasn't just his arm that felt better. Their escape to the waves brought relief. Being unreachable, and on their way at last, eased his nerves.

'It's funny,' said Phee. 'For so long I've wanted to leave the woods and see the world – but two nights in Blanbor and I can't wait to get home!'

Jayben said, 'Maybie, do you think your magic could work on my head? You know, stop me from having seizures?'

'Hmm,' Maybie said, looking into his eyes. 'I'm not sure. If it's deep inside you, then I don't think my magic will do anything. Gan-Gan always said dusthealing can't heal everything on the inside. But we can try.'

She licked her hands and held them over his head. The glowing specks passed into his forehead.

Jayben grinned, hoping as hard as he could that it might work. 'Thanks, Maybie,' he said, giving her a hug.

'Fingers crossed . . .' she said. 'It depends on what the Moonmother writes for you. Mamma says not even old magic can shift the Moonmother's quill. I can't wait to get home and read the ancient spell books! Imagine if I could do proper spells!'

Why would the Moonmother write seizures into my

story in the first place? Jayben wondered. He was glad that she had let the old magic out of Maybie's blood. He wondered again what Null's old magic might be, what clan he was part of. A Spritewood like Snaggis, able to duplicate anything? Could he move things with his mind like a Trollwood? Make himself invisible like a Dragonwood? Maybe he could do Fairywood spells, or had super-strength like a Giantwood? Whatever charm Null wore, it was a terrifying thought.

Jayben's left arm started to tingle. 'My arm feels funny,' he said.

'Oh,' said Phee. 'You said that yesterday, before it happened.'

Jayben's heart thumped. Would he have another seizure? He couldn't afford to lose any more time.

'How's your hearing?' asked Peggro. 'Any funny smells? You had them in Blanbor too, before your seizure.' He paused, seeming to realise that this wasn't what Jayben wanted to hear. 'But you're probably just tired,' he said finally. 'It's normal to be really tired with your condition.'

Soon, the worries whirling around Jayben's head were dulled by the rocking ship and the warmth of the sun, and he closed his eyes and slipped into a long nap.

CHAPTER 22

Last Rock

Jayben sat up with a shiver, rubbing his eyes. The sun had disappeared. They were under the ceiling of a dark cloud, the boat rising and dipping as it cut across the swell.

'You okay, Ben?' said Phee, standing at his feet in a spray of seawater. 'Feeling better?'

Jayben nodded, but if he was honest he didn't feel quite right. He felt agitated, like everything – every sound and movement – was too much. Phee talking, the flapping of the sails, the metal fixings clinking against the mast, Yespa whistling a tune from the helm, and, above the crashing waves, the sound of distant bells and people shouting. Inside, he knew

Maybie's magic hadn't fixed him.

Maybie cheered from the bow of the boat, 'There it is! Last Rock!'

Jayben gasped. The Rock was immense. It rose a dizzying fifteen hundred feet from the ocean, twinkling with purple crystals. From the castle at its peak, the capital city sprawled down its slope, a sea of pointed roofs and chimneys spilling out to the countryside.

'Wow!' he said, holding on to the mast to pull himself up. His elation at finally being here was immediately replaced with dread. The enormity of the problem he was expected to solve was closer than ever. He would soon face Null, and in doing so, decide the fate of two worlds. And before that he had to find the chord.

He edged closer to Phee and Maybie, and saw the large ships, weaving their way through the choppy waters in one direction: away from the city.

'I can't believe I'm actually seeing Last Rock,' said Phee.

'Nowhere quite like the Rock,' said Yespa from the helm. 'I used to work here.'

'But what's happened up there?' said Maybie. 'There's so much smoke!'

Phee looked worried. 'It's coming from the castle

gardens. You don't think the townsfolk *actually* think the Queen's a Dream Thief? They wouldn't burn—'

'The castle gardens?' said Peggro, who still looked very green. 'And take all those Free-Dreams? But of course they will. The Queen sent her army of marshals to defend the forest. And Null told the Agents to collect *every* Free-Dream for his new city—' He stopped to retch over the side of the boat.

'Not the gardens,' said Phee, flaring her nostrils. 'Not the ancient helicorn tree.'

'We need to concentrate on keeping Jayben safe,' said Yespa firmly. 'We've made good time, but there will be other Agents with those glasses. We can't let them spot you before you face Null. I know a safe way to get you to the Guard. Now, make sure you've got everything . . .'

Jayben turned to Phee with fearful eyes. She gave him a hug. 'We can do this.'

Peggro was still struggling not to throw up. 'But the Rock is miles from the docks. It's going to take us *ages* to get up there.'

'Ha!' Yespa laughed, steering past the busy harbour, heading straight for the Rock. 'We're not docking *here*.'

'Then where?' said Peggro, heaving again as they plunged down from a large wave.

Yespa bit his pipe between his teeth. 'You might want to hang on to something . . .'

They were approaching another dock at the foot of the immense cliff. Phee caught Russog, fastening him into her backpack, then huddled with Maybie and the boys around the mast.

'Here we go!' said Yespa, gripping the helm.

CRASH!

They slammed against the stilt of an extremely tall pier. Yespa skilfully tied a rope around the post, then grabbed a rope ladder dangling from the platform, some eighteen feet above them.

'You must be joking!' said Peggro.

'Come on, Jayben,' said Yespa, with one foot on the ladder. 'Up here!'

Jayben and the girls stood in the cold spray from the crashing water.

Peggro looked like he wasn't sure which was worse, riding the turbulent waves or dangling above them on a rope ladder.

'It's okay, Peggro,' said Phee, grabbing hold of the ladder. 'It's sturdier than it looks.'

'Wheeeee!' Maybie cheered, swinging about behind Phee. 'Come on, boys! This is fun!'

Peggro muttered to himself, 'It's going to be all

right. It's going to be all right.'

'Come on,' said Jayben. 'I won't leave you, Peggro. Let's climb it together.'

Peggro shut his eyes and stepped on to the bottom plank, gripping the tatty rope with white knuckles. Then, slowly, he began to climb.

'You're doing great!' said Jayben, following behind.

'Keep going!' said Phee from the top. 'And don't look down.'

Peggro slowly climbed the ladder, swinging like a pendulum, but as he reached the top step, the weathered slat snapped under his foot, and he opened his eyes. 'AAAH!' he yelled.

'Almost there,' said Jayben.

'Get a move on!' Yespa bellowed, grabbing Peggro by his satchel and hoisting him up on to the pier.

Peggro crawled to the middle of the deck, turning from green to red, taking shallow breaths.

'He would have been fine, you know!' said Phee. 'He just needed a moment.'

'That's all very well,' said Yespa, putting his earplugs in, and pulling Jayben over the top. 'But the day is half gone. We don't want to meet sundown. Now, let's go!'

Yespa whisked them up the pier, and a group of

men ran past in the opposite direction, their bags spilling their belongings.

They were in such a hurry that they weren't bothering to pick up what they had dropped. How bad was it up there? he wondered. For a moment, he imagined turning and running. But he remembered the children back in Ampelwed, the flaming Rackem barn, the scorched ruins of Jonningwed, Peggro's dad, Maybie's dad . . . He was doing it for them. He couldn't stop now.

'In here,' said Yespa, opening the metal door to an old warehouse.

'At last!' said Maybie. 'Is there somewhere in here I can shrink down and change? I need to fly!'

'No time,' Yespa grunted, hurrying forward.

'Oinff! Oinff!' said Russog, unsettled, as they followed inside through a dark maze of wooden crates until, finally, Yespa stopped in almost pitch black.

'Hang on to the railings,' he said, and as they did, Jayben heard the clang of an iron gate shut behind them.

'I can't see anything!' Peggro panicked, before the floor shook and they started moving. 'What's going on?'

There was a loud *BANG!* and a hatch burst open above their heads, and the dim daylight flooded in.

Jayben shielded his eyes. They rose up through the roof clinging to the thin platform. Jayben realised they were standing in some sort of cargo lift.

'Wow!' said Maybie, as it winched them above the rusty warehouse roofs of the dock – the next best thing to flying.

Peggro shuddered, the chains stretching high above them, almost disappearing into the sky. 'Surely this thing doesn't go – it can't go – all the way to the top of the Rock?'

Yespa nodded, relighting his pipe in the whistling wind. 'All the way. I used to take parcels up here every day.'

Peggro sat down and closed his eyes, clinging to the railing. Jayben and Phee sat either side of him, while Maybie, no stranger to heights, peered over the edge.

'Oinff! Oinff!' said Russog, wriggling with excitement to see hundreds of tiny creatures nesting on narrow ledges in the cliff face. 'Leave them be, Stinkbomb!' he said in Tedrik's voice. Phee tightened his straps.

The winch raised them higher up the rockface. Yespa took his jacket off and draped it over Jayben, covering his head.

'Keep this on until we're across town. It will

hide some of your light. There's a backstreet that should be safe enough, but we'll need to cross the avenue. If we're quick we can get away with it. Then I'll get you safely to the Observatory. That's where the Guard are.' He drew a deep breath through his pipe. 'Until then we need to keep you alive – and hidden from Agents.'

Soon, the harbour ships looked no bigger than bath toys, and there was a loud *CLONK!* The lift jolted and swung them sideways, into a hole in the rock: the entrance to a tunnel.

Jayben looked around at the sides of the passage, purple crystals flickering in his eyes as the daylight faded.

'The Rock really is full of amethyst,' said Peggro, opening his eyes at last as the lift slammed to a halt, his legs like jelly.

'Remember what I told you,' Yespa whispered, 'stay hidden.' He opened the gate to a platform, Everyone followed him to some large double doors, beneath some gold letters:

CASTLE GOODS
Very Important Deliveries Only

He took a baton from his belt and knocked the door twice.

The children hid, pressed against the sharp points of the cold crystal wall.

A muffled man's voice spoke through the door. 'Codeword?'

'Rejon's Revenge,' said Yespa, standing to one side, out of sight.

A dozen locks clinked and clonked. The doors opened and a short man in a scarlet coat stepped out, clutching a logbook.

'Who's there?' he said. 'State your—'

WHACK!

Yespa struck him on the head with his baton. The children gasped as he fell to the ground.

'Is he okay? Jayben asked, kneeling beside the unconscious man.

'Oinff! Oinff! Oinff!' said Russog, then he said in Fudd's voice, 'Nobody move!'

'Why did you do that?' said Phee.

'You kids don't get it,' said Yespa, grabbing the man by the arms to drag him inside a storeroom. 'This isn't a game! There's no time for procedures. We can't risk Jayben getting caught by Agents and taken to Null before his time. Now, come on! And somebody silence that skoggle.'

Phee shoved a nomseed in Russog's snout.

Jayben was shaken. Yespa hadn't mentioned attacking an unarmed man in the plan. But he also knew it was a life-and-death situation. It was all too real now.

'But . . . but . . .' said Maybie, visibly troubled. 'I could fix the bump on his head with my magic, and then maybe—'

'No time!' said Yespa, cutting the man's keys from his belt and tugging Jayben's hand, leading them through, between stacked packages. He unlocked another entrance, and they hurried through, down a long corridor, up some steps, and into a high-ceilinged hallway with marble tiles.

Jayben tripped on a line of fine silk.

'You okay?' said Phee, getting caught by another strand of it, stretched across a doorway.

Jayben looked up. Something was crawling down the silk from the ceiling, like a large furry caterpillar. It was the size of a rat, with teeth just as sharp.

'Grollits!' said Peggro.

'*Where?*' Yespa flinched, swinging his baton.

'On your back!' said Phee. 'They're on webs!'

Yespa twisted around and shook off the creature.

'Filthy dirt-curds!' he shouted, running across the squeaky marble as more grollits spun their webs at him. 'Always hated these things!'

Before Yespa could reach the door on the other side of the room, the handle was turned from outside and it was flung open. Grey smoke billowed in from the street, followed by a young man carrying two small children.

'Stay inside!' the man spluttered, wiping soot from his brow. 'It's madness out there!'

The grollits scattered to the corners of the room to escape the smoke and the man ran past them.

'Come on,' said Yespa, herding them into a cobbled street of mayhem. A frenzy of panicked locals were dashing about in the smog, cradling their possessions.

Jayben noticed an abandoned market stall, lying on its side, with a damaged sign that read:

SOUVENIRS!
Bookmarks of Famous Free-Dreams
2 for an inch!

The bookmarks scattered around it each had a picture of an object Free-Dreamed from Earth, and a few facts about it.

Phee clutched her Giantwood charm.

'Please, Yespa,' Maybie begged. 'I need to shrink so I can fly. Could we just stop somewhere for a moment?'

Yespa didn't answer. His earplugs were well screwed in and his expression was set, determined as he hurried them through the crowd.

Jayben's arm was tingling and he felt as though he could hear every noise all at once.

Phee was calling to him but he couldn't make out what she was saying. She grabbed him by the hand, her other arm around Peggro and Maybie. 'We *have* to stay together!' she said.

There was comfort in having his friends close but no time to tell them how he was feeling. They lost sight of Yespa as they turned a corner into an alleyway, and the smoke blew thicker.

'Quick!' Phee cried, struggling through the crowd. They were pushed and shoved from all directions, until Yespa reappeared.

'Stay with me,' he urged, grabbing Jayben by the arm. 'I've seen an Agent already!'

They joined a crowd of a different nature: thousands of angry townsfolk, holding signs with the names of loved ones who'd been null-headed. They were marching up a broad avenue of grand buildings and ancient trees. Some carried clubs, others brandished hammers – and they all looked furious. Dotted amongst them were Null's Agents of the Ninth, handing out placards, homemade firebombs, and leading the mob's angry chant:

> *Stop the Dream Thieves.*
> *Stop the Queen.*
> *Save the Woods.*
> *Burn them clean!*

CHAPTER 23

The Smoking Garden
of Free-Dreams

The crowd repeated the chant, over and over, smashing ornate windows and tearing down the Wenden flags on their way up the Rock towards the castle gardens.

> *Burn them clean!*
> *Burn them clean!*
> *Burn them clean!*

'How can they burn the woods clean?' cried Phee as they forced their way through the crowd behind Yespa. 'Like we're some kind of disease? Do the trees, with all their memories, mean nothing to them?'

263

'Those windows have been there for centuries!' shouted Peggro. 'And why are they tearing down the Wenden flag? It belongs to all of us!'

'Hush, keep it down!' said Yespa, pulling his coat halfway down over Jayben's face. Then he said, in a louder voice, 'They're angry. The Queen's been defending forestfolk. They just want their Energy back so their friends and family can recover. The Queen is hoarding enough Free-Dreams in that garden to keep half the country going.'

'But it's a lie,' said Jayben. 'Isn't it, Phee? Nobody's stealing Free-Dreams. At least not forestfolk or the Queen. The Jarmaster said. It's Null's curse, spreading these lies. It's the whispers.'

'*What did he say?*' a woman with a placard growled.

'Nothing,' said Yespa quickly. 'The boy's in shock. He can't believe how wicked those rotten Dream Thieves are – especially the Queen.'

'No,' said Jayben, then he staggered.

'See?' said Yespa, holding his arm. 'Boy's delirious.'

The woman shook her head. 'Poor mite. Don't worry, son. They're no match for us. We're getting them Free-Dreams, and then getting that thieving old crook of a queen. It all ends today!' She marched on ahead.

Yespa bent down to Jayben. 'You can't say things like that,' he whispered. 'This isn't a game. Your life is at stake. We just need to make it to that turning, up there – then we can get to the Observatory.'

Jayben nodded. Seeing the effects of Null's lies and whispers was terrifying.

He noticed a young woman standing calmly by the side of the road, knocked about by people marching past. Her eyes stared at a window, expressionless, her mouth mumbling. *A nullhead!* He looked to the other side and saw an old man in a doorway with the same blank expression, whispering mindlessly.

'They're everywhere, Phee!' he said.

'It'll be okay,' she said, squeezing his hand. 'It'll be—' She gulped, like she couldn't keep saying the words, however much she wanted to stay positive.

'Will it?' he said, looking up at the tall buildings in the smoke and feeling more doubtful with every step. 'How can I possibly fix all of this?'

'None of this is your fault,' said Peggro angrily. 'Adults are just really stupid sometimes.'

The old trees lining the avenue started drumming over the racket of the mob.

'Is that the Museum?' said Peggro, spotting a huge stained-glass window above the crowd. 'The

Wendenian Museum?'

Jayben looked up. Suddenly the museum's doors blew open, and the window shattered. The crowd cheered, and the trees drummed faster.

'ANIMALS!' Peggro shouted, watching helplessly as some of the mob rushed inside, smashing exhibitions as they went. 'This can't be happening!'

'That way!' said Yespa, as they passed the entrance to another backstreet. There was a narrow break in the crowd. 'Quick, Jayben!' he said, rushing through the gap. But the gap closed and they were separated.

'*Yespa?*' Jayben called.

But he was gone.

Burn them clean!
Burn them clean!

The menacing chant was stabbing in Jayben's head, and then came a smell in the stinging smoke – a foul stench, like burning blood. He held his nose, but it got worse. He looked frantically around but realised – only he could smell it.

It was another alarm bell wailing inside, sending his heart racing.

'There it is!' Maybie called, with a cough. 'The big

gate to the castle parade ground, Jay-Jay!'

The bright curve of the archway Maybie had described shone above the placards. It had a wide frame of bright moonstones. To one side was the water of the city stream, and either side were two tall trees. Beyond the parade ground was the spectacular Last Rock Castle, its turrets and towers soaring high into the swirling, murky sky.

'Is this really it?' said Jayben. He could hardly believe it. 'The arch from my dream? Have we actually made it?'

They heard Yespa calling desperately, over the buzz of the crowd, 'Jayben! Where are you? We have to take the backstreet!'

Jayben hesitated. Phee clutched her clanband, as the crowd pushed them forward, reaching the gate. 'Third time lucky, Ben.'

Jayben looked up at the arch, trying to ignore his doubts and steady his head. Was this the moment his memories would return? 'It's not here,' he said, as they came closer. 'Just like the other arches. Just a pointless dream.'

'But, Jayben, look!' said Peggro, pointing through the arch to an enormous glass dome beside the castle. 'The Observatory!'

Jayben's eyes welled as they were pushed through the gate, filing into the vast grounds. They had actually made it.

From the corner of his eye he saw an Agent stop in her tracks. Had she spotted him? Was she going to raise the alarm? Her mouth opened and formed words, barely a sound coming out. Her eyes glazed over. She was whispering Null's spell.

The young man next to her dropped his placard. He stopped chanting and began whispering the same spell.

He looked around to see another null-headed woman in the crowd.

The man next to her dropped his hammer and copied.

The man opposite dropped his club and repeated the curse.

It was spreading like a forest fire.

'They're forgetting!' cried Jayben. People's memories, their identity – everything gone, in a single moment. 'Put your earplugs in!' he pleaded, 'Please! Put them in!' But nobody could hear. 'They're forgetting, just like me.' He couldn't bear it. 'I have to light the Torch!' he said. 'Right now. It could be enough Energy to break the curse on them. It would show them who I am, before it gets any worse.'

'How?' said Peggro.

'Do you remember how you did it before?' said Phee.

'No,' he said, 'but I know I have it in me. I did it when I needed to, and I can do it again.' He looked around for somewhere high, where the Torch's Energy could go further, and noticed a gigantic statue of a woman in robes on top of a monument, wearing a crown and holding a torch. They'd all see the flame, if he was up there. He pushed his way grimly through the crowd.

You can do this, Jayben thought to himself, climbing the plinth to the enormous marble feet of the statue. The plaque read:

QUEEN SOJAN
The First Dreamer

The statue of Sojan towered above the crowds, facing the castle, her cape of purple canvas hanging from her giant shoulders all the way to the ground.

He turned and saw Phee following, Russog still in her backpack.

Jayben smiled, trying his best to hide his terror.

He was glad she'd come. The awful smell eased for a moment, but there was flashing in his eyes, erratic pink and yellow dots. *Make it stop!* He blinked in the hope of subduing them, terrified that this might be his final warning before a big seizure.

He turned and saw his reflection in the polished monument. He lifted his hand to his cheek. The boy in the mirror copied. *I can still move and think*, Jayben thought. *As long as I'm conscious, I'm in charge.*

He felt calmer, stood up straight and turned to Phee. He could do this.

'Get down!' he heard Yespa shout, fighting through the crowd. 'You can't be seen!'

'When I've done this.' Jayben nodded. Then he grabbed hold of the cape, locked his knees around it, and began to climb.

Phee hoisted herself up behind him, Russog still on her back. 'Yikes!' She coughed into the smoke. 'It's higher than it looked!'

'You're nearly there,' said Jayben, crawling over the top, on to the Queen's great shoulder. The angry townsfolk looked like a sea from so high, waving their placards and hurling the bottles stuffed with lit paper into the castle garden, exploding with fire. They were led by the Agents and chanting over and over:

Burn them clean!
Burn them clean!
Burn them clean!

Jayben stood up slowly. He could see over the castle railings to the smoking garden of Free-Dreams, with the Queen's marshals ringing it. At its centre, surrounded by small glass domes of what he assumed were ancient Earthly objects, was the oldest helicorn tree, holding hundreds of glowing coloured jars.

'We're so high,' said Phee, reaching the top and gazing up at Sojan's giant face, speckled with droppings, her golden crown hidden in the swirling cloud.

Russog was trembling and mumbling in Phee's bag. 'Wish this . . .' he said in Jayben's voice. 'Wish this . . . Wish this . . .'

There was a smash from below and the crowd roared, pulling down the lamps from the castle walls and crashing at the gates.

Burn them clean!
Burn them clean!

'We have to stop them from getting to the Queen and the Guard,' Jayben said firmly. 'I need them to see.'

He reached into his pocket, pulled out the Golden Torch, and held it up.

Nothing happened.

He shook it about and held it higher.

Still nothing.

'*Come on!*' he groaned. Had it been a fluke on the moor when he lit it? A chance error in the pipeline? The other Dreamers had all found their chords before lighting it . . .

'Light!' he shouted. 'Please light! Come on!'

But not a single spark flew.

> *Burn them clean!*
> *Burn them clean!*
> *Burn them clean!*

He looked down. He could just about see Yespa, with his arm around Maybie, and Peggro hugging his satchel.

Jayben was despairing, tears in his eyes. In his mind he kept seeing his empty jar in Ampelwed. He was nothing – no memories and no powers.

'It's not working!' he shouted, exasperated. 'I don't remember how I did it before. I want to remember, but I can't. I can't remember anything!'

Sojan's face vanished into the cloud, and there was a crash of thunder. The castle gates finally succumbed, the crowd rushed forward and the marshals inside drew their swords.

CHAPTER 24

The Boy on the Queen's Shoulder

'*For moon's sake! No!*' Phee shouted with a sob in her voice. 'This cannot happen!'

Russog was still mumbling on her back. 'Wish this . . . Wish this . . .' he repeated in Jayben's voice. 'Wish this . . .'

'Shhh, Russog!' said Phee. 'Ben, I know it's horrible. I know it feels impossible, but it's not, because you did it before. *If it's not impossible, then you can do it.* You need to believe that now.'

There was a loud bang from the castle, and the statue shook.

'How?' Jayben said, tears of frustration and fear running down his cheeks. 'How can I solve everything

when I know absolutely *nothing*?'

'Nobody knows nothing!' Phee retorted angrily. 'You've got something inside. You're just not looking at it the right way.'

Suddenly Jayben remembered the motto, chiselled into the log on the Feller house. '*Always check your pockets,*' he whispered, '*before you search the woods.*'

What was it Tedrik had said? *Sometimes what we need is closer to home that we think.*

Was the key to lighting the Torch something obvious?

Russog poked his green snout out of Phee's bag. 'Wish this . . . Wish this . . .'

They heard an Agent shouting from below. 'Up there!' He was holding a pair of purple lenses.

'I know, Russog,' said Jayben, 'we all wish this could just—' He stopped and then he realised Russog was saying the words in *his* voice. He, Jayben, had said them. 'That's it. That's it, Russog! *Wish this.* That's what I said when I lit the Torch!'

The first Agent broke through the castle gates, aiming his flashpin at a Guard's head.

Jayben pulled Yespa's coat off, held the Torch up with both hands and closed his eyes. 'Wish this.'

BOOOOOM!

Flames exploded into the air, sending a shockwave through the crowd to the gates.

Silence fell. The people turned and froze, wincing at the blinding light shining from the top of the statue.

'WHOA!' Phee yelled, crouching to shield herself from the flame. She held Jayben's ankle in case he slipped.

Then there was a loud *CRACK!* The violet flame must have reacted with the green tree gas in the cloud, and purple lightning ripped through the sky.

Jayben laughed in disbelief, holding the vast flame. 'I wished! I wished, Phee! I said the words, and it worked! Good boy, Russog! I couldn't have done it without you – without any of you.'

He looked down at the thousands of eyes staring up in wonder. All around, people were dropping their placards, firebombs and swords. Nobody was whispering any more. Their eyes were wide in the light of the Golden Torch. They were remembering, released from the shadow of Null's curse by the intense burst of Energy from the Torch. And then –

FOOMPH!

The torch puffed out.

The lightning ceased in an instant. The cloud stopped churning and then it emptied, drenching the kingdom in violet rain.

Jayben turned to Phee and they laughed again.

The sky cleared, and sunshine flooded down to reveal the golden crown on Sojan's head. The castle's colossal towers emerged with their scaly, dragon-like roofs. And the glass dome of the Observatory sparkled in the sun. Jayben felt a longing to draw it, to capture it in his mind.

'Now *that* is cool,' said Phee.

Jayben stood up straight, the Torch in his hand, looking down at the stunned, rain-soaked crowd.

'I'm the Ninth!' he said loudly. 'The real one, I mean. The Ninth Dreamer.'

People gasped, pointing up at the boy on the Queen's shoulder.

'The fake Ninth who sent you here has been lying to you. He is Null, an imposter, and *he's* been the one making you and your families forget. Not forestfolk. Not the Queen. They're not stealing Free-Dreams. Null has been whispering a curse, and you've been whispering it to each other, a spell that stops your brain absorbing the Energy. *That's* what makes you forget.'

The Agent with the purple glasses nearest to the statue was listening reluctantly.

'Null is hungry for power,' Jayben continued, 'to conquer not only this world but Earth World too. He doesn't want to mend the Torch, he wants to break it! He wants to close the pipeline for good.'

Gasps spread through the crowd.

'The city of Free-Dreams is a trick. He plans to put both worlds in darkness, like Maejac did once – but this time for ever.'

Jayben opened his hand so they could see the Rainbow crystals glistening in the sun.

'But he doesn't have the Golden Torch,' he continued. 'I do.'

Jayben looked at Phee. She was beaming. His head was still stinging. He was still running out of time to find his chord. But he needed everyone to believe in him, and it seemed to be working. He turned back to the crowd.

'I am the Ninth Dreamer. And like the Book says, I will mend this Torch, there will be Energy for everyone. A New Magic Age.'

The crowd erupted, cheering and clapping.

Phee threw her arms around him. 'You did it! I knew you would!'

'*We* did it.' He smiled, stroking Russog's head. 'The five of us. Wait, what's happening to your charm?'

Phee's red pine cone charm was glowing.

'Your old magic?' Jayben said. 'You were holding my leg when I lit the Torch.'

Phee's eyes widened. 'Do I really have it? I can't wait to try!'

Jayben slipped slightly on the wet marble.

'Let's get down now,' Phee said, and they crawled back to the thick canvas cape and slid down.

Maybie rushed over to hug them, and Peggro gave him a giant grin.

Only Yespa looked anxious, his face pale and tense. 'Well done,' he said, rushing to put his arm around Jayben. 'But we're running out of time. You're nothing without your chord. We need to go.'

'I know,' said Jayben, 'to the Observatory.'

'Yes, I know the safest way,' he said, pulling him in the direction they'd come. 'Now put the Torch away until—' He stopped, interrupted by the sound of trumpets.

People scrambled for a glimpse of the Dreamer, and a man shouted, 'Clear! Clear!' He was one of a dozen marshals in scarlet cloaks, weaving across the parade ground on white trox. 'In the name of the Queen!'

Yespa frowned. 'I don't like this, Jayben. It's not

safe yet. We have to go this way, to the Guard. Trust me.'

Jayben followed with Phee, Peggro and Maybie close behind.

'Out of the way!' Yespa said to the crowd, and the people parted for them.

The soldiers on troxback followed but were slowed by people trying to catch a glimpse of the true Ninth Dreamer. 'Come back!' one of the soldiers shouted. 'By order of the Queen!'

Yespa shook his head. 'I trust no one till we get to the Observatory,' he said. 'Hurry.' People moved out of their way, recovered nullheads applauding the young Dreamer who had freed them from the darkness.

Yespa rushed them away from the avenue, leaving the crowd for an alleyway, then turned into a deserted backstreet and a railway, where a line of small wooden carriages awaited, the sort you might use to transport animals.

'Where now?' said Phee.

Russog was growling, his snout in the air.

Yespa exhaled. 'Nearly there,' he said, swigging from his hipflask.

'*Now* can I shrink?' said Maybie.

Yespa led them to one of the carriages. Inside it was

dark, with no windows but for a peephole in the door. Yespa poked his head through the open door. 'Are you there?' he called.

Nobody answered.

Jayben peered in behind Yespa and noticed something red in the corner of the inside. It was a postbox, like the one on the moor. 'A Free-Dream?' he said.

Russog suddenly became very excited. 'OINFF! OINFF!' Then in Tedrik's voice, he said, 'Stay here, boy.'

'What's up?' said Phee.

'Hey!' somebody yelled, running down the street. 'Stop! Get away from there!' It was a man wearing grey, Null's badge on his arm.

'*Agent!*' cried Phee, and they all hurried into the carriage, except Yespa, who turned to face him, grabbing something from his hip-case.

'Bad luck,' he said to the Agent.

'Careful, Yespa!' Jayben shouted. 'He's got a flashpin!'

BANG!

Maybie screamed and looked away.

The Agent fell to his knees.

'Get your own Dreamer,' Yespa smirked. He

turned, clutching a flashpin of his own. A pair of purple glasses dangled from his hand. He snatched the Torch from Jayben's hands, then just as quickly ripped Phee's fishdart from her belt and yanked Maybie's charm off her chain. Then he shoved all four of them to the floor and slammed the door shut, plunging them into darkness.

CHAPTER 25

Protect Us From What?

Jayben thumped against the door, hearing the heavy bolts locking and distant cheers as the city celebrated.

'*What are you doing?*' he shouted, stretching up on tiptoes to the peephole.

'Taking you to the true Ninth,' said Yespa. 'Did you really think none of us would see your light when you came to Blanbor? All of us undercovers have lenses now, and I got you out to sea before any of the others came to snatch you. Knew this train full of Free-Dreams would be here, where I once used to load the mail – quickest way to Bramalan and too fast for the competition!'

'You're an agent?' Jayben yelled. 'But you were helping us!'

Yespa continued, 'Of course then you had to run off and make a scene just to save a few stupids. Pity it won't save the world.' He laughed bitterly, taking a small glass bottle from his back pocket and tossing it through the peephole, where it smashed on the floor in the corner. 'Sleep tight. Another long journey for you.'

'NO!' shouted Phee. 'Let us go! Let us out! My aunt will never forgive you for this! Somebody help us! Anyone! HELP!'

Maybie and the boys joined her, shouting and screaming, but they were drowned out by the jubilant crowds at the castle as Yespa hurried away to the front of the train.

Russog was shaking and charging into stacks of hay in the corners. Then he stopped suddenly and slumped to the floor.

'Russog?' said Phee, crawling over to him. 'What's wrong, boy?' She looked up at the others. 'He's passed out.'

Jayben's head felt fuzzy and he stumbled as Maybie and Peggro collapsed.

'The bottle!' said Phee. 'He chucked it in here! Where is it, Ben?'

Jayben looked around, but it was hopeless in the dark. The carriage suddenly shook, sending Phee flying.

'What's happening?' she yelled, and it shifted again. Before she could stand, she too slumped to the ground at Jayben's feet.

'Wake up!' he shouted, shaking her shoulders. 'Phee! Stay awake!' But she was already under. There was a chuffing noise and the carriage rolled forward. He hurried back to the door for fresh air, stretched up on his toes and yelled at the top of his lungs, 'SOMEBODY HELP!'

The carriage slowly rolled away. As Jayben felt woozier, he got one final glimpse into the castle garden as they passed a gap in the wall, and he saw the bright blue feathers of an enormous creature, looking straight at him. It had giant ears, tusks and a long trunk.

'*Zalbanope!*' he gasped. He remembered Peggro saying they were highly intelligent and needed lots of Energy. He held his Rainbow crystals to the peephole and shouted again: 'HELP!'

The last thing Jayben saw before the fumes overwhelmed him was the creature spreading its immense wings, and then the carriage rumbled around a bend, picking up speed, and he fell down next to the others into a deep sleep.

Jayben yawned, rubbing his eyes to see the low evening light shining in through the peephole. He groaned, slowly kneeling and crawling across the rocking carriage. 'Phee!' he said. 'Wake up! You need to wake up! Yespa's got the Torch. He locked us—'

WHAM!

They were thrown forward into the hay. The vehicle was braking hard.

EEEEEEEE! The wheels screeched, and then the carriage hit something heavy and slid off the tracks, crashing on its side and skidding to a stop.

Everything was quiet until Russog came to. 'Oinff! Oinff!' he said, licking Phee's face.

'Stinkbomb!' she cheered groggily.

'Peggro? Jayben?' Maybie moaned. 'You okay?'

'I'm fine,' said Jayben, coughing in the dust. His head was actually feeling better for having had a rest. He could focus. 'You?'

'What happened?' said Peggro. 'Did we crash?'

'My leg's trapped,' cried Maybie, struggling beneath a broken panel of wood.

'Here,' said Peggro, reaching over to her, his handkerchief to his mouth, and he lifted the plank.

'Thanks, Peggro!' she said, freeing herself, and to her surprise, he gave her a hug.

Russog started chewing chunks of wood away from the damaged door.

'That's it!' said Phee, tugging at the slats. But the door was jammed by the heavy postbox. She crouched down, and with a loud groan she lifted it out of the way, ripping the door off its hinges.

Everyone was stunned. Phee's red Giantwood charm was shining.

'*What the moon?*' She gasped. 'It really works!'

'Where is Yespa?' Jayben whispered, struggling to see through the dust as they climbed out of the carriage. They had come to a stop near the edge of a cliff. 'He has the Torch!'

Maybie was frantically sniffing for her golden charm, unable to see much through the dirt. They heard footsteps approaching.

'Pheetrix!' a woman's voice cried.

They looked around. It was Gwennal and Nilthan.

Jayben was astonished. 'How did you—'

'Thank logic!' said Gwennal, running to them. 'You're alive! I'm so sorry, Jayben! It was the only way we could stop him, the only thing we could think to do – we didn't expect it to be moving so fast!'

The dust thinned, and the tall silhouettes of Keylo and Woodge appeared in the evening sun, sniffing at the leaves of a felled tree, lying across the track. It started to make a clicking sound. Jayben scanned the dust and rubble, searching for Yespa – and his Torch.

'How did you find out where we were?' asked Phee.

Nilthan was beaming. 'Mother rode a trox!' he said. 'I found Yespa's map, and his plans in the sack of post he left behind. He's an Agent! Undercover. We knew he was going to use this strange road, to take you to Bramalan, so we rushed here and felled that tree – just like Uncle Tedrik showed me. Look, Phee, the roots are all there.'

'*Where is Yespa?*' Jayben snapped.

Nilthan pointed to the cliff. 'The engine went over. Good riddance!'

'NO!' said Jayben. 'It can't have. He has the Torch!'

'Wait, what?' said Nilthan.

Through the dust, Jayben saw some bushes between the trees. 'Maybe it fell out somewhere here?' he said, desperately. 'We could start searching—'

Then he froze, noticing someone else in the haze, walking slowly towards them. The tree's clicks turned to drumming. It was a young woman in grey, holding a pair of purple-tinted glasses.

'She's back!' cried Maybie. '*Run!*'

But Jayben didn't want to run any more. He was tired of running. He took a deep breath and faced the figure.

'No more,' he said. 'You want us? Come and get us.'

'Get you?' said the woman. 'I'm trying to protect you.'

'Protect us from what?' said Phee fiercely, standing between them.

The woman looked over Phee's shoulder at Jayben and answered, 'Him.'

CHAPTER 26

The Crystal Shilling

Jayben laughed. 'You must be confused.' He showed the woman his hand. 'I'm the true Ninth Dreamer.'

'I know,' said the woman with a sigh. 'I'm sure you meant no harm. But until you control your power, it can do terrible things.'

'He's done no harm at all!' Phee snapped.

'Really?' the woman said. She took a step closer so they could see her more clearly. 'So nothing bad has happened since you first met?' She turned to Jayben. 'Nothing since you woke up as a Dreamer?'

'Well, of course it has,' said Phee with a nervous laugh. 'But that's because of Null's Agents.'

The woman shook her head. 'Agents don't have

powers like you,' she said to Jayben. 'They can't bring fears to life. But you can. Your power is strong, like Maejac, the Eighth Dreamer. Until you harness it, it will wreak havoc. Make nightmares come true for those around you.'

Everyone was quiet.

'Think about it,' she said gently. 'How many nightmares did you face on the journey here?'

Jayben thought back.

He remembered Tedrik after the skallabore fled 'Feared 'em since I was wee,' he had said.

He remembered Phee and Larnie's shock at seeing the barn in flames.

He remembered Maybie's fear of hemniks on the moors. She'd said she had 'always been scared of hemniks'. Peggro's panic on the Iron Road when the Agents appeared. 'Just my worst fear coming true,' Peggro had said.

Then he remembered the strange fungus in Blanbor, a true nightmare for the residents. The grollits attacking Yespa, 'Always hated these things!'

And the unusual darkning strikes following them around, and Phee's words after the first strikes: 'I've always feared darkning.'

The trees started hammering their alarm again.

'The trees,' Jayben whispered.

They had clicked and drummed everywhere he had been, telling everyone to 'run.' The Fellers' house had groaned, and the big red trees had tried closing their roots the day he arrived at Ampelwed. He thought they had been warning them about Null – but they were telling everyone to run from *him*.

Phee looked at Jayben. 'The fire never burned past those big reds before,' she said slowly. 'And we never actually saw the Agents, the day the barn caught fire.'

'Get away from me,' he said, feeling sick. He should have trusted his instincts, he should have travelled alone, should never have allowed them to help him. He'd been depending on his friends, and all the while causing them harm. 'I'm dangerous,' he said. 'Stay away!'

'You didn't know,' said Peggro. 'It's not your fault.'

'Yes,' said Maybie. 'You were trying to help.'

'He did help!' said Phee, frowning at the woman. 'How come you know so much about Dreamers, anyway?'

'Because I study them,' the woman said calmly. 'I'm in the Chordian Guard.' She held her purple-tinted glasses out to Jayben. 'These chordical glasses let us see the light from far away, the chordian light that

Dreamers and Free-Dreams give off. Here . . .'

Jayben held them to his eyes and immediately pulled them off again. The light was blinding.

The woman smiled. 'Your light is strong. Several pairs of these went missing from the Observatory last year,' she said. 'We've been compromised, someone is working for Null, but we don't know who. All we know is someone made copies for Agents everywhere.'

Jayben nodded. 'That'll be Snaggis.'

'Yes,' she said. 'The witch who put one of Null's Rainbow crystals in her enchanted staff, connecting him to the North, giving him the power to curse. That stick is how he's null-headed so many. And since everyone saw the lights align, the Agents have been using their chordical glasses to try to find you – as have I.' She shook Jayben's hand. 'I'm Raynor. I grew up in the Observatory.'

He noticed she had a Trollwood charm. 'We thought you were an Agent,' he said. All this time they'd spent running . . . If they had talked to Raynor days ago, perhaps they'd have found his chord by now. He wouldn't have done so much harm.

Raynor shook her head. 'It's my fault. I was wearing grey to get past the Agents but of course you assumed I was one of them. We need to help you, Jayben. Your light is bright, like you've found your chord, but it's wild, which means you can't have done. And we need to find it, fast!'

Jayben looked back again. There was still no sign of Yespa in the dust. 'Yespa has the Torch, and a flashpin. He was taking us to Null.'

Jayben looked at the sky with despair. The sun was winding down. 'And there's no time.'

'We can't give up,' Raynor said.

'If Jayben doesn't have his chord,' Phee asked suddenly, 'then how come he lit the Torch?'

Raynor looked baffled. 'Impossible,' she said. 'You don't control your power. Your memory hasn't returned, has it?'

'No. But I *did* light it,' insisted Jayben. 'It's how I saved Last Rock. And I lit it before then, too.'

'No Dreamer has ever lit the Torch without finding their chord and, with it, their memory.'

'Well, they had help from the Book,' Jayben said, annoyed to have it pointed out yet again. 'They had maps, instructions, a prophecy. I only have a missing page. It's been hard, but I needed to light it – and I did.'

'That's . . . that's extraordinary!'

'Yeah,' said Phee. 'I know it sucks that you don't

294

remember, Ben, and the Book isn't much help. But in a weird way, maybe that missing page sets you free a bit? It can't define you. You get to write it.'

The words shifted something in his mind. Phee was right. Unlike the other Dreamers, he didn't have to follow everything the Book said.

'And you saved Last Rock!' added Peggro. 'You broke the curse on those nullheads and stopped the townsfolk invading the castle. They saw you and the light from the Torch.'

'But how?' asked Raynor, visibly excited. 'How did you do it?'

Jayben thought a moment, 'I just said, "*wish this*" – I didn't get to say what I wanted.'

'Ah!' she said, staring at him. 'Of course. *Wish this.* That phrase was used in the Magic Ages when the old fairies used wands. Sojan once said, *If you believe in yourself, you needn't wish out loud.*'

Jayben smiled. 'Is that how I managed a Free-Dream too?'

Raynor shook her head, dumbfounded. 'I don't understand how you're absorbing so much Energy if you haven't found your chord. Maybe you got very close to it. Can you remember when it started?'

Jayben cast his mind back to the evening on the

moor. 'We had found the first arch,' he said. 'With moonstones in its frame . . . I hoped it was my chord, but it wasn't. I remember Peggro's moondial lighting up . . . After that I was able to light the bushes on fire . . . Then I saw the moon, like it was dancing . . . I remembered seeing it just like that somewhere once before, in a kitchen . . . That was before I lit the Torch. And then I Free-Dreamed the postbox.' He ran through it again. 'The moonstones . . . The moondial . . . The moon . . .' It clicked. 'Wait . . . the moon?' he said slowly. 'Is the moon my chord?'

'But,' said Phee, 'if the moon is your chord, how come you haven't got your memory and you can't control your power? We see the moon every night!'

Jayben thought again. 'You said the blue moon isn't really blue, right? It's just a full moon. I think the moon I saw in the kitchen, the one I can barely remember, was full.'

'Hang on,' said Raynor. 'So then—'

Jayben continued, 'I saw the moon from the moor only two nights after that. It was so nearly full, but not . . .' Then he realised. 'I *did* see my chord. But not quite.'

'That's it!' said Raynor, beaming. 'That's incredible! I had no idea it was possible. You have come into your

powers – but not completely. It will surely be enough to save you tonight, Jayben. To keep you alive long enough to see the next full moon – your chord.'

Peggro did the sums in his head quickly. 'A hundred and fifteen days, I think, until the next one.'

It was a long time to wait – but knowing that his chord was waiting for him was a huge relief.

'I'm here to help,' said Raynor. 'You'll need to hide, until the Observatory is safe again.'

'Thanks,' said Jayben. 'But we still need to find Yespa and get the Torch back.'

There was a distant *thud* from the woods and a flash of shadow, and a tree turned to ice.

'Not again!' said Maybie, diving behind Phee, hearing another darkning strike.

'Is it me again?' Jayben cried. 'How can I stop it?'

'Here,' said Raynor. She took a little box from her bag and handed it to Jayben. Inside was a large, transparent coin. 'It's a crystal shilling,' she said. 'Put it in your pocket and keep it there. It won't last for ever, but it will help – for now.'

Jayben took the coin out of the box and the darkning stopped instantly.

'It will absorb your power and dim your chordian light until you can control it.' She put her chordicals back on. 'Much better.'

Jayben felt uneasy. 'How can you be sure? I can't risk hurting my friends again.'

Raynor insisted. 'Keep the shilling with you and you'll be safe, until it turns opaque. If you can still see through it, it can still absorb your power. It will last you until the next full moon.'

'Thank you,' he said, stowing the crystal shilling in his pocket.

Then a deep voice emerged from the haze behind him. 'Very impressive.'

The mist cleared. It was Yespa, appearing from the trees, blood trickling from a cut on his forehead, his loaded flashpin aimed at Jayben's back, and the Golden Torch gripped tightly in his other hand.

'Oinff! Oinff!' Russog shouted. Phee held on to him.

Raynor froze. Her weapon was no match for a flashpin.

Jayben tried to stay calm and think of a way out. He knew Null needed him alive to take his crystals, so Yespa likely wouldn't harm him. But he didn't want to test Yespa's patience at this point.

'How could you?' said Gwennal. 'The whole town trusted you. All this time, you were one of them?'

Yespa grabbed Jayben by the back of his shirt.

'We're just doing what needs to be done. Unlike your dear old Hanno, I'm not comfortable doing nothing with my life.'

'You shut your mouth about my dad!' Nilthan snapped, lunging forward.

Gwennal held him back.

'Everyone stay calm,' said Raynor. 'Yespa, the boy is no use to Null if you hurt him.'

Maybie sneezed behind Phee. 'Sorry,' she whispered. 'It's the dust.'

'Yes, you're really doing something with your life aren't you, Yespa?' Phee retorted. 'Living a double life? Kidnapping kids? What a guy!'

Russog suddenly wriggled free and bolted for Yespa.

'No!' Raynor shouted.

BANG!

Russog dropped in his tracks, thrashing about and crying in pain. Yespa had shot him in his front paw.

'RUSSOG!' Phee yelled, rushing to her skoggle.

In Maybie's voice he screamed, 'I wanna fly home!'

'Ah-choo!' Maybie sneezed.

Yespa laughed, dragging Jayben towards the railway.

The air cleared to reveal an enormous rail bridge

stretching from the cliff edge for three miles, across the channel of sea to Bramalan.

Raynor looked alarmed at the sight of the bridge. 'It's not safe,' she called. 'It's made of treddolwood. Come away and let's talk.'

'Yes,' said Gwennal. 'He's just a boy.'

'He's no boy,' said Yespa, pulling Jayben on to the bridge, between the two tracks. 'He's a Dreamer. And when I hand him over to the Ninth I'll be—' He stopped, distracted by a gentle clinking noise from the rails beside him.

He looked over his shoulder, to the Bramalan end of the bridge and saw a dark plume of steam on the distant shore, from a long grey train snaking its way on to the bridge. 'Perfect!' He laughed. 'They're coming. *He's* coming. He'll be here any moment.'

CHAPTER 27

The Treddolwood Bridge

The sea wind blew, and with it came the ominous chuffs and a shrill whistle from the other end of the bridge.

Jayben tried to stay calm. He could feel the Torch pressing into his chest, still firmly in Yespa's grip. Jayben needed it. He couldn't face Null without it, and he couldn't risk Yespa giving it to Null.

'If you help me, Yespa,' he said, 'I'm sure the Guard would reward you.'

Yespa ignored him, pressing the flashpin into his back. 'I'd run and hide, now, if I were you.'

Jayben saw Phee spot her fishdart under a bush, where it must have been thrown in the crash. She slowly reached over and grabbed it.

'Drop it!' said Yespa, moving his flashpin to the back of Jayben's head. 'Any of you shoot me and he dies. And I'll still have the Torch.'

Raynor shook her head and Phee dropped her weapon in despair. Peggro, Nilthan and Phee's aunt were all huddled together, looking equally lost. But where was Maybie?

Yespa took another step back, and there was a flicker of fuchsia pink behind him.

'*Yoink!*' said a miniature Maybie, buzzing up from under the bridge. She yanked the Torch from Yespa's hand, dropping it at Jayben's feet, then she fluttered around, jabbing Yespa in the face. Her gold charm hung on her neck once more.

'Get off!' Yespa shouted, waving his arms to swat her. In the chaos, he dropped his flashpin.

Jayben broke free, stumbling further out on to the bridge, gripping the Torch with both hands. 'Thanks, Maybie!'

Yespa landed a punch on her, sending her spiralling back to the others, collapsing at their feet. Then he turned in time to see Jayben gripping the Torch with both hands.

'Don't be stupid, boy,' he said, reaching for his

flashpin on the wooden sleepers. 'For North's sake, this bridge is made of treddolwood!'

The train's chuffing grew louder.

'I'm not just a boy,' he said, remembering the crystal shilling in his pocket that would mute his powers. He took it out and put it on the bridge by his feet. 'I'm a Dreamer.'

Phee looked horrified. 'Ben! No! *Please!*'

Yespa reached his flashpin. 'I wish you'd learn.'

Jayben grinned. 'Wish this.'

BOOOOOM!

The flames erupted from the Torch, throwing Yespa to the ground.

Jayben looked over his shoulder. The dark tower of soot from Null's distant train was charging ahead. He looked back to the others, Russog whimpering in Phee's arms, Peggro clutching Maybie.

He had two terrible options, but only one would protect his friends.

'Please, Ben!' Phee begged, shielding her eyes from the light. 'You don't have to do this!'

'I do.' He nodded, the rails rattling by his feet. 'And I can.'

He swung the blazing torch around to light the bridge between him and Null's train.

'*NO!*' Yespa cried, climbing to his feet as the flames ripped into the treddolwood sleepers.

Phee stumbled back with the wave of heat, and somebody rushed past her. It was Peggro, swinging his portapedium and running on to the bridge.

'Take that!' he yelled, swiping Yespa in the back of the legs with the heavy cylinder, knocking him down and hurrying down to Jayben.

'Peggro!' Jayben shouted. 'What are you doing?'

'We're friends, aren't we?'

Jayben smiled. 'We sure are. Let's go!'

But the wind blew and the flames spread around them, ripping through the bridge in both directions. Now the boys were trapped.

Then a hook on a long wire landed on the track by their boots.

'Grab hold!' Phee shouted, clutching her fishdart, attached to the wire.

Raynor followed Peggro, leaping over the flames. She picked up the crystal coin and put it in Peggro's pocket. 'As soon as the Torch is out . . .' she said, nodding at Jayben. Then she ran past them, further down the bridge, leaping over the flames, and heading towards Null's train. 'Grab the hook on the wire!' she called back. 'And jump off the bridge to get down to the rocks. I'll stop the train!'

Peggro attached the hook to his portapedium and ran to the side of the bridge. 'Oh!' he gulped, peering down at the waves crashing on the rocks far below at the foot of the cliff. But there was no time to be scared. He held one end of the portapedium out to Jayben.

Jayben took hold, the Torch still blazing in his other hand, as the fire on the bridge closed in.

There was a loud bang, the frame of the bridge buckled beneath them, and the boys fell into the air, yelling with every breath in their lungs, until the line jolted, caught on the twisted rails, leaving them swinging beneath the crumbling structure, high above the sea, the Torch still blazing in Jayben's other hand.

With all the adrenalin it didn't feel real.

He looked up and could see Phee on the cliff edge, beside the end of the flaming bridge, holding the wire, which was still caught on the rails above the boys. Her red charm was shining. She was groaning, slowly pulling the line up. But the wire was wearing thin on the hot rails.

'We're going to die, Jayben!' Peggro yelled, struggling to hang on as they ducked to avoid falling debris.

'No,' Jayben shouted, desperately clinging to hope. 'It's gonna be okay.'

The wire snapped, and Phee screamed from the cliff. Everything seemed to slow down. The portapedium slipped from Peggro's hands, Jayben put his arm around him, and together they fell towards the rocks.

Down and down—

Until suddenly they weren't falling any more. They had landed on a soft, feathered surface.

'We're dead,' said Peggro, 'we must be dead.' They looked up to see the bridge and cliffs vanishing away, leaving only pink fluffy clouds in the sky.

Jayben raised the Torch, about to extinguish it, and they were shaken by a loud trumpeting noise and a deep rumbling.

'Peggro! Look!' He gripped the feathers with one hand and crawled forward on his knees.

There was a whoosh of air, and two immense wings rose on either side of them.

'ZALBANOPE!' Jayben realised, and they soared into the sky and across the sea. 'It must have followed us from the castle! Must have followed the Energy!' He climbed on to the giant creature's shoulders, holding the blazing torch in the air.

'How?' yelled Peggro, gripping the pale-blue feathers for dear life, the wind whipping their faces. 'How did it know?'

Jayben could barely hear him over the noise of the Torch and the wind. He just laughed, overwhelmed by the breathtaking view of the Southern Mountains, their snowy tops shimmering in the sunset. It felt amazing.

But the amazing feeling didn't last long. As the zalbanope turned above the Bramalan cliffs it was attacked by a swarm of hemniks, flying up from the coast. They swiped at its wings and stabbed their fangs into its feathers. Jayben couldn't help remember that the last time he had seen so many hemniks was when Snaggis was around too.

'Get off!' Jayben shouted, spinning the Torch around, catching some of the creatures in the air. The zalbanope was struggling to fly, flailing its trunk and groaning in pain.

They spiralled down towards the Bramalan cliffs and the other end of the bridge, where hundreds of armed Agents wielding flashpins were gathering. They had abandoned Null's train on the bridge, chased back up the track by the fire.

'Don't let go, Peggro!' said Jayben as they swept

over the heads of Agents, before awkwardly thumping down at the top of a grassy bank, overlooking the burning bridge.

As the wounded zalbanope thrashed about, Jayben lost his grip on the Torch and it dropped to the ground, puffing out.

'NO!' he shouted, sliding down the animal's silky shoulder, grabbing the smoking Torch from the grass. He turned to its giant face, stroking its feathers. 'Thank you.'

Peggro winced, clutching his satchel, and jumped down after him.

Jayben felt his arm beginning to tingle and he was filled with dread. He couldn't have a seizure. Not now.

He turned back to Peggro – and froze.

Someone was hunched behind the zalbanope.

The tatty cloak, white matted hair to the ground, frosted blue eyes, and long strands of drool from a cracked mouth – it was Snaggis, wearing a new glowing Spritewood charm on her wrist. She held her enchanted staff, with its Rainbow crystal embedded.

She clicked her bony fingers and a dozen more hemniks appeared and set upon the blue-feathered giant.

'Stop it!' Jayben shouted. 'Leave it alone!'

He raised the Torch to relight it but it moved, as if pulled by a powerful magnet. Some kind of force was pulling on it – tugging it towards . . .

There on the bridge was a foreboding figure. A figure wearing a black hooded cloak and a white mask of porcelain, depicting a face with no expression, and large back eyeholes with no visible eyes behind them. A figure carrying a silver imitation of the Torch in a leather-gloved hand.

Null.

Jayben felt a chill down his spine. The Torch shook in his hand as the force tugged again on it.

Peggro gripped the back of Jayben's shirt, trying not to look.

'Get back!' Jayben said, with a quiver in his voice. He raised the Torch again, but Null didn't stop.

Jayben stepped back as Null reached the top of the bank.

This is it. Be brave. You have to be brave. But it was easier said than done.

'Light the Torch, Jayben!' Peggro cried, gripping tighter. 'Light it, now!'

Before Jayben could say the words the Torch jolted and he almost dropped it. Again, it was tugged towards Null and pulled Jayben with it. Then, with a startling force, it was ripped from his hands and flew through the air.

Null tossed the imitation torch to the grass and caught the Golden Torch.

Jayben froze, paralysed by fear. Null had Trollwood magic. Null had the Torch. And Jayben still couldn't control his power. How could he fight Null?

Snaggis cackled as her hemniks drove the zalbanope away, unable to fly with the pests clinging on.

'Here he is, Ninth . . . The child who dares challenge your greatness . . . The obstruction to our plans . . . His crystals ripe for picking . . .'

A loud explosion came from the bridge and Null looked back to see the train consumed by the fire, and the treddolwood bridge crashing into the waves. The Iron Road was broken, the channel for transporting Free-Dreams washed away in moments.

Jayben shivered. He had done that. Witnessing his own power in the scale of destruction was a terrifying thing, but he was proud that he'd been able to protect his friends, protect innocent people. But there was no sign of Raynor. Had she survived? And now he didn't have the Torch. Now what powers he had could only make things worse. He whispered to Peggro, 'Give me the shilling.'

Peggro put the shilling back into Jayben's pocket, still clinging to his back. Just in time.

Null's wrist flicked and the boys were dragged forward by Peggro's satchel and tumbled down the grass bank, past Null, spilling Peggro's belongings everywhere until the boys stopped by the tracks.

Jayben climbed to his feet, not feeling his grazes. Peggro had lost his glasses and gripped Jayben's shirt even tighter, as Null marched down the bank towards them, followed by Snaggis.

'Come here, little grubs!' said Snaggis.

The boys were backed on to the railway, towards the broken bridge. Their friends were far away, the Torch lost to the enemy. They were just two children against a witch and a powerful Dreamer. And now every noise was piercing Jayben's head, and the tingling in his arm intensified. His brain was sounding the alarms at the worst possible moment.

'It's okay, Peggro,' Jayben said. 'It's all gonna be okay.'

Null reached them. He looked down at Peggro's things strewn in the grass, then focused on the precious logbook. It started to shake and—

CRACK!

In a flash of light it turned into a laptop.

I've seen one of those before, thought Jayben, somehow recognising it.

Null pointed at Jayben and the computer flew through the air towards him.

Jayben raised his arms to shield his face and the laptop hit him hard, knocking him and Peggro on to the bridge.

'Yes!' Snaggis hissed, 'Disable him for the removal . . .'

Null continued towards them, looked at Peggro's book of medicine and –

CRACK!

Another flash and it turned into a large TV.

I know what that is too! thought Jayben. How did he know these Earthly things without any clear memories?

Null hurled the TV towards them.

Jayben gritted his teeth, stood up straight, raised his right leg and kicked the TV as hard as he could to one side. He felt a pop in his leg and it went stiff, but still he felt no pain as they stumbled back further.

'*What was that?*' cried Peggro. 'We need to get off the bridge!'

But Jayben was seething, full of adrenalin, flaring his nostrils at Null. 'Those weren't yours! Leave his stuff alone!' He felt so close to remembering something. The emotions were so familiar, the feeling of having your precious things snatched away . . .

If only he could remember . . .

CHAPTER 28

The Fifth Sundown

Null glanced down at Peggro's broken glasses.

CRACK!

Two flashes and they became a motorbike.

How did Jayben recognise these things? He knew exactly what they were and yet he was sure he'd never seen them before.

'Peggro! *Duck!*' he yelled, pulling him down as Null threw the bike, which missed Peggro by inches. It smashed along the rails behind, falling off the snapped end of the bridge.

The crystal shilling slipped out of Jayben's pocket on to the track.

'I'm scared, Jayben!' Peggro whimpered, feeling the

fragile treddolwood ruin swaying and hearing the motorbike crash on the waves far below.

Jayben wanted to tell Peggro that they would be okay but he couldn't. He tried reaching for the coin but he was starting to feel fuzzy. They were trapped. Another familiar feeling, a bad one.

That awful feeling jogged something inside. It felt like the memory was banging on a little door in his mind. 'We're not alone,' he said. 'That's the important thing. We're friends. That's better than any memory or any magic they can throw at us.'

Peggro grabbed his hand. 'But we've got nothing. NOTHING. It's hopeless!'

Hopeless?

Jayben *felt* that word.

Null looked at Peggro's monocular.

CRACK!

Three flashes and it turned into a big black London taxi, and everything seemed to slow down again.

Peggro closed his eyes as the heavy vehicle bounced down the track, a snarling grey hemnik flying in front of it.

Jayben shut his eyes too, squeezing Peggro's hand, but he couldn't stop feeling that word.

Hopeless . . .

        Hopeless . . .

                Hopeless . . .

HOPELESS!

The door in his head burst open and he opened his eyes to the hemnik.

CRACK!

In a blinding flash of white light the creature turned into a silver sports car, bearing the logo *Lipworth Lettings*, and it rammed into the taxi, smashing up the track towards Snaggis and Null.

Jayben stared, breathing hard.

Null jumped out of the way, tripping down the bank, and dropping the Torch.

Snaggis was hit and fell to the ground.

There was a noise behind the boys and Jayben turned.

They saw Raynor, heaving over the end of the bridge. 'Sorry I took so long . . .' She looked at Jayben. 'Somebody burned the bridge down!'

The boys laughed, giddy with shock. They carefully edged over to help her up, and Jayben noticed Peggro's green Dragonwood charm was glowing around his neck.

'The Torch!' cried Raynor, seeing it roll down the bank towards the cliff edge.

Jayben limped back to the bank as quickly as he could.

Null clambered up, raising an arm to pull the Torch back, when Raynor picked up the crystal shilling from the bridge and threw it, skilfully landing it in Null's cloak pocket.

Jayben grabbed the Torch before it reached the ledge. He turned to see Null stretching out a hand, summoning it.

Nothing happened. The Torch remained firmly in Jayben's grasp.

Raynor whispered to the boys, 'The shilling is strong, see?'

Jayben stood up straight. This was it, he thought. Now he would stop Null once and for all.

Null tried with the other hand, then marched towards Jayben, gesturing to the Agents for support. But the Agents stayed where they were and lowered their flashpins.

Were they affected by the Energy from the Torch and the Free-Dreams? thought Jayben. Was the burst of Energy bringing them to their senses?

Null stopped and looked back. The black hood had

slipped slightly and Jayben could just see the glint of an eye in the dark eyeholes of the white mask.

Emboldened, Jayben took a step forward. 'Get away from the Agents!' he said. 'I just burned down that bridge. Want me to use this again?'

Null didn't budge until the Agents started dropping their weapons.

'Move!' said Jayben. 'Get on to the tracks.'

Null slowly walked past Raynor and Peggro, then stood on the tracks in the final rays of the setting sun.

Jayben lowered the Torch. Null's charm was dimming. Angry as Jayben was, he wanted peace, for all elves; that was his mission from the Book, after all. He walked forward. 'I don't want to hurt you,' he said, 'but you have to stop this evil.'

Null said nothing. Jayben wondered what Null's expression was like behind the creepy, emotionless mask.

Null hesitated, then swiftly shook the cloak and the crystal shilling fell out and rolled towards Jayben.

The boys gasped. Raynor pulled them back.

Null's charm lit up.

'You can't kill Snaggis!' Snaggis yelled from behind them. They didn't see her coming, waving her

long stick. She spat her corrosive green bile on to Raynor's arm.

Raynor screamed and spun around. She grabbed the witch by her hair and swung her on to the bridge.

Snaggis dropped her enchanted stick as she and the Guard wrestled.

Jayben stood in front of Peggro and Raynor and held the Golden Torch in his right hand, opening his other hand to Null to show his Rainbow. *I have to show him*, he thought. 'I am the Ninth Dreamer,' he said. 'Not you.'

Null stood up, raising one sleeve to reveal a long Rainbow wound, darker and more jagged than Jayben's.

From a device in Null's mask came a distorted voice, 'Pity you were late.'

Then Null pointed at the Torch and it flew out of Jayben's hand.

'NOOOO!' cried Jayben, freezing with fear as Null grasped the Torch.

'Wish this . . .' said Null.

THUD! THUD! THUD! THUD!

Darkning struck all around, turning some of the Agents to ice.

'At last!' said Null. 'I shall seal all Energy from both of these wretched worlds, for ever!'

The Torch sucked light from the sky as Null began closing the pipeline.

Peggro and Raynor fell to their knees.

Jayben looked back with horror to see them starting to lose consciousness. The Energy was draining away. 'You can't do this!' he shouted.

Snaggis howled with laughter.

THUD! THUD! THUD!

The darkning continued and the other Agents ran for their lives.

There was a horrible smell. The stench of burning blood. The same Jayben had smelled at Last Rock. Just as he had feared, some kind of seizure was beginning.

He had no weapon. No magic. No luck. He was powerless to stop Null taking his crystals. But the thought of all the people in both worlds losing their memories, unable to think – it was too much. He couldn't allow it. He would rather die fighting Null with his bare hands.

He left Peggro and ran towards Null, yelling at the top of his lungs, but was knocked to the ground by a force. He felt dizzy, and pressure in his left hand. Everything seemed to happen in slow motion.

Null pointed at the Rainbow in Jayben's palm, the

crystals glistening in the last rays of the sunset. Then one of the crystals detached and flew to Null's arm, bonding with the darker crystals.

Jayben felt weak.

A second crystal was ripped from him. He felt cold, and heavy.

A third was taken. His vision blurred and his ears were ringing.

'NO!' he cried as the sun finally set.

This was it. **The Fifth Sundown**.

Darkness fell on both worlds.

Jayben collapsed. His whole body was numb. Lying on the ground he could see Wenden in the distance, engulfed by darkning. And there was nothing he could do.

And then he saw a cool, white light on the horizon.

The moon was rising.

And yet Jayben was still here. It was after sundown and he hadn't perished.

It hasn't happened, he thought, *I'm still here. I'm still awake.*

And as long as he was conscious, there was something he could do.

Another crystal broke off and flew to Null's arm, and Jayben felt icy cold and ten times heavier. His eyes wanted to close, every muscle wanted to rest. But he couldn't. If it wasn't impossible to stop this then he *had* to do it. And there were still a few tiny crystals left in his hand.

He dug deep for any last drops of strength.

'Come on,' he groaned. 'Move.'

Then he saw a strand of drool and long white hair brushing the ground, moving towards him.

He looked up. Snaggis was approaching with a crooked grin. She picked up her enchanted staff and held it high, aiming its sharp end straight at his head.

'It's over,' she hissed. 'No use fighting now.'

A part of him, so heartbroken and worn out, felt like she was right. How was Jayben ever supposed to have won? Life had stacked the odds against him from the start. It made more sense for him to give up.

There was just one problem: he wouldn't.

As Snaggis swung her stick down, Jayben yelled, heaving himself to the side, and the point stabbed into his shoulder.

He felt dizzy – but still felt no pain.

Snaggis ripped out the staff and raised it again.

He felt the last crystals begin to leave his hand.

Null roared with laughter to see Jayben wounded on the ground.

With just one last crystal in his hand, Jayben looked up at the sharp point, glistening in the moonlight, and he said to Snaggis, 'I'll decide when it's over.'

An image flashed up in his mind and—

CRACK!

A flash of light, and the stick turned into a huge red vehicle that he recognised – a London bus!

It knocked Snaggis and Null back on to the damaged bridge. The bus stayed upright, teetering on the wooden structure, side-on to Jayben, with Null and Snaggis on the other side – trapped.

On Jayben's wrist, the Jarmaster's blue charm shimmered.

He felt a surge of power and climbed to his feet.

He saw Null through the windows of the bus and focused on the Golden Torch. With a violent tug it flew out of Null's grasp, smashed through the bus windows, and landed into Jayben's right hand.

Jayben let out a wild yell of fury with every breath in his lungs, and his stolen crystals were ripped from Null's arm, taking a clump of the darker crystals with them, which came flying through the broken bus windows.

Null cried out, as half of the dark crystals were absorbed into Jayben's palm.

The treddolwood structure buckled under the weight of the bus and the bridge broke away from the cliff, taking the bus, Null and Snaggis with it, screaming as they fell to the waves below.

Jayben exhaled, shaking with relief. He felt woozy, overwhelmed by Null's crystals. But the sky was growing darker still and the darkning intensified.

THUD! THUD! THUD!

He had to stop the pipeline from closing. He had to light it.

He held the Torch tightly and whispered, 'Wish this.'

The Torch went out. The darkning ceased.

He heard Peggro and Raynor coming to stand beside him.

'What's happening?' said Peggro. Jayben turned to see Peggro – or rather his jacket, because his head and hands weren't there. His green charm was still glowing. He had gained his old magic, the power to turn invisible.

'Peggro?' uttered Jayben.

Peggro reappeared, looking surprised and scared. Which was normal for him to be fair, Jayben thought.

Then Jayben lost his balance and collapsed in exhaustion. 'We did it,' he mumbled.

Raynor wrapped her jacket around Jayben's wound. Then she and Peggro helped Jayben on to the zalbanope's back, to return to their friends in Wenden. Jayben dreaded what state they might be in.

Peggro put the crystal shilling in Jayben's pocket with the Torch. And the colossal beast spread her vast wings and soared into the twilight sky.

He looked back to see the half-submerged double-decker bus, and a bright orange boat beside it, an inflatable dinghy. Null had Free-Dreamed it as they fell and was inside it with Snaggis, paddling to shore.

'We're too high for them now,' Raynor reassured them, 'and they won't cross the channel at night.'

Jayben smiled at the moon and everything went dark.

'Morning, Ben,' said a voice.

Jayben opened his eyes and was delighted to see Phee sitting by his bed.

'You're okay!' he said. 'I was so worried about you all.' Then he carefully opened his hand to see a swirl of Null's darker crystals bonded with his. His shoulder and his leg were fully healed.

Phee drew some curtains to let the bright sunshine in. 'Maybie fixed you up,' she said. 'We're at the inn. Raynor brought us here, after you came back on that *amazing* zalbanope.'

Russog bounded up on to the bed to lick Jayben's face with his wet snout. His wounded paw was healed too. Then in Jayben's voice he said, 'The five of us!'

Jayben laughed. 'But what about Yespa?'

Phee sighed. 'He wouldn't be helped,' she said. 'He fell.'

It was a horrible thought, but Yespa had tried to kill them all.

'Here,' said Phee, handing him a light-blue zalbanope feather. 'It was in your hand when you passed out. Now you have a keepsake for your jar on the helicorn tree. And what a story it tells!'

Jayben grinned, delighted to have something to remember the friendly blue giant by. 'And,' he said, remembering the charm lighting on his wrist, 'I must be a Trollwood.'

There was a knock at the door. Peggro and Maybie poked their heads into the room.

'Jay-Jay! You're awake!' Maybie cheered, rushing to hug him.

'Want some breakfast?' said Peggro, sipping from a warm gribblenut. He wasn't wearing his glasses. Jayben remembered they'd been broken in the fight with Null. 'Raynor says we need to get back now.'

'Back?'

'To Ampelwed,' said Phee, lacing her boots. 'She's coming with us, to protect you. She says she'll help get some medicine for your head. The crystal shilling's in your pocket. It absorbs your power, remember? So there won't be any more random horrors, and the Agents won't see your chordian light.'

'What about Null though?' He remembered Null and Snaggis escaping in their orange dinghy. He hadn't defeated them. Null was still a threat.

Raynor came in the door. 'Null's power has been halved,' she told him. 'Thanks to you, taking those crystals. You sent that enchanted staff to the Earth World. Without that stick, he and Snaggis can no longer spread the curse. You've seriously weakened them, Jayben. And with half of Null's crystals in your hand, you are now twice as powerful. Once you can control—'

'But they're still out there,' said Jayben. 'They still have Agents all over. I can't hide in the woods for ever, can I?'

'You won't have to hide for ever,' she said. 'Just until you see the full moon – your chord. Then you'll be ready for them. Until then, you must be patient. You still don't control your power yet, remember? We need to figure out how to mend the Torch and keep it lit, too. And your crystals could switch you back to Earth again. It says so in the Book. *Until you find your chord you may switch back and forth between worlds, without much warning.*'

'Really?' said Jayben, suddenly worried. 'When? Soon? How much warning?'

'We don't know,' she explained. 'It varied for the other eight in the Book, but it was just until they could control their power, when they found their chord. But don't worry, you'd know if it was about to happen. You would start to feel pain, for the first time in this world.'

'So *that's* why I don't feel pain?' he said. 'It's a Dreamer thing?'

Raynor nodded. 'You'll only feel pain when your mind is returning to Earth World. For now, let's get to the woods. With your Jarmaster's help, I can report to the Guard from there, until the Observatory is secure.'

'You've done so much already, Ben,' said Phee. 'So many nullheads here will have seen the Torch's light yesterday. And you destroyed the bridge they were using to take away our Free-Dreams, our Energy.'

Raynor helped Jayben with his jacket, then bandaged his hand to hide his Rainbow. 'One day everyone will see your light. You'll write your story on that missing page, and everyone will read it.'

Jayben felt much lighter on their sunny ride back to the Giantwood. His past was still a mystery and his future uncertain but now he had some treasure for his jar. Now he knew who he was, and no one could take that away from him.

CHAPTER 29

Miraclest Eve

Far away in the Earth World, a sleeping Ben Thomson began to stir.

A doorway between the two boys was beginning to open again.

Jayben woke, the most excited elf in Wenden. Since the autumn he had been counting down to this moment: Day One, the last day of the year and the most important in the Miracular Calendar: Miraclest Eve.

He opened his eyes to the extremely pink back

bedroom in the Fellers' house, now decorated with drawings of the first eight Dreamers, and a silver Rackem medal hung by the door.

'Peggro!' he shouted across the room to a new little bed. 'Wake up!'

'Go back to sleep,' Peggro groaned, pulling his blanket over his face.

'But it's today!' said Jayben, leaping out of bed and grabbing the now-misty crystal shilling from his bedside, knocking a pile of papers on the floor. They were pictures he had drawn, of strange buildings from his dreams. He loved creating new buildings. It was like another part of himself.

He put the shilling in his pocket and threw open the curtains, startling something red and furry clinging to the outside in the early dawn. 'A sorrybob!' He grinned, squishing his nose against the frosty glass to see the small, four-legged woodland creature tumble into deep snow, a bright spot of colour amid the white forest.

'It's still dark,' Peggro grunted. 'You're letting the heat out.'

'Get up, grumpy guts, it's Miraclest!'

Peggro put his new glasses on and squinted at his moondial. He grabbed his dressing gown and hurried to the window to watch the red ball of fluff scurrying into the twinkling woods. Every tree was glowing with hundreds of tiny frostlight berries.

'Must be mid-morning already!' said Peggro. 'Shortest day of the year!'

Loud singing came through the floorboards – a cheery Tedrik. They scurried out to the landing as Phee dashed out of her room, bouncing a ball with one hand.

'Merry Miraclest, guys!' she said.

'Come on!' said Peggro, racing them downstairs.

On the way down, Jayben paused to look at the new memoring on the stair. Carved inside the circle was a picture of the Feller family in their garden, running with their arms outstretched to welcome Jayben, Peggro and Maybie. He wondered how Maybie was celebrating with her family. She hadn't been back to visit since she had flown home in the autumn.

'Merry Miraclest!' Tedrik bellowed, stomping snow off his boots, back from having fed the trox.

Jayben gazed in wonder at the sparkling sitting room. It had been transformed for the winter holiday, a riot of crimson bows and gold beads around the fireplace, but it was the kitchen he wanted to see.

'*Breakfaaast!*' Russog sang in Larnie's voice,

hopping with excitement.

'Merry Miraclest, little ones,' Larnie smiled, dusting sugar over a bountiful breakfast, lovingly styled and stacked into a delicious edible castle, modelled on the one at Last Rock.

'Best one ever!' said Phee, licking syrup off a turret of pancakes and doughnuts.

Tedrik filled mugs from a bubbling pan labelled: *Never Mind Wine*.

Everyone sat at the table and Tedrik raised his mug. 'To Jayben,' he said. 'Without you, lad, we wouldn't be sitting here today, together again. Miraclest is always special, but after what you've all been through, having you home is everything.'

Larnie nodded, wiping a tear from her eye. 'To our Jayben.'

Jayben beamed. It was hard to believe that he had not long ago met the Fellers. Now he couldn't imagine life without them.

Everyone dug into the fortress, all but Russog, who was leaping about by the front door. In Tedrik's voice he said, 'Leave them be, Stinkbomb!'

'Did you invite someone?' said Tedrik.

Larnie shrugged. 'Silly fluff-nugget. Leave those poor sorrybobs alone.'

Tedrik put down his mug and plodded out to see what all the fuss was about. Holding Russog back, he opened the door.

'Te-Te-Te-Tedrik!' a tiny voice shivered.

It was Maybie, hovering in the bitter air, in a tiny white-feather coat and hat.

'You poor mite!' said Tedrik, holding his hands out to her.

She dropped her bag and crashed into his palm, shaking, her wings half-frozen.

Larnie wrapped her in a warm cloth from the oven and sat her on the table with a hot gribblenut.

'Tha-tha-tha-thank you,' she said, rubbing her tiny hands in the chocolatey steam and gawping up at the breakfast castle. 'Oh, my wings!'

'We missed you!' said Jayben, delighted to see her.

'I missed you guys too,' she said, controlling her shivers.

'Wait,' said Peggro. 'You flew here this morning? In the dark?'

'It was freeeeezing,' she said. 'But the frostlights got me here. I've been so excited to see you all again, and see Ampelwed at Miraclest!'

Phee grinned at her parents. 'Loveliest village in all the Memory Woods.'

Maybie gobbled the sticky crumbs of the castle, then picked up her bag. 'I'll just go and de-shrink. I kinda like being on the ground with you guys.'

Larnie found her a small red coat, long outgrown by her daughter.

'I love it!' said Maybie, full-sized again.

Everyone wrapped up for the cold.

'Always check your pockets . . .' Tedrik chuckled.

The children plunged their hands into their coat pockets and found warm gingerbread cookies.

Larnie wrapped their chins with colourful scarfs and Russog in a little red skoggle coat. 'Time to look festive . . .' She tied silver strings around their heads and hung their charms on their foreheads, an elf tradition on special occasions.

Jayben picked up a heavy sack of red jollyboxes, little parcels of goodies. He dropped it on his toe and to his surprise, he felt it. '*Ouch!*' He flinched.

'You okay, Ben?' said Phee.

Peggro frowned. 'Raynor said if you feel pain, it means your crystals might be going to switch you back to—'

'Earth?' said Jayben, feeling a pang of anxiety in the pit of his stomach. The thought of not being here any more was scary. Then he pushed the worry aside.

He just wanted to enjoy Miraclest. 'I'm fine,' he insisted, 'it's nothing.'

'Course you are, lad!' said Tedrik, packing a flask of hot Never Mind Wine. 'Just the excitement. Fresh air will sort you out. Only twenty-one days to the full moon!'

Peggro patted Jayben on the shoulder. 'Don't worry,' he said. 'Even if you do switch back, Raynor said you just need to see the full moon in Earth World again, same as it appears here. Then you'll come back here again.'

'But I still won't have my memories and my power,' said Jayben. 'I need to see the full moon on *this* side for that to happen.' He didn't want to think any more about it.

'Poor little one,' said Larnie. 'You must tell us if you don't feel well.'

Tedrik put his felling gloves on. 'You gonna navigate, Jayben?'

Jayben smiled and took his compass from his pocket, then stopped.

'*How?*' he said.

The crack in his compass had gone. He could read his parents' message clearly. There was not a scratch or dent on it. It looked as good as new. All of a sudden

Jayben felt a lump in his throat and his eyes felt hot. He looked up at Tedrik, but found he couldn't form words.

Tedrik winked. 'If it's made of tree, it's no trouble. Merry Miraclest, lad.' Then he flung open the door and led everyone out into the blinding winter scene.

The whole family fed the hungry sorrybobs and rode the trox into the frostlights, their antlers jingling with silver bells, down the snowy spiral lane. In the village, dressed with colourful whimtrees dripping with spiced sap, they met their friends for games and hot dropcorn, beneath a banner that read:

Gribblenuts for Charity!
Avoid holiday sugar crash!
Keep the kids topped up!

Jayben loved every moment. The trees around the village were still scarred from the fires, and the school was still being rebuilt, but the wood was at peace now.

Soon the lanterns were lit, the sun already setting on this shortest day and on the Year 6 minus 8. Jayben noticed a banner hung from the helicorn tree.

Eight Years Tonight...
The Sixth Miracle
Merry Miraclest to All!

They gave half their sack of goodies to their Ampelwed neighbours, then took the rest to the market town of Breckles, joining Gwennal and Nilthan at their new, more colourful home. They had moved to be closer to their family – and Nilthan's new bookshelf was packed with his father's storybooks.

Tying their trox to a post, they wandered the small town, delivering jollyboxes to neighbours they didn't know.

'This street seems familiar,' said Tedrik, as they turned the corner on to a narrow lane leading back up to the woods.

'Oinff! Oinff!' said Russog, his snout sniffing prints in the snow.

With just one box left, they came to a sorry-looking cottage behind an overgrown garden. Jayben plodded up its unshovelled path, and Larnie handed him the last jollybox.

He knocked, but there was no answer.

'Never mind,' he said. But then he recognised the doorknob. He'd been here before. The garden was obscured by the snow but he knew the door. Suddenly he remembered leaving this place and running up the lane, into the woods. Could it really be where he had woken up . . .

Then the handle clinked, and the door slowly opened; behind it stood an old woman with silver hair and rosy cheeks. Her eyes widened when she saw him. '*Jayben!*' she cried, rushing out and wrapping her arms around him. 'You're safe! You're awake! *My stars!*'

Jayben stared, trying to make sense of what the woman had said. Did she . . . did she *know* him?

The woman looked over his shoulder with tears in her eyes. 'It can't be,' she whispered. 'Peggro? Little Peggro? It is! And my, how you've grown!'

Peggro shrugged at Jayben then walked slowly forward, and the woman bent down and pulled him against her red cardigan.

'Oh! My boys!' she cried. 'You're all right! But where is your father?'

'Father?' asked Jayben, now completely baffled. 'You mean Peggro's dad?'

'I mean, your father,' said the woman. 'Both of yours.'

Phee's jaw dropped. '*You're brothers?*'

The woman beamed. 'My grandsons! You were so little, Peggro, when you left, all those years ago.'

Peggro looked bewildered. 'I don't have a brother,' he said, removing his glasses. 'My dad never mentioned a brother. Only my mum, and grandparents.'

'Oh,' the woman sighed. 'It must have been so hard – after what happened. I suppose he was waiting for you to be older. But you're here now, and you've found Jayben. *My stars!*'

Jayben was bursting with questions. 'You were here the whole time?' he said. 'Just outside the woods? Since I woke up before the autumn? Weren't you looking for me?'

She nodded. 'Your Grandpa Mandon has been looking for you all this time,' she said. 'He's still searching now. I couldn't leave in case you came back.' She peered around. 'So, where is he? And your father?'

'Dad was bringing me this way to meet my grandma,' Peggro explained, 'but then he got – wait! *You're* my grandma?'

She grinned. 'You were so little. Too young to remember. You don't remember Jayben at all?'

Peggro blinked over at him, shaking his head.

Jayben was stunned. *Could it be real? Was this*

his family? Had this unfamiliar place been his home all along?

He looked at Tedrik and Larnie, who were speechless, taking it all in.

'Remember, Peggro,' said Jayben, 'you said your dad was bringing you to a town near a market, to find your grandma . . .' he said slowly. 'You said he took you away six years ago, when you would have been only three. And your dad wouldn't talk about it.'

Peggro nodded.

It made sense, Jayben realised. He had actually found his family! Bursting with excitement, he grabbed Peggro's shoulders. 'I have a brother, Peggro! We're brothers! I found you! All this time!'

'But how?' said Peggro wonderingly. 'How did you not know about me? How did I not know about you?'

'Jayben's been asleep since it happened,' said their grandmother. 'All those years ago.'

'Asleep for *years*?' said Jayben, struggling to take it in.

She turned to Peggro. 'And you and your father never returned since that awful night. The night when your poor mother passed away, when Jayben went to sleep. I never stopped hoping to see you come back one day, and hoping that you, Jayben, would wake up.

Oh! The fright I had when I came home from market to see you had gone from your bed, on your birthday of all days! After all those years waiting to see you wake again.'

'Tedrik found him in the wood,' Larnie explained. 'He had forgotten everything.'

'Thank you,' she said, 'for taking such good care of them. A thousand times. Thank you! My name is Fay.'

Jayben was overwhelmed. Finding his grandmother changed everything. But it was bittersweet. He was exhilarated to find his home, to know where he came from, and who his family were. But his father was missing, null-headed, and his mother – their mother – had died when they were young, when he had gone into a deep sleep. And this revelation wasn't jogging any memories. No memories of his childhood with his lost parents. It hurt. A lot.

'You said I've been asleep "*since it happened*",' he said with a frown. 'What did happen?'

Peggro looked up at Fay. 'Dad always changes the subject.'

Fay shook her head. 'I suppose you're old enough now. You deserve to know.' She took a deep breath of the crisp air. 'Let me get my coat.'

Fay led everyone into the woods, to a vast frozen lake nestled deep in the forest. It was a silent place, no other boot prints in the snow. Millions of frostlights encircled the ice, reflected on its surface like a giant mirror beneath the stars.

'I've never seen so many lights,' said Phee.

'I've never seen ice like this,' said Peggro.

'It's the prettiest thing ever,' said Maybie, wandering towards the bank.

'Stay away from the edge!' Fay called. 'It's beautiful, but it's not safe. Karpergen is no ordinary lake.'

'This is Karpergen?' said Peggro. 'An eternally frozen lake? I thought it was a myth.'

'The ice never thaws,' she explained. 'Not even in summer.'

Jayben felt the Golden Torch in his pocket heating up. He took it out, but it didn't light. It just felt warm.

'My stars!' Fay gasped. 'Where did you get *that*?'

Jayben shrugged. 'It was in my pocket when I woke up,' he said.

'Hey,' said Maybie, looking across the lake. 'What's that? That little house covered in frostlights?'

Russog seemed unsettled by the lake. 'Stay here,

boy,' he said in Tedrik's voice.

'The everhouse?' said Fay. 'I'll take you to see it when it's not so cold. Those are moonstones in its bricks.'

Jayben was drawn to the ornate structure. He was still wonderstruck by every building in the Elf World. But not because they were whole, unlike his life. Not any more. Now he realised that what he loved about these structures was the bold colours, the odd shapes, and how they fitted together to make something special. As much as he hoped to get his memories back, he didn't need them for his life to feel whole. It was friendship and love that made him complete.

'I love its twisted roof,' he said, admiring the everhouse. 'Who lives there?'

'Nobody,' said Fay. 'An everhouse is built when somebody dies, a home for their spirit, with no doors or windows. This one's been here since I was young. Those are troll jinx tiles, the pillars are dragon jaws, and there are star glass gems all the way around. You don't remember this place?'

Jayben tried hard to think but nothing came.

'Me neither,' said Peggro.

Fay crouched between her grandsons, wrapping her arms around them and facing the shimmering lake.

'This is where it happened,' she said with sad eyes. 'Where you hurt your head, Jayben, and where your poor mother Merriju rests, below the ice, in this beautiful place.'

Jayben's eyes welled and he knelt in the snow.

Peggro took a small blue shell from his pocket and handed it to Jayben. 'Here,' he said, 'if I'd known we were brothers, I'd have shown you this a long time ago.'

'You still have the balloshell?' Fay smiled.

Jayben was curious. He held it up in the air, and the moonlight reflected from the ice. The shell quietly whistled, and in the whistle came the soft, sweet voice of a woman humming a lullaby.

That's when it came to him.

He remembered sitting on a strange blue floor, staring at a silver stereo, and heard a woman call, 'Happy Birthday, Ben!'

Somehow he recognised the voice. He knew it was his mum, her earthling in the Earth World. He was her little boy, and it was real. After all this time searching his brain for a meaningful memory, he had found her at last.

Tears streamed down his hot cheeks.

It was just one short memory, but it was his. He

could face the rest of his story with something of the beginning in his mind.

'I remember her,' he said, standing up.

He felt a surge of power. Another image popped into his head. The small frostlit tree in front of him started to shake.

CRACK!

In a flash of light, it turned into a bright red phone box.

Everyone was stunned.

'What is it?' said Maybie. 'I love it!'

Another memory appeared in his mind. Jayben saw a blurry image of his mother taking him inside the phone box. He could hear them both giggling. He stepped towards it, desperate to remember more, dropping the Torch on his foot. It hurt. 'Ouch!' he said.

'Ben?' said Phee. 'You're feeling it again?'

He felt heavy and extremely tired. 'Sorry,' he said slowly. 'I just need to—' He stopped. The Rainbow was glowing in his hand.

And then he collapsed in the snow.

'We'll get you more medicine,' said Larnie.

'I don't think it's a seizure,' said Maybie.

'Your crystals are glowing!' said Peggro.

Jayben's ears were ringing. What was happening? He felt scared and trapped. His legs and arms felt numb. His vision blurred, and he felt something cold on the end of his nose. It was starting to snow.

'It's your doorway, isn't it?' said Peggro. 'It's opening again. Are you going back?'

Jayben said nothing. He could hear them but he couldn't respond.

He saw Phee cross her arms. 'It's not fair! It's Miraclest, for moon's sake! He won't get to check his pockets tomorrow, and it's just twenty-one days to the full moon! What if he misses it? He needs to see it in *this* world to get his power and his memories.'

Miss it? The full moon? No! He couldn't!

He couldn't feel the cold on his face any more, but his eyes were open, staring up through the snowflakes to the stars and the dancing near-full moon. All he could think about was the memory of his mum and the phone box, and he was suddenly filled with hope.

If his mum was still alive in the Earth World, he would find her there somehow.

He thought of the Miracle, at the turn of the century, and remembered that a Miracle is something that bends the rules of the worlds. *Please, Moonmother,* he addressed her in his mind, *if you really do Miracles, please help me remember. Please help me find my mum.*

The moon followed him through the frostlights, carried by Tedrik, all the way back to his grandma's house.

Jayben recognised the doorknob and staircase, at last remembering where he had woken up before following the skallabore into the woods.

Before closing the door Tedrik stopped. 'Your compass!' he said, lying Jayben in a chair by a window. 'I can see it out there in the snow. You get warm, lad. I'll be right back.' He hurried outside to retrieve it, closing the front door behind.

Jayben smiled, watching him through a window as snowflakes gently settled on his coat sleeves.

Phee placed a small package next to him. 'I was gonna give this to you tonight,' she said. 'You can open it when you feel better.' Then she joined the others by the fire.

Outside the snow came heavier. Jayben saw Tedrik picking up the compass, his back to the house, but then he dropped it, as if distracted.

A young man was shuffling past the gate. He had no expression but his lips were moving. Jayben's heart raced. *NO!* he cried in his mind. *Tedrik! Get away from him!*

He tried everything to alert the others but he couldn't, he could just feel a tear trickle down his cheek as softly as the snowflakes falling outside. He was trapped, watching helplessly as Tedrik faced the whispering nullhead. *Put your earplugs in!*

Tedrik finally moved, but he didn't turn around. The wind blew stronger, and Jayben could hear branches snapping against the window, trying to warn him. Tedrik was shuffling out through the gate and away from the cottage, leaving Jayben's compass on the path.

Curled up by the fire, Phee was unaware that her beloved dad had gone.

It was too much to bear. Jayben screamed internally, *Tedrik! Come back! Please, Tedrik! Come back!* But Tedrik had disappeared into the flurry.

His grandma spoke. 'Merry Miraclest, Jayben,' she said. She hadn't noticed Tedrik was gone. She kissed Jayben on the forehead and the Rainbow crystals in his hand shone brightly. His eyes closed and his mind was pulled away to another world.

CHAPTER
30

Cake After Midnight

Ben opened his eyes to the muffled sound of a woman's voice.

'Ben?' she said softly. 'Can you hear me?'

Then came a different woman's voice:

'Benjamin Thomson,' she said sharply. 'Answer her, please.'

He peeked out, and there she was, Samantha, at the foot of a hospital bed, tapping her black leather boots.

The other woman clicked a pen and ticked a box on a clipboard. 'My name is Dr Sahni,' she said. 'You're in hospital. You had a seizure this evening. You were awake earlier but not quite with us. Do you remember?'

Ben was baffled. He knew he had been away, far

away, and for a long time, so how could it be the same evening? Sitting up, he reached for Phee's present, but it wasn't there. He looked around for the snowy window, but there were no windows at all. Where was Tedrik? He had to get back there. Tedrik was in danger. It was real, wasn't it? Jayben could still remember it, though it felt blurry. Phee, Peggro, Maybie and Russog were there, and he had hazy visions of skallabores and zalbanopes. It couldn't have been a dream.

He noticed the TV on the wall, showing the news, on mute, and beneath an image of a bus depot, the rolling text read:

. . . Double-decker bus vanishes . . .

'*Snaggis's stick?*' he muttered under his breath.

'Remember something?' said the doctor.

Samantha scowled.

He couldn't tell her any of it. She would only accuse him of making up stories, and she'd punish him.

'I'm not sure.' He shrugged, pretending he was confused, 'I mean, I don't know. Sorry.' He noticed a birthday card tucked beside him on the bed. It was from somebody called June. A name he didn't recognise.

'That's okay,' said Doctor Sahni, leaning forward to examine his eyes. 'It's normal to forget a few things. Don't worry, it'll come back. You were muttering in your sleep. Something about a fire?'

'Oh, that's just Ben,' said Samantha, trying to soften her voice in front of the doctor. 'He's always had a wild imagination, Now, when can we go? It's late and it's a school night.' She slowly pulled the card from his hand. 'I'll keep this safe for you,' she said, zipping it into her bag. He knew what that meant: she would hide it. But why? Who was June?

'I'm sorry, Ms Vaughan,' said the doctor, 'but we'll need to do a few more checks.'

Samantha gave Ben a frosty look, then feigned a smile for the doctor. 'Whatever's best.' She left the room, clutching her phone.

Dr Sahni continued, 'We're doing some tests and we might increase your medication. How are you feeling?'

Ben felt surprisingly good for someone who'd just woken up in hospital, he thought. He'd been in another world on an adventure. He wondered where his other Free-Dreams might have popped up. The toxic rock from Snaggis . . . her enchanted staff . . . the frostlit tree from the frozen lake . . . and what about Maejac's gramophone? Where would that stack of magical turnstones be?

He remembered the strange green rock he had seen in the kitchen that morning, where Samantha's tablet used to be. Had he somehow Free-Dreamed her tablet to the Elf World? And where were Peggro's things? He was determined to get them back.

His stomach rumbled.

'Hungry?' said the doctor. 'Can you tell me what date it is?'

His mind was still foggy, but he remembered the morning. 'Fifteenth of September?' he said.

She nodded. 'Your birthday, for five more minutes.'

A tall nurse came in with a big chocolate cake and a small blue candle. 'Awake just in time!' he said in an Australian accent. 'I've told his aunt we're doing cake, doc, but she's on her phone again.'

Ben grinned from ear to ear. Was he really going to eat cake after midnight? He couldn't imagine what Samantha would say.

'Happy birthday, big man!' said the nurse, setting the cake on his tray and lighting the candle. 'Make a wish!'

Ben took a moment. He knew he'd been to the Elf World, in the life of his elfling. He knew he had friends there and a family. He felt a confidence he'd never felt before. He looked up to the corridor, where Samantha was talking on the phone, probably to Marcus.

'What do you mean your car's gone?' she said, frowning. 'Slow down— *What? A flying cat?* Have you lost your mind?'

Ben couldn't help but laugh a little. If anyone deserved to have their car swapped for a hemnik . . .

Samantha glanced into the room, and for the first time, Ben didn't shy away. He stared back at her, and then he saw something in her eyes. It was fear.

'I've got to go,' she said to Marcus.

What were Samantha and Marcus up to?

Suddenly, as Ben watched, her hand that was holding the phone began to shake. 'Ouch!' she cried. She dropped it, but before it hit the floor –

CRACK!

In a flash of light, the phone turned into a gribblenut, splattering hot chocolate on her boots.

Samantha froze. She looked at Ben. He grinned, and she turned and scurried away.

'Come on,' said the doctor, putting her clipboard and pen down on the bed. 'You can wish for anything. Quick, before midnight!'

Ben shifted the cake closer and noticed some paper

poking out of his pocket. It was his unfinished doodle, the half-started house, torn in two by his aunt. He recalled her words from that morning: *These stupid drawings won't get you anywhere. You are hopeless.*

And then, he remembered the weird roofs of Last Rock Castle and the wonderful living beams of the Fellers' house, and these words:

If it's not impossible, then you can do it.

Going back to life with Samantha wasn't going to be easy, but he wasn't afraid of her any more. He was no longer 'Just Ben'. He was also Jayben.

'Make a wish!' said the nurse, gesturing to the cake. 'It's nearly midnight.'

He glanced up at the ticking clock. In his mind he saw the Golden Torch.

I needn't wish out loud, he remembered.

'Wish this,' he whispered, and before he could blow, the flame of the candle was gone.

ACKNOWLEDGEMENTS

Thank you, dear reader, for joining me on this adventure. I hope to see you again soon when Jayben returns.

This book would not be here without my fabulous agent, Abi Fellows, Callen Martin and everyone at The Good Literary Agency. Thank you for believing in me and for helping me to reach my dream. I couldn't be more grateful to my marvellous editor, Polly Lyall-Grant, and to everyone at the joy factory that is Hachette Children's Group, especially Emily Thomas, Beth McWilliams, Jennifer Alliston, Ruth Girmatsion, Joey Esdelle, Katherine Fox and Annabel El-Kerim. A special thank you to Jenny Glencross and Genevieve Herr for all your amazing work, and to Teo Skaffa for bringing Jayben and his world to life with this stunning cover and beautiful map.

I cannot imagine getting here without my wonderful, enormous family. Thank you to my parents, Jacqueline and Tony, and my wife, Sophie, for believing in me, no matter what. Thank you to our Phoebe and Lucy for kindly napping sometimes so I could write when you were little, for all the giggles and hugs, and for inspiring me every day to be the best possible me. Thank you to Dom, Lizzie, Phil, William, Rosie, James, Rich, Jo, Jack, Ed, Tom, Nelly, Pete, Susan and Jim, Liz, Mark, Harry, Seren, Julia, Paul, Sarah, Isla, Jacob, Esme, Emily, Tom, Annabelle, Effie, James, Lauren, Ray, Maeve and all our aunts, uncles and cousins. I couldn't wish for a more loving, supportive family.

On the real adventure behind this story there are two great friends who have stuck by me since the beginning, no matter what. Shevanne Karajian and Chris Stansell, because of you I know true friendship. Trying to be a writer when you're a stay-at-home parent with a brain injury has been a challenge and I couldn't be more grateful to my fab friends Laura Kyriacou, Molly Walker, Misha Whittaker and Kelly Whelan for being there for us any time, rain or shine.

An enormous THANK YOU to everyone who has supported me on my writing journey, especially Beth Rose, Mahi Cheshire, Tom J Cull, My Ly, Nacho

Mbaeliachi, Sarah Collins, Andy Duffy, Reece Finnegan, Janine Hammond, Joe Wells, Emma Layfield, Lydia Barram, Gillian Sore, Steve Antony, Alexandra Strick, Nikki Marsh, Isabella Sharp, Dan Beasley-Harling, Alice Church, Esther Harris, Giles Paley-Phillips, Nazar Horokhivskyi, Mauricio Prada, Angela Myers, Kerry Asquith, Monica Larson, Peter Ellis, Anna Larson and the wonderful Skoog family. I'm so grateful to our friends Sarah, Ann and Gary, Kate, Lewis, Jayne and Steven, Karen, Mick and Julie, Rob, Nigel, Pat, Kirsty and Jeni, for all your encouragement.

A special thanks to the fabulous Jacqueline and Vida of Jacqson Diego Story Emporium, and to Anke of Anke's Tea and Coffee Lounge in Westcliff-on-Sea, for your kindness and the beautiful, quiet space where I finished this book.

To Headway, Epilepsy Society, and all the hard-working people of our invaluable NHS, without you this story would simply have no author – thank you.